C1 C

CW01657913

The Mother-in-Law's Secret

Melanie Price

Books by Melanie Price

The Mother-in-Law's Secret

My Perfect Family

For S x

Published by Wendlebury Ltd in 2023

20-22 Wenlock Road
London N1 7GU

Copyright © Melanie Price, 2023

Melanie Price asserts the moral right to be identified as the author of this work.

All rights reserved. No part of this publication may be reproduced, stored in any retrieval system, or transmitted, in any form or by any means, electronic, mechanical, photocopying, recording or otherwise, without the prior written permission of Wendlebury Ltd.

This novel is entirely a work of fiction. The names, characters, businesses, organizations, places and incidents portrayed in it are the work of the author's imagination or are used fictitiously. Any resemblance to actual persons, living or dead, events or localities is entirely coincidental.

ISBN: 978-1-7384652-1-7
eBook ISBN: 978-1-7384652-0-0

Prologue

If I'd made better choices, maybe I would never have had to kill the person I love most.

But here I am, standing over their unmoving body, a pool of red starting to bloom across their back. If I shut my eyes, perhaps I can imagine it's just a terrible stain.

And then I can pretend that they'll get up laughing, and I'll finally see that bright smile again.

I blink my eyes open in hope, but my daydream vanishes as swiftly as the life I've just snuffed out.

They're still there. Still dead on the dark wooden floor.

The cold light of early morning slips through the open window and I know my time is running out.

My grip tightens on the cool glint of metal in my palm. There's no going back, no undoing what I've done. What I *had* to do.

But you have to understand, there was simply no other choice.

That's what I'll say to the police when they come – and I know without a doubt that they will.

I should have realised that all the secrets, all the lies I'd worked so hard to keep buried over the years were going to catch up with me eventually.

But it was never supposed to come out like this.

And no one was ever meant to get hurt.

I try to switch my attention, and look over towards the only other person still breathing in this otherwise deathly silent room. I stare straight into their wide, haunted eyes. The eyes of the life I chose to save.

As I wait to face what will come next, I wonder if this life I'd had up until now was all worth it.

The answer?

You'll have to decide.

PART ONE

Chapter One

Izzy

Today is the day my life will change forever. I gaze up at the white-bricked mansion, my eyes open wide, taking it all in. Because it is frankly huge – I can't even count the number of windows and balconies studded across its expanse. Neat hedgerows protect it from any unwanted onlookers, and there's not a single speck of grass out of line. So this is what growing up in Chelsea was like.

It's the biggest and most beautiful house I've ever seen. I have to try hard to stop my jaw from dropping open in awe. And from bursting into tears.

Because I *know* she is going to despise me.

No way will a woman who lives in a home like this be happy with a girl like me as her daughter-in-law. Let alone a woman like Cassandra King. Standing in front of this intimidating mansion, adorned with towering hedges and perfect porticos, my stomach plummets. This was all one big mistake.

But then I hear a voice behind me. The only voice that could bring me back to the present. My fiancé, Miles.

'Hey, you okay?' He smiles down at me as he takes my hand in his, squeezing it tight. His warmth and the sparkle in his eyes send a rush of relief through me. My breathing eases a little. After all, I remind myself, I'm doing this for him. For us.

I twirl my necklace with my other hand and try to give him a reassuring grin back, but it must look more like a grimace because the next thing I know I'm being swept into a hug.

'Don't worry,' he whispers into my ear. 'They're going to love you.'

I gulp and hug him back as my head tucks into the safe place between his neck and shoulder. I try to squeeze him even closer but my hands barely meet around the stretch of his broad back. 'I just don't know... I'm seriously not from this world.'

In this moment of weakness, right on the precipice of meeting his entire family, I let this slip out. But he doesn't miss a beat as he leans back from the hug to look me square in the eyes.

'That's a good thing.' I can detect no hint of irony. His ocean blue eyes burrow deep into mine as he tries to make this message sink in. We had this exact conversation before we made the leap over here.

'Miles,' I'd said earnestly when he suggested the move, 'are you *sure*?' I had been gazing around his gorgeous apartment. It was everything I'd ever dreamt of with its floor to ceiling windows and bird's eye view of Sydney Harbour. I'd felt like enough of an imposter when he'd first brought me there, and just as I had started to get used to it, he wanted us to move to London. 'I just don't think I'll fit in over there and your parents definitely won't be happy – you're their only son and set to take over all of King & Co. – they never wanted you to end up with your latest *assistant*.'

Miles had scoffed, wrapping me closer until our cheeks brushed. 'You're the best thing that's ever happened to me. And you are *not* "just" an assistant.' He'd drawn me even tighter to him. 'You're amazing at your job and I literally couldn't have functioned without you when I first moved to Australia to run the fund. And now...' He'd pulled back to look at me with surprising vulnerability in his eyes. 'Now, I can't live without you in all parts of my life... And so, Miss Isabel Atkinson, will you do me the honour of becoming my wife?'

I had been speechless as he'd dropped down onto one knee in the middle of his sun-speckled apartment, the sunset creating a blaze of red across the sky.

I hadn't responded for a minute, my wide-eyed expression frozen.

'Look, I'm sorry I don't have a ring or anything yet,' he'd continued in a rush, getting to his feet and running his fingers through his soft brown hair. 'But it's back in England. It's my grandmother's ring...' he'd mumbled, and it was seeing how nervous he was that had jolted me out of my daze.

My Miles was always confident and self-assured; it was one of the things that first attracted me to him. I had needed stability in my life after the childhood I'd had. To see him so uncertain made me relax and I'd pulled him towards me in an instant.

'Yes,' I'd said, 'of course I'll be your wife!'

We'd celebrated in style with a bottle of Cristal champagne and a sleepless night in his bed. To me, that had been perfect. Just us, in our own little sun-drenched bubble.

The next day, I'd told him I'd do it – I'd move to London for him. Back to his home to start our new life together.

He had been so excited that he'd picked me up and spun me round in a full circle like I was as light as a feather.

'You'll love it, Iz,' he'd said breathlessly, dropping me back onto the floor. 'This will be the start of us; I'll do anything to make you happy.'

And I'd known he was telling the truth as I kissed him back.

But now, I am being hit by the reality. Not about my love for Miles, that's in no doubt. But whether I'll actually be accepted into his family, his world here in London.

And that *has* to happen. No matter what.

I shiver in spite of myself, the cold of a British November morning contrasting with the bright sunshine and promise of summer back in Australia. Everything that we'd just left behind.

The shiver that runs down my spine isn't entirely due to the cold though. And I try to take another deep, reassuring breath.

Because if I'm being honest, there's a lot more at stake than just breaking up if his parents don't like me.

My life would be on the line too.

I know who his parents really are, and what they're capable of.

To the whole world, the Kings look perfect. Successful. Beautiful. And rich beyond anything.

But I know their darkest secret.

And my darling Miles does not.

I'm thrown back into reality by the sound of approaching footsteps behind us. Our driver has started to carefully bring our suitcases out of the car and up towards the secure black gate that I'm frozen in front of. The gates are so large that it feels like once I'm inside them I'll never be able to get out.

'Come on,' Miles says, squeezing my hand once more. 'Let's go inside.' He sounds excited, as opposed to my terror, but I can't let him see how scared I really am.

Sure, he can know I'm nervous to meet his parents. That's only normal. But he cannot know the real reason why I'm terrified. Not until he sees it with his own eyes.

The true monsters his parents really are. He would never believe it otherwise – no one would.

When I met Miles six months ago, we weren't supposed to fall in love. But now we have, I realise that exposing them for the liars they really are is not just for me, but also for him. For us, and our future family.

But I need proof first. Until then, I have to hide the truth.

As I take my first steps towards the threshold, I feel sick to my stomach remembering one of the reasons *why* he loves me so much.

'You're so different to anyone I've ever met,' Miles had told me once as we lazed intertwined on our secluded corner of a golden beach. We'd just been swimming, and we were lying in the late afternoon sun, fresh from the exhilaration of the cool water. He'd twirled a strand of my hair away from my face as I'd smiled at the taste of saltwater and sunshine on my lips.

I didn't think I'd ever been happier. But then he'd said, 'You're so honest. No one in my life has ever been honest with me.'

My smile had faltered and the taste of salt turned acrid in my mouth. I'd studied his expression. Did he know *my* secret?

But his face was serene as he leant down to kiss my forehead. 'I trust you completely, Iz,' he'd said into my hair.

'Me too,' I'd replied, too quickly.

I try to put this out of my mind now. Or rather, concentrate on the fact he *trusts* me without question, as he should. When I eventually tell him – when he knows the whole truth – then he'll see that he was right to place his trust in me. And not in his dangerous family.

I'm only keeping this secret from him to protect him – to protect us. Everything will be revealed when the time is right. And then he'll understand.

So I'm doing all this for the right reasons. For Miles and me, and the life he deserves to have.

Away from the influence of his terrible parents.

For now though, I need them to like me. I need them to trust me.

Most of all, I need them not to recognise me.

Chapter Two

I shake away my doubts as Miles helps me through the towering gates and up the white stone steps. The rich mahogany door looms ahead. I'm surprised when it's not immediately opened by a sombre butler straight out of *Downton Abbey*.

Instead, Miles locates a discreet keypad blended into wood panelling and places his finger on it. I frown and chew my bottom lip. This high-tech situation was not what I was expecting. A flicker of doubt crosses my mind as I wonder who has access to this house. And how can I be included?

But before I can ask, the door swings open to reveal an ornate entrance. Miles pulls me inside with an excited tug.

He sweeps his arms wide in an extravagant gesture as he cries, 'Welcome home!'

It takes me a second to register the richness of my surroundings. I gaze around the vast room. Pearly white marble tiles stretch along the breadth of it. It's pretty much as large as my entire house growing up. And this is just the front hall.

The room is framed by two wrapped staircases that sweep down and around from the first floor. They tower so high that I can barely make out the level above. A magnificent crystal chandelier sparkles in the cavernous ceiling overhead. It casts a soft light across the room, making the floor almost glow. And at the opposite end of where we stand, there is a yawning alcove entrance to another gigantic room – where an elegant grand piano takes centre stage.

I'm in complete awe, but there's a tinge to the opulence. Everything is too clean, too perfect.

I turn to Miles in disbelief.

'You grew up here?' I try to keep judgement from creeping into my tone. My childhood home was absolutely nothing like this: a small bungalow on the outskirts of a forgotten town. Of course, I knew that he and his family were wealthy – King & Co. was an investment hedge fund after all, and I had worked at one of their offices. But I now realise how much of a satellite office Australia had been to them. The level of luxury oozing out of the Kings' life here back in their home city appears to be on a whole other level to his life – our life – back there.

He rolls his eyes, turning to look at me with an earnest expression.

'Yes, it's a lot. But this is my parents' place, not mine. And honestly I was barely here anyway. Shipped off to boarding school at the age of seven.' He must see the pity in my eyes because he adds, 'Oh don't worry, it's just what was done. Stiff British upper lip and all that.'

I nod, but I catch the touch of bravado in his voice. It must have been hard leaving home at the age of just seven, no matter what he says.

'I know it's different in the colonies,' he says with a wink.

'Hey!' I swipe at him playfully. 'Don't be such a posh Brit!'

He laughs and before I can protest further, he swings me up into a passionate kiss, his strong arms squeezing me tight as one hand starts to travel down my spine. I begin to lose myself in his embrace, feeling a little flurry of relief that at least I've made it this far.

But then a deafeningly soft 'Ahem' cuts through us like a knife.

We spring apart fast as a flash and I look up in horror to see a figure at the very top of the stairs: an impeccably dressed woman, towering over us with a look of utter disdain.

So *this* is the one, the only, Cassandra King.

And this is how we *officially* meet.

I want the floor to swallow me whole.

Chapter Three

'Oh, Mum,' Miles cries up to her. 'There you are!'

Cassandra doesn't happily shout back down to her son. That would be too undignified. For a moment she just stands at the very top of the stairs.

Imposing.

Statuesque.

Perfect.

All the things I am not.

Then she begins her descent, gliding along like she's floating on a cloud.

My heart beats faster in anticipation.

Please like me. *Please* don't recognise me.

I've gone over the plan a million times and there's no reason she should recognise me. But my breathing becomes tight anyway. This is the moment of truth.

I turn to see Miles smiling up at her, and so I try to put my best charming face on too.

There's a sharp click clack of heels on the tiles as she at last reaches the bottom of the stairs and makes her way towards us. Miles breaks apart from me to meet her halfway.

'Darling,' she says drily as they air kiss on either cheek. It looks like a frosty greeting to me, but Miles doesn't seem to notice.

As they embrace, Cassandra's eyes never leave mine, staring me down with a pincer-like stare. Her eyes are icy blue.

Miles must have inherited his features from his father, because there appears to be absolutely nothing soft about this woman. She is all hard angles, from her sharp, short platinum blonde haircut to her sophisticated high-heeled boots. She is exquisitely appointed, not a hair out of place. Just like her house.

My chest tightens as those eyes bore into mine.

I tug at the ends of my jumper and absentmindedly play with my necklace as I wait to be introduced. It always gives me a bit of comfort, as the heart necklace was given to me by my grandmother before she died. I never take it off.

I must look like a mess in comparison to Cassandra's perfection, having just got off a twenty-four-hour flight. I smooth my clothes down and tuck my hair behind my ears as I keep my eyes directed away from her, uncomfortable to meet her stare.

'Mum,' Miles finally says, turning to face me with a huge grin on his face. 'Meet Izzy!'

She releases him with another casual 'Hello, darling' and breezes over to me. Miles is seemingly oblivious to her sub-zero stare.

My heart pounds with every step she takes and I'm sure she must be able to hear it. It takes everything in me not to turn around and run.

But I have to do this, I have to try. For Miles and our life together.

For a moment I think I've done it. She doesn't recognise me.

But with one small step to go, she lunges.

Oh god, this is it already.

As I'm about to run back out of the imposing door, she pulls me into another one of those air kisses with a fixed smile.

I could cry with happiness when not a single flicker of recognition passes her face, and I frantically try to remember to bob to either side of her cheek at the right moment. I have to be *normal.* I have to act like this is the first time I'm meeting her. And it's true in a way – I've never *formally* met her before.

Her razor-sharp nails pinch into me as she says, 'I've been *so* looking forward to this.'

Caught off guard by the unexpected wince of pain and potential threat in her words, I accidentally bob one too many times as she pulls back, and I end up flailing in the air alone.

'Oh dear…' She laughs in a twinkling, mirthless tone. 'I guess things are done a bit differently in Australia.'

Miles joins in with her laughter for a moment and I feel my confidence shrink. There's no way I'm going to be able to fit in here.

'Oh come on, Mum,' Miles says, pulling his arm around me protectively when he catches the look of confusion on my face. 'In Australia things are much more straightforward, aren't they Iz?' He gives me a squeeze, and all I can do is nod along, glad that Miles has read my panic as just being nervous. My relief at somehow passing this first test of recognition has rendered me temporarily speechless.

But I must be sweet and charming. I try to venture for something to say. 'Thank you so much for having us,' I mumble out in a rush.

She waves a hand in the air and rolls her eyes.

'It's no trouble; we have enough room.' The clear understatement makes me feel, if possible, even smaller. 'And I've been *dying* to meet you; the mysterious woman who has stolen my boy's heart so quickly.' She says it with a smile, but there's no mistaking the hidden feeling in her words. At least, not for me. Miles seems oblivious as he beams happily between us. I try not to frown. Getting her to like me might not be as easy as I thought.

'Hey Mum,' Miles jumps in with a tinge of excitement in his voice. 'So actually, we have some ne—'

Oh no. I panic. He's going to tell her about the engagement, and I instinctively know that this is *so* not the moment. She's just met me, and I've made a terrible first impression. I look a mess, and besides, this is not part of my plan. I need to try and get her on my side first.

Grasping for a distraction, I blurt out, 'You have a beautiful home!' even though it's a bit of a foolish thing to say, considering I've only seen the entrance so far.

'Yes, we like it...' Cassandra drawls as she fiddles with the charm bracelet dangling from her wrist. It's full of different shapes and colours I can't quite make out.

Miles glances sidelong at me with a quizzical expression. I ignore it as I continue with my attempt at a distraction. 'Miles says you've filled some of the rooms with your own paintings and photos. I'd love to see them sometime.'

I'm expecting to see her smile: I thought this would be the perfect thing to show an interest in and bond over. When I'd asked him to tell me more about his mum, Miles had mentioned that she adored anything to do with literature or art, and even painted herself.

But instead Cassandra glares at Miles, and flicks her narrowed eyes at me. 'They're not really for show,' she says in a low voice, and then remarks to Miles in a frazzled undertone, 'Did you tell our guest about what's in my private study too?'

Wow, in a matter of seconds I've turned into just a 'guest' and Miles is getting told off for mentioning her hobby?

'No, of course not, Mum,' Miles says with an exasperated huff.

'Good,' she snaps. 'Just to be clear Isabel, you can go anywhere in this house, but my study off the library is my private space, understood?'

I nod, confused. At least I've managed to shift the conversation, but I feel like I have whiplash from the strange way it has turned.

'Right,' Cassandra continues, back in her confident stride. 'You both better get settled in and cleaned up. You've arrived at just the right time to join my charity event tonight.' She beams at Miles, her smile almost blinding. 'Everyone will be so happy to see you.'

I see a flicker of hesitation cross Miles's face. I don't think either of us were expecting to go straight into a social event from a long-haul flight. But he won't want to disappoint his mother.

Cassandra pouts and says in a sickly sweet voice, 'Oh Miles, please say you'll come... And it'll be so wonderful to introduce Isabel to everyone too,' she adds after a beat, and even turns her pearly white smile in my direction – a smile that doesn't reach her eyes. She swivels back to Miles. 'Please, for me? You've been gone so long...'

A small sigh escapes him but I'd noticed that his eyes had become bright with excitement as soon as Cassandra mentioned me. 'Of course Mum, you're right, it'll be great to introduce Izzy to your friends. We'll be there.'

'Wonderful!' Cassandra claps her hands together in delight. 'The car will be here at six. Your father promised he'd be there too, so we can have dinner in town afterwards.'

'I'll believe that when I see it,' Miles mutters under his breath as Cassandra starts to walk away.

'Miles,' she says in a low voice, turning around again to face her son. It's as though she thinks speaking quietly will stop me hearing her. 'He said he'd be there so I'm sure he will, and he won't want to miss seeing you.' She twists the ring on her left finger but looks straight at him with a bright smile.

Miles just huffs a little and Cassandra shakes her head. This clearly isn't the first discussion of this kind they've had. Already, I'm learning a lot about Miles's family dynamic. He'd praised his mum in Australia but had always been quiet about his dad, except when it related to work. I'm beginning to understand why.

He takes my hand and pulls me towards the stairs. 'We'll see you at six then.' All I can do is be led along by Miles as Cassandra slips away out of sight into one of their many magnificent rooms.

Finally, I can breathe again. At last that first meeting is over. And at least she didn't recognise me.

Plus, I've learnt one other useful thing. She doesn't want anyone going into that study.

And I want to know why.

Because I'm certain that's where I'll find the proof I need.

I just have to find a way in.

Chapter Four

The car arrives promptly at six. Somehow I'm ready to go, having dug out what I hope is an acceptable outfit from the depths of my suitcase. We hadn't even had enough time for a proper tour of the house, let alone a chance for me to sniff out any evidence in this secret study, before Miles had half-dragged me out the bedroom door.

Old habits apparently die hard and he'd insisted we had to be prompt for his mother. The doting son always.

We arrive in the entrance hall just as Cassandra appears at the top of the stairs and floats down. She has changed into another incredibly chic but understated outfit: a black pantsuit with an elegant jacket, paired with classic pearls. Matte black heels complete the ensemble, and underfoot I spot the trademark red Louboutin sole.

Of course.

I feel acutely unfashionable in my sweetheart neckline knee-length black dress and sensible matching heels. I wish I were already wearing my coat to hide myself away in. But this really was my only outfit option: as I was rummaging through my bag, I discovered that I had a severely limited wardrobe for a 'charity event'. Back in Australia, I'm more of a shorts and T-shirt kind of girl. At a push, I'd opt for a summer dress or the classic jeans and a nice top combination for going out. When I was a teenager, I'd experimented with a lot more make-up and different styles; these days at twenty-six I opt for a more natural look. It's just easier.

For tonight though, I really had tried to make an effort – after a quick shower to wash off the long journey, I'd even tried to apply some rarely used eyeshadow. I'd hoped it would brighten my tired chocolate brown eyes, and I'd also dusted some sparkly blush on my cheeks in an attempt to add a little glow to my sun-kissed but weary face. As I'd looked into the mirror while taming my wavy long blonde hair into an appropriate low bun, I thought I would pass the test.

Apparently not though as Cassandra flicks her gaze up and down my body when she arrives at the bottom of the stairs. A look of concern crosses her face and she bites her lip – evidently to stop herself from remarking upon my 'look'. She towers over me in her high heels and I try not to shrink into nothing as my cheeks flare red hot. She just says with a shrug, 'Ready? Let's go then,' and sweeps out the front door.

Miles doesn't appear fazed as he helps me into my coat before following her out the front door. I guess he's used to it. I hurry behind, and bite down on my embarrassment. I try to remember that Miles thinks I'm beautiful as I am, and that's all that matters – right?

Miles is already down the steps and near the gate, and Cassandra is out of sight. No one has locked the door.

'Hey,' I call after Miles before he disappears around the corner too. 'What about locking the door?' I gesture behind me.

'Oh, don't worry about that,' he shouts. 'It locks automatically.'

'What?' I ask, catching up with him by the ornate wrought iron gate.

'Yeah,' he says, swinging it open. 'You can only get in *or out* if you're set up on the system.'

'Wait, you mean, I couldn't just open the door and leave the house?' I pause midway through the gate, needing him to elaborate before we can carry on. It is just so strange. If I can't leave of my own accord – then what?

'Don't worry,' he says with a wink. 'Only joking. That side of things isn't enabled, it could be if the admin wanted it to, but *normally* it's not. You can leave anytime you want – but it's fingerprint activated to come in. So I'll ask Dad to set you up on the system.' I chew on my cheek but he says, 'Seriously, don't worry about it, Iz. Anyway, let's go. Mum will be in the car by now.'

He presses his hand into the small of my back as he leads me out into the road and towards the car. Sure enough, his mother is already arranged in the black Range Rover, a bored expression on her face.

I slip in as quick as I can and wonder what the implications of this controlled door mean. Miles seems relaxed about it, but I've never had to navigate something like this before. I'm probably over thinking it though – I would just have to get access and all would be fine. I frown at my expression in the glass as I remember Miles saying it would be his father, William, that had to set me up on the system.

While Miles thinks that won't be a problem, from what I know about his dad, I fear it could be.

I'll have to insist. It might even give me easy access to this secret study of Cassandra's.

I smile at this thought as we rush through the streets of London. The quirky beauty of the city strikes me as we twist and turn on the busy roads glistening under the golden street lights. Part of me is in awe at the old, statuesque buildings, and how they are all tucked so neatly into this ancient city.

But I am also a little overwhelmed at the luxury of this moment: inside a car I could have only ever dreamt of once, being driven to a glamorous event through the streets of Mayfair. Oh, how the other half live.

I don't envy Miles; I'm glad he had this amazing life. He is wonderful and kind and smart. But his parents? They don't deserve their freedom, let alone all this.

We pass the journey in silence as Cassandra taps away on her phone, dealing with some last-minute problems for the event that she has to sort. I think she's trying to frown but the Botox she must get freezes her brows into a smooth line of perfection. I wouldn't be surprised if there's not really an emergency and she just wants to avoid making small talk with me.

I desperately wish we could start again. Everything in my plan would be *so* much easier if she already liked and trusted me. I'll have to just try harder.

Unconcerned by the silence, Miles scrolls away on his social media feeds with one hand and holds my hand in the other as I continue to watch the world go by.

As we near to the event, I try to stop my heart from beating faster and faster in my chest.

Cassandra might not have recognised me. But what if William does? Or any of their friends?

Because I have met them all. Once before.

And if anyone does recognise me, I'll be exposed before I've even had a chance to prove or explain anything to Miles.

And he would never believe my story without proof.

But I don't have time to panic for long: we arrive at an incredible Victorian building that stands in the heart of the city, stretching up and up, further than the eye can see. Glamorous people file their way in. We must be at one of these private members' clubs that I've heard about but never dreamt I would actually step foot in.

There's a first time for everything though. I just hope I can fit in. My life depends on it.

CHAPTER FIVE

As I step inside, I'm struck by how the candelabra floats across the ceilings and my eyes are drawn to the array of famous portraits lining the walls. Beautifully dressed women and expensively tailored men mill around exchanging pleasantries and sharing tinkling laughs. They echo around the room and all I want to do is hide away from their inevitable ridicule.

In complete contrast to my automatic response, Cassandra strides into the centre without a backwards glance. She sparkles her platinum white smile on everyone she comes across as she begins to thank everyone individually for coming and for their contributions to her charity this year. She's come to life and looks at utter ease in this room full of glimmering people.

Before I even have a chance to turn to Miles for comfort, he swoops away to find some friends for us to greet and I can't see where he has gone as he's swallowed up by the crowd.

Shrinking against the wall, I aim to make myself as invisible as possible until he returns. It's abundantly clear to me that I don't belong here, and perhaps that's exactly what Cassandra wanted me to see when she insisted on us coming tonight.

All this is a world away from a typical Wednesday evening for me: a night in, or at a push having pizza and wine out with my cousin and best friend, Gemma. I feel a pang of sadness at how much I miss her.

A waiter appears interrupting my thoughts and thrusts a glass of something sparkling and gold into my hand. I blink but accept the overflowing flute. I look around to make sure no one is watching as I take a sip of the ice-cold champagne, letting the bubbles fizz on my tongue. There's a bitter taste left in my mouth that I can't seem to shake, no matter how many sips I take. I finish the drink and place it on the tray of the next waiter that bustles past before anyone can spot me.

I try to stop thinking about Gemma and instead while away the time by studying the shiny people milling around. I'm hovering behind a loud and oblivious group of tipsy women. They're all around Cassandra's age and as well turned out as she is, all the way from their freshly highlighted hair to their manicured nails that catch the light as they swirl the champagne in their glasses. I edge a little closer to catch fragments of their conversations.

'Isn't this a *wonderful* evening?' a woman with chocolate-coloured hair in a crisp, stylish bob says, taking a delicate sip of her drink.

'Oh yes,' another one with bright red nails and lipstick purrs in response. 'A Cassandra King classic indeed.' She nods over to where Cassandra stands, in the middle of one of her air kisses as she greets yet another guest.

'We would expect nothing less, would we?' This comes from the third woman, with an elegantly twirled bun and a light Hermes scarf flicked over her shoulder, but her voice is laced with sarcasm. 'But *where* is her darling husband, William?' She raises her eyebrows in amusement.

'Ah.' Red Nails leans towards the others, her voice lowering, and I have to shuffle nearer to hear more. 'I heard from Francis that William's been finding things tough at home again. Apparently, Cassandra's not been making life easy. You know with all her "house rules", it's no wonder he's feeling a little stifled. But honestly, I'm still surprised he even stayed with her after the breakdown...'

Chocolate Brown Bob nods. 'The breakdown is ancient history now, but I wonder if sometimes it's hovering just below the surface. I mean, we all like a clean ship, but I think Cassandra's expectations are beyond. I was over at the Boltons' once and she *completely* lost her temper at their housekeeper when she noticed that one of her paintings was askew.'

'Oh, the *paintings*.' Elegant Bun groans dramatically. 'I don't know why she bothers – did you know that she refuses to let *anyone* go into her little studio space? Isn't that bizarre? Once, I enquired where the door off their sitting room went and I've never seen anyone turn so frosty. She practically accused me of nosiness. I mean, is she hiding something in there or what?' She laughs, and I can practically *hear* her roll her eyes. 'Surely Cassandra can't value her art skills that highly.'

The other two echo her laugh and then Red Nails sighs, her voice becoming more sympathetic. 'I guess it all started after the breakdown so we shouldn't be too harsh. But see what I mean – poor William.' They nod in agreement.

My mind is spinning with questions. What breakdown? Miles has never mentioned it – does he even know?

'And,' Chocolate Brown Bob adds, 'it's not like that son of theirs is making things any easier for their marriage.' My pulse quickens. My Miles. I don't think there's anything they can say about him that I don't already know – he values honesty so highly – but my heart beats faster in spite of itself.

'What do you mean?' coos Red Nails, clearly fascinated by any King family gossip.

Chocolate Brown Bob responds, adding an edge of drama to her voice: 'You know how he's been working over at the office in Australia for a while?'

'Yes,' they echo in unison.

'I hear he's brought someone back with him.'

As they both oooh I feel my cheeks start to flush, and I press myself closer against the wall, hoping to blend in.

'You can imagine how Cassandra must feel about that,' she continues. 'Especially after the last girl and what she did, Cassandra must want to practically vet them. She obviously can't trust Miles's judgement.'

A last girl?

'True,' replies Red Nails, 'but that whole thing was quite strange, wasn't it?'

'How do you mean?' says Elegant Bun. 'I don't think I really know what happened.' A bolt of panic races through me, because neither do I.

'So,' Red Nails begins, 'it's just like with this whole Australia thing. After school Miles went on a little gap year, and returned with this mysterious new girlfriend that he had started dating in Peru or something. Apparently Cassandra was *not* impressed.'

'Can you blame her?' Chocolate Brown Bob interjects, and I bristle at the nerve of these women so shamelessly discussing Miles and his family. But I'm also rooted to the spot and can't stop listening.

'Anyway,' continues Red Nails, 'she was from some remote part of the UK and had fallen out with her family.'

'If that's not a red flag, I don't know what is!' Elegant Bun scoffs under her breath, and I scowl into my drink. What gives them the right to judge other people's personal lives?

Before I have a chance to become too disgruntled, I see Red Nails shooting daggers at Elegant Bun for interrupting and she continues in a terse voice. '*Like* I was saying, apparently the plan was that until they found a place of their own they would live in the King family home initially.'

That sounds familiar, I realise with a tinge of unease.

'Truly, I don't *really* know what happened but I do know that I met her a couple of times at an event or two, and she seemed sweet but *not one of us*. Poor girl. She was like a lamb for slaughter, so adrift in all this.' She waves a hand around the room as though to illustrate. They all nod. The word *snobs* springs to my mind unbidden. I bite down on my tongue as she continues. 'And then I didn't see her again. She just disappeared from the scene and was never mentioned. Not even once.' She finishes with flair, taking a sip of her champagne.

'But...' Elegant Bun begins, her tone uncertain, 'what's so strange about that? Plenty of people meet on a gap year and then the relationship doesn't work out. Why would you expect any of them to mention her again to you?'

Red Nails huffs and adds with a flicker of irritation, 'that's just what I was about to get to. All in all, it's not that strange, *however*, I heard from Brigitte, who heard from Marissa, who heard from Allegra, that she was apparently paid a sum of cash from the Kings to leave.'

Elegant Bun laughs in a loud, derisive shriek. '*That's* your explanation? It's a little convoluted, isn't it? Cassandra's son probably just tired of her.'

I had to agree: the story seems a bit too far-fetched. I take a deep breath and force my heart rate to ease a little.

Red Nails flicks her hair over her shoulder in annoyance at the reception of her story. It's like she'd been expecting a round of applause. 'It's what I heard, and Allegra is very close to them, so if anyone would know, it's her.'

'I did hear something too,' Chocolate Brown Hair admits softly, 'but not that. I heard that she was forced to leave because she *stole* something – or that's what it sounded like to me. My housekeeper is a little bit of a gossip, and she said that the girl "took something that didn't belong to her".'

'There you are!' I jump and try to stifle a shriek as an arm slides around my waist, wresting my attention back into the buzz of the rest of the party.

It's Miles. He'd been smiling broadly, but now looks puzzled by my reaction. 'Sorry I left you so long, I couldn't get away from the Fortescues – they're dying to meet you, though. Everything okay?' He frowns as he sees the concern that must be written on my face.

I shake my head, unable to phrase a proper response, still reeling from what I've just overheard.

Miles and I hadn't really gone over our dating history in detail. Especially from that long ago. But something like that, a girl vanishing from his house, that's something that he should have mentioned. Unless it is all just gossip?

The parallels of the situation with mine aren't lost on me though, and Cassandra's frosty welcome makes more sense if the last time Miles brought a girl home things had not ended well.

'Hey,' I whisper up at him through gritted teeth, 'can I talk to you for a second?'

I have to know more about this mysterious ex-girlfriend. *Now.*

Chapter Six

'Sure,' Miles responds, a little uncertain. But he lets me lead him across to a corner of the room.

I drop my voice into a whisper. 'Just now, I couldn't help but overhear some ladies discussing your family. And…' I pause as I find the right way to phrase this so it won't sound like I'm accusing him of something. 'They mentioned an ex-girlfriend of yours that apparently disappeared under "suspicious circumstances".' I add in air quotes to suggest that I think the whole thing is a little ridiculous. 'So, what's all that about?'

A shadow passes his face as he glares over at the extravagant ladies I'd been standing beside.

'Ah, of course they were.' He runs his hand through his styled hair, making it stick up to one side. 'I'm sorry about that. I should have known that *some people* would still be talking about it. Even though it was almost ten years ago.' He shakes his head.

'Don't worry,' I whisper. I can see anguish etched along his forehead and I hate that I've caused it. After all, it's not like I've been entirely honest with him either.

'No, Iz, it's not right. I should have told you about what happened with her – with Maya.' His voice drops so low I almost miss the name. 'It's just,' he gulps, 'a bit painful for me to relive it all.'

He scans the room once more to make sure no one can hear us. 'Can I tell you properly later? When we're not surrounded by a roomful of the worst gossips in the country? But I promise it's nothing for you to worry about now. It's just sad and ancient history.' And the far-off look in his eyes makes me believe that he's telling the truth.

'Of course.' I bob my head up and down – maybe too enthusiastically. Whatever happened between him and this ex-girlfriend many years ago is bringing back some hard memories for him. He must have been around twenty-one at the time, having just celebrated his thirtieth birthday last year. Ancient history indeed.

Our whole relationship has been full of happiness, ease and fun. As far as he's concerned anyway. But if we're going to be forever, it is time for both of us to start bringing our secrets to the surface.

Before we can have that particular conversation though, I have to make it through dinner with his parents.

So I stare up into his beautiful blue eyes, those eyes that always make me feel safe – reminding me of the deep blue of the ocean that surrounds the country I call home. I flash my brightest smile back up at him, and his shoulders instantly relax when I squeeze his hand tight.

Returning to the throng united, I just hope that he'll remember how understanding I was when he finally learns the truth about me.

Chapter Seven

I'm sitting in an elegant restaurant with a 'modern French-style' cuisine – whatever that means – fiddling with the napkin bunched up on my lap. We're all waiting for William to arrive and I'm beginning to sense the rising tension in the air. Cassandra looks down at her watch and Miles sighs, but he looks unsurprised.

Cassandra purses her lips and glances towards the door, disappointment etched on her face. It looks like William is going to be a no-show. And this isn't her first disappointment of the night as far as her husband goes.

After Miles had introduced me to a couple of their 'closest' family friends, who had nodded politely, and asked me questions devoid of any actual interest in my life, Cassandra had given a short speech. She'd thanked everyone for coming and had passed on her regrets that her darling husband, William, couldn't make it. I'd wondered where he was and what publicly admitting that he wasn't there had cost her. I didn't know her at all yet, but well enough that I'd suspected it would not have been something she was happy about. Especially when he'd said he would be there.

Now, we're supposed to be meeting for a late dinner, which William had said he *would* be here for. But he still hasn't shown, and it is past nine o'clock.

I stifle a yawn and blink my eyes open. The jetlag is starting to hit and all I want is to be in bed. I'm feeling a little delusional with the lack of sleep mixed with the exhaustion of trying to be perfect.

'Right,' Cassandra declares, stirring me awake. I sit up straighter in my plush seat. 'Let's just order, shall we, it's getting late and he's evidently in one of his *unreliable* moods.' She flips her menu shut with a snap. This flash of annoyance is to disguise her disappointment, I'm sure of it. And the fact that she can keep a tight control on all other elements of her life – except for her husband.

'It's *classic* him,' Miles responds, slamming his menu shut too. The edge in his voice is also one of disappointment. It's clear that William King doesn't value his family commitments as much as his son and wife do.

As we wait for the food to arrive, we somehow manage to carry a conversation and make small talk. Cassandra is back to her polite self. Trying to get her on my side, I compliment her event and ask as many questions as I can think of about the charity and her work with it. Really, the chat is going so well that I almost forget about how cold she was when we met earlier. *Almost.*

But I should have known it was all too good to be true, because when we finish our incredible meal and Miles slips off to the bathroom leaving the two of us alone for the first time, it all takes a turn for the worse.

I feel like a deer caught in the headlights as she focuses her laser-sharp eyes on me.

'So...' She begins swirling her wine in her fine glass, as the restaurant continues to hum around us. 'It must be a bit strange having to stay with us initially. Perhaps even a little overwhelming, meeting the parents for the first time?'

For a moment I'm taken aback by her astute observation. I'd had her pegged as someone who was more self-absorbed. I'll have to be even more careful around her.

'A little, perhaps,' I say and her smile falters. Maybe admitting that has insulted her. I try and backtrack. 'What I mean is that it's so kind of you to let us stay – we really appreciate it – and it's so special to finally meet you all. But I guess it is a lot at once, yes.'

She nods and taps a finger to her lips. 'Hmm yes,' she says drawling out her words, 'especially after what Miles must have told you about life growing up in the family home.'

I shake my head in confusion. 'I don't know about that...' I manage to mumble out. 'What would he have said?' I ask, falling for the bait.

'Oh, has he *not* told you?' she manages a cool, twinkling laugh as if to brush off her question, but there's an edge to her voice and I'm sure she must be trying to test me. Then again, if I didn't know any better, I would say that she sounds almost insecure. Surely someone like Cassandra King can't ever be insecure.

'Told me *what*?' I fidget with my napkin under the table, twisting it round and round.

'I just assumed he would complain to *all* his friends about it.' She's trying to sound casual, but I can see the glint in her eye. This information is important to her somehow.

I also don't miss the deliberate use of the word 'friends'. I ignore it.

'About what?' I ask again.

'About his unfair and difficult childhood; I'm sure he must drone on about it to anyone that will listen.' She takes a sip of her wine.

I'm thrown by her revelations. Thinking back, I suppose Miles hasn't told me that much about his childhood, other than he went to boarding school when he was very young. But it seemed like he was still close to his mum – he always mentioned her whenever we came across something she might like, and they spoke often enough on the phone. Had I read the situation all wrong?

Why would a mother even bring this up to a new girlfriend? Was Cassandra trying to make her own son look bad?

Questions chasing around my mind, I try to respond positively. 'No, he hasn't mentioned anything like that. From what I've heard he had a very happy childhood.' This isn't strictly true, but he hasn't ever said he was *un*happy.

'Oh, never mind then. I'm glad he hasn't. But you must know he was a *very* difficult child, and men, well, they don't always grow out of these things, do they?' She says it with a little look, as though she's sharing an innocent secret between just us girls.

I work hard to keep my face neutral – there's certainly nothing innocent about her words as she continues. 'And, it's just good for you to bear that in mind as you get to know our family. It would be no reflection on you if you found fitting in to our way of life a bit too much. So don't feel badly if that happens – it would be better for you to leave quietly and quickly after all. And I'll take good care of my boy, I always do.'

She leans over to deliver her parting blow. 'But I'm sure everything will work out *just* as it should. I tend to find, for me, it always does.'

I blink for a moment in shock as I try to take in her thinly veiled threat.

Before I can respond, she sits back upright and says, 'Oh Miles, good you're back. I think the jetlag is starting to hit poor Isabel. Can you wave a waiter down for the bill, please? Thank you ever so much.' And she smiles at me, a winning look in her eyes as Miles does her bidding.

Oh, she knows exactly what she's doing. She is trying to scare me off her son. She wants him all to herself. It's so obvious. But this just makes me more determined than ever to free him from the Kings' toxic world and her vice-like grip.

And so I smile back at her, letting her think she's won this round. But really she has played right into my budding plans.

Because this has been a very helpful conversation, with three things now abundantly clear to me:

Cassandra King will do anything to get her way.

She has a weakness: her husband.

And she has no idea that her trying to drive a wedge between Miles and me is *exactly* what I want her to do.

CHAPTER EIGHT

On the way back to the house, Miles falls asleep, and I pretend to as well so I won't have to talk to Cassandra. I need silence to consider everything that has happened tonight.

I don't know if Cassandra was telling me the truth about Miles's childhood, or just trying to use it to scare me off. But either way it wouldn't do me any good to ask him directly about it. He would just laugh it off, like he did earlier today when he mentioned boarding school. And unhappy childhood or not, without the proof I need, I doubt Miles would believe what I have to tell him about his parents.

My whole heart is at stake if I don't pull this off properly. I can't risk losing Miles. And I owe it to more people than just the two of us to show the world what the Kings are really capable of.

My thoughts are also being pulled in another direction: towards Miles's ex-girlfriend and the whole sad story that he promised he'd tell me. I have to know *everything* before I can figure out what to do next.

But the jetlag is hitting me hard, my brain barely functioning. I don't think I'm in the right frame of mind to have the conversation about his ex tonight. I don't have it in me to be the understanding girlfriend, or rather fiancée, that I need to be.

Back at the Kings' too perfect house, I collapse into the comfiest bed I have ever slept on in my life, and fall into an exhausted, dreamless sleep.

I wake with a start to absolute pitch black, my mind a total blank trying to remember where I am. I start to panic before I hear Miles's soft breathing beside me and I remember that I am in his parents' house. But that definitely doesn't mean I'm safe. For right now though, I'm in control.

It's dark out, so it must still be very early. I feel wide awake though. The joys of jetlag.

I reach for my phone that I hope I placed on the bedside table last night. I had been so spaced out, I can't quite remember going to bed. Luckily, it is there and as I tap it once, the screen flashes up at me. Five thirty in the morning. The spots from the light remain in my vision as I close my eyes again, deciding to remain in the comfort of the bed for a minute.

It's not too early in the grand scheme of things, but with Miles fast asleep I have no idea what to do with myself, and I'm thirsty. Surely no one else will be up yet, so a trip down to the kitchen can't hurt. If I can find it. And maybe I'll be able to find Cassandra's secret study along the way too.

I slip out of bed and shiver at the chill of the morning. I grab the oversized jumper that I can just about see the outline of on the little armchair where I left all my stuff.

In the dim light, I feel along the walls to the door handle and tiptoe my way out. I pause for a minute in the corridor and blink, disorientat-ed. Which way were the stairs again? But before I can bring my phone flashlight up, a soft glow begins to stretch along the corridor, lighting my way. Of course they have automatic sensor lights.

I pad down the hallway. I know that Cassandra and William's room is down the other wing of the house as Miles pointed it out to me briefly yesterday. But as we're on the floor above that, I don't want to wake them up with my footsteps. Then again, this house is probably soundproofed.

The light is eerie and the corridor feels endless. A sense of claustrophobia begins to creep up on me. But I push past it and finally arrive at the incredible staircase. In the dim light, the cavernous space that I can just about see feels hollow and empty. A stark contrast to the glittery and sparkly feel it had in the day.

I hasten down the stairs in my bare feet, careful not to trip. The polished floor is slippery underfoot, and an image of me tumbling down the stairs flashes in my mind. I grasp the handrail and make it to the foot of the stairs, pushing my negative thoughts aside. Now I just have to find the rest of the way to the kitchen. Miles said it was down *another* floor.

I venture towards the double doors that I saw Cassandra disappear into yesterday and I'm met by an enormous sitting room. Even in this light all I can see arranged in there are the outlines of two enormous sofas facing each other, and beyond them two glassy arches. They must be double doors that lead to the garden. Copious amounts of art and little statues line the walls but I can't make out any of them properly in this light. Just a blurry, colourless mass. It gives me the creeps.

I spy to my right another set of large double doors. During Miles's brief run through of the house, he mentioned that this floor led through to the library. And then into Cassandra's private study. But when I reach the doors I find them locked. *Damn.* Is it always locked or is it just because I'm here? Then I notice another one of those discreet keypads to the side of the door. The fingerprint access. My way in. I have to get on William's good side when I finally meet him to gain access.

At last, I see the set of stairs I'm looking for and make my way down. This must be the way to the kitchen. Down in the very depths of the house. Where there is definitely no way out except back up these stairs. According to Miles it's very common to have a kitchen in a lower ground floor of these old Victorian homes. But it feels a little wrong to me – like the life and soul of his family home is hidden away out of sight.

I gulp and try not to make any sound as I emerge into the room. All is quiet and still. And totally pitch black beyond. I feel across the wall and find a soft-touch button. As soon as I press it, a warm glow illuminates the enormous room. Although it is still dark outside, the room suddenly feels bright as the natural morning sun.

And my mouth drops open. Because 'kitchen' is a serious understatement – it's more like a palace of white marble and stainless steel. State-of-the-art cabinets line the upper walls and luxury appliances are artfully dotted in between. Then, there's the ginormous island right in the centre. I take a step closer and notice the impeccable light grey veining running through the pearlescent sheen of the countertop. It screams expensive, and in the bright overhead lights it sparkles as I place a finger on the surface edge. It's cool to the touch as I walk around its edges, running my hand along the shimmering surface.

I take a deep breath as I approach one of the endless soft-touch cupboards. After rummaging through what feels like thousands of high-end kitchen utensils, I find a regular glass. *Thank goodness.* I had almost given up hope of finding anything 'normal' in this house. But then I turn to look at the tap and my heart sinks. There are multiple different handles sticking out of the shiny silver faucet floating out of the countertop. Which one is just regular water?

As I reach down to try the first one, a voice cries out, 'Ah, the damn taps.' I jump back in shock, the glass tumbling from my hands and straight into the sink. It's a miracle that it doesn't shatter, but it does make a metallic thumping sound as it hits the bottom. I wince at the unreasonably loud noise before glancing up to see a man framed in the doorway.

For a split second I think it's Miles, but as the man steps forward into the bright light I see that it's just an older version of him. The same tall height, strong, broad stature and thick brown hair, except this man has a slight peppering of grey that becomes more noticeable as he steps further into the room. *This* must be William King.

And I'm frightened to my core as I stare into the eyes of one of the most powerful men in the country.

The man that I will do *anything* to bring down.

He just doesn't know it yet.

And that's how I need it to stay.

Chapter Nine

'Oh, I'm terribly sorry to frighten you,' William says as he strides over to meet me, his long legs closing the distance in a matter of seconds. And then he's above me, looking down with concern in his eyes. They are exactly the same shade of ocean blue as Miles's. But in Miles's eyes, I always feel like I'm being understood – in William's, it feels like I'm being forensically examined. William also sounds a little different to Miles, with his accent as posh and clipped as you might hear from the lord of the manor in a period drama. It's almost like he's practised it over the years to hone it to perfection.

'No worries,' I stammer, turning away to reach for the glass. He needs to think I'm sweet, weak and innocent. This isn't hard to achieve since I am genuinely frightened.

'So, you must be the famous Izzy,' he says with a broad smile, side-stepping to my left and sticking out his hand. It feels like a challenge and I collect myself enough to return his handshake, hoping my palm isn't too sweaty. This is certainly a friendlier reception than his wife's. But even snakes can be charming.

'Yes, I guess,' I try to match his easy grin with a light laugh, but I worry that it sounds forced. I step back to put a bit more distance between us and notice his clothes for the first time. He's dressed in what must be exercise gear, with sleek black shorts, top and trainers. And I suddenly realise that I'm in fairly threadbare pyjamas with only a light jumper to cover me.

This isn't how I wanted our first meeting to go. But at least it makes me look weaker and as though I'm not a threat of any kind.

'Sorry that I'm in such a state, and thank you so much for letting us stay with you.' I tug my jumper further down to try and cover my bare legs, to no avail.

'Oh, not at all, Miles knows he's always welcome, and certainly he's *always* welcome when he brings someone as lovely as you.' William smiles in his dazzling way once more and I try to ignore the odd undertone to his words even as they spider up my back.

'I was sorry to miss you last night,' he continues on oblivious. 'Was the event frightfully dull? Oh and here, let me get that.' I can't help but feel flustered as he whisks the glass out of my hand and selects the correct tap for cold water.

At least it gives me a chance to think, as I am not really sure how to reply to his question. It was his wife's charity event: wouldn't he have wanted it to be a success? There is a chance he is trying to catch me out on Cassandra's orders, so I just reply to the first part. 'No problem, it sounds like things were very busy for you.'

He turns round to hand me back the now full to the brim glass of water. I take it murmuring my thanks, but it's so icy cool to the touch that I almost drop it again. I place it down on the countertop as he leans back against the edge of the cabinet. 'Yes,' he drawls. 'There is always something that crops up to keep me busy. But never mind. Now, I hope dear Cassandra didn't scare you off at all?' he asks, winking and cocking his head to assess my response.

And another shudder goes through me at the wink.

'I... umm, we had a great time.' I settle upon this diplomatic response, not wanting to say anything that could cause offence to Cassandra. Surely if I did, it would get back to her.

He looks at me in a knowing way and I try not to shrink from his challenging stare. 'I'm sure you did.' And after a moment adds as he scans me up and down, 'The old girl can be a little... intimidating to some perhaps, but she's harmless really. I would know.' He finishes with another flash of his perfectly straight and whitened teeth. I can't decide whether his words are meant to be reassuring or sinister. I can't trust them either way.

'Oh...' I stammer, not really sure how to respond once more, 'truly, it's been lovely.'

He nods. 'Ah, I can tell you're more than a match for her, Miss Isabel Atkinson, so you'll be absolutely fine.'

I'm scrabbling for a reply to his dramatic statement when I hear footsteps on the stairs, and a moment later Miles emerges, looking dishevelled and bleary-eyed in his pyjama top and boxers.

'Iz, is that you?' He walks into the kitchen and then stops short. 'Dad,' he says in a flat tone, sounding surprised to see his dad in his own home.

'Why hello, son,' William responds in a starkly different tone of voice to the one he had just been using with me. This one sounds more stern and possibly... patronising?

William walks over to meet Miles, and they both extend a hand in a formal handshake. I try to stop my face from contorting into a confused expression. They seem so awkward in each other's presence, but I barely knew my parents. Maybe it's normal.

'Good to see you, Dad,' Miles responds. 'Shame we missed you last night.' This time, I can't mistake a hint of bitterness in his words.

'You know how it is, work has to come first – as you should know. Right, I have to get this workout done if I'm going to have any chance of fitting it in before the markets open.' He turns to face me again, his expression softening. 'Lovely to meet you, Isabel.' As he walks out of the room he calls over his shoulder, 'And see you later in the office Miles – unless you want to join me for a workout?' His tone is light but there's an edge to his words.

'I'll see you in the office, Dad,' Miles says through gritted teeth, and William strides out with a casual wave of his hand, disappearing around the corner to what I suppose must be some sort of gym room that I haven't seen yet. What did this house *not* have?

I see Miles visibly relax as he rolls his shoulders. 'Hey…' he reaches me in a few long strides and pecks a chaste kiss to the top of my head. 'I didn't know where you'd gone when I woke up, all okay?' He draws back and looks deep into my eyes as though he's searching for something. I blink, confused. What did he think could have happened to me wandering this house alone?

He clears his throat and when I don't respond asks, 'What were you doing down here anyway?' He leans back on the island as though to appear more casual. But I can see straight through it. And as an afterthought, as though to explain his strange behaviour: 'Sorry if he was bothering you.' A frown is forming across his forehead, and I want to stop it in its tracks. I don't like seeing him like this.

'I couldn't get back to sleep and came to find some water – I wasn't searching him out if it's what you think,' I add with a little laugh, but his frown doesn't disappear.

'Hmm,' he muses, and I wonder what it is about my run in with his father that's made him so jumpy. His face is flushed pink – this isn't like my Miles at all.

'Honestly honey, in fact he was quite nice actually.' I lift up on to my tiptoes to plant a kiss on his cheek but he still seems distracted and stares into space.

'Yes, he's good at being nice to anyone that's as beautiful as you... Or anyone to do with me,' he mutters under his breath. He rubs at his forehead hard as if torn between exasperation and concern.

'What's that supposed to mean?'

'Oh, nothing, nothing.' He shakes his head. 'I'm sorry. He just rubs me up the wrong way sometimes. All my life he's always had somewhere better or more important to be. He knows how much I wanted to introduce you to him last night. But hey, he always does things his own way, always has done. I guess that's why King & Co. is so successful.' He shrugs, resigned. This is the most I've ever heard him open up about his feelings towards his father. In Australia it seemed like he'd tried his best to be his own man – but here, back at home, among his family, already things appear a bit different.

I stand there, waiting for him to continue, but he tries to close the conversation. 'Anyway, doesn't everyone have a tricky relationship with their parents?' I flinch, crossing my arms instinctively. 'Oh, Iz, I'm sorry – I'm such an idiot, of course you wouldn't know.'

'Don't worry about it, I understand – it was the same with my grandparents sometimes. We didn't always see eye to eye.'

He hugs me tight, and I let him, trying to hold at bay the wave of sadness that still hits me when I unexpectedly think of my parents. I bury my face into his neck. Even though my grandparents had cared for me growing up, I'd always missed being in a 'normal' family. And more than anything, that's what I want with Miles.

As my thoughts turn to the future, the thing that I heard last night returns once again.

'Miles...' I look up at him. 'Can we talk about your ex-girlfriend now?'

I feel him tense but eventually he raises his chin. 'Yes,' he says in a soft voice. It's like he hopes no one will overhear us.

I try to scan the bright kitchen for any movement or hidden shadows as he takes me by the hand. 'Let's go back to our room.'

Chapter Ten

We creep back upstairs, the house casting ghostly shapes from the half-light caused by the streetlamps. Sunrise is still far off. The perfect time for a secret conversation.

I close the door with a quiet click and turn to see Miles sitting on the edge of the bed, his head hanging down as though in prayer as he clasps his hands together. He's trying to psych himself up.

Padding over, I slip down next to him.

'So...' he stretches out his hands before placing them on his knees. He looks at me once, then away. At last he begins, 'I had a girlfriend way before I met you, before I ever came to Australia.'

'Okay.' I nod to encourage him.

'And, long story short, it didn't end too well.' His face crumples and I just want to hug him. But I need the full story first.

'Maya and I met when I was travelling in Southeast Asia. I'd just finished university and for the first time I felt like I'd found a bit of freedom, and someone I could be myself with. For different reasons, we were both trying to get away from our lives back here. For me, I guess I was twenty-one and trying to run away from who I was and the pressure of my father's expectations for a while.'

This is the first time he's openly admitted anything like this, and I hold my breath, hardly daring to believe what he's telling me. I thought King & Co. had always been everything to him, and that his number one goal in life was to succeed his father. It's good for me that there was a time when it was not.

I twirl a strand of loose hair away from my face and lean in closer to catch the rest as Miles continues. 'As for Maya – at the time, she told me she'd left the UK to have an adventure and start a new life away from her controlling family. Then she'd met me and things changed – she said she thought I was her future, and that we should start our own life together back home in England. I thought we were both working towards the same dream. But after everything that happened later, I understand now that I don't think that was ever her real reason for wanting to return with me...' He shakes his head as though to remind himself to stay on track.

'Anyway,' he continues. 'When we'd made the decision to return, I knew that I needed to come back and prove myself at King & Co. It was time to grow up and create a life for us. I'd hoped I'd be able to buy a house of our own quickly, but good old Dad insisted that a deposit wasn't just going to be handed to me and that I'd have to earn every penny of it. Of course, I didn't *want* it to just be given to me – I welcomed the challenge – but if that was going to be the case, I'd need to live at home and save up. Which meant Maya would move in too – she couldn't go and live with her estranged family, and there was no point her paying rent somewhere else either. So it was the best plan for us, and she said it would be a good chance to get to know my family. And at first, everything *was* great. She seemed to slot into our whole world easily – she and Mum even seemed to be becoming fast friends. But then some weird things started happening.'

He looks away, lost in memories of the past.

'Like what?' I prompt, trying to bring him back to the present. I try to stop myself from frowning at the idea of this other girl somehow managing to impress Cassandra enough to become her friend. I doubted it. Miles has rose-tinted glasses when it comes to his mother.

'It happened in stages. So small I didn't catch it at first. I guess it was taking me a while to find the right place to buy for us, and I became extremely busy at work – Dad was really ramping everything up. But eventually I noticed she was becoming distant with me. We used to share everything and anything, but then she started disappearing at random times of the day, and not telling me where she was going or where she'd been. I tried not to worry – of course I wanted her to have her own life – but there was something about it that didn't sit right with me. Why wouldn't she tell me what was going on?'

He looks baffled, as though he's still trying to process it all now.

I twirl my necklace between my fingers a little too much. Of course, I'm not sharing everything with him either.

He doesn't notice my nervousness. 'And then it all came to a head when Mum realised that some of her jewellery was missing. She keeps everything important to her in her private study – I shouldn't be telling you that really, but I think it helps explain why she's so funny about it now. Anyway, one day when she was looking for something, she spotted that a few pieces were no longer there.'

He looks away from me and begins to tap his foot on the floor too. It's as though the next part of this story will be particularly painful and he wants to distract himself. 'And then my grandfather's Rolex watch went missing. I thought I'd lost it really – because I'd worn it maybe once since I got back from travelling. I remember putting it on pretty much just to show Maya. Mum had given it to me for my twenty-first birthday and she'd made a comment about how I never wore it anymore. So I *had* to find it – I knew she'd kill me if I couldn't. I started looking everywhere, and began digging through all the drawers in our room – including all the ones that were Maya's. I worried that I might have accidentally left it in one of them before I gave them to her. And that's when I found it...' Colour drains from his face as he looks down at his feet.

'I found some strange chunky envelopes at the bottom of the furthest drawer. I took them out, and inside I found one of the missing sets of Mum's earrings. And the watch. It's like she was just waiting to smuggle them out.' His voice drops dangerously low. 'I couldn't believe that Maya would actually steal from us. But there it was, proof in black and white. I wanted to give her the benefit of the doubt and see if I brought up the fact that Mum was missing some things, she might own up. And maybe explain *why* she felt the need to steal. I would have tried to understand.' He turns to face me so suddenly I almost jump back. His eyes are full of pleading, as though it's the most important thing in the world to him that I understand too.

'And so I approached it in a really casual way, when we were just out at lunch one day. Explained that Mum thought she might be missing a few pieces, and asked her if she'd noticed anything at all. But Maya's face was blank, not uncomfortable in the slightest. She looked me straight in the eye and said that she had no idea. I thought she might be the best liar I had ever known.' His voice is bitter, and a flush rises up my cheek. If only he knew about his parents. But also, me.

I try not to look guilty as he continues. 'Then she got a mysterious message and had to leave lunch halfway through. I couldn't believe it. So, and I'm not proud of this...' He locks his eyes on mine. 'I followed her.'

He throws his hands up in despair and apology, but I reach over to take one and give it a reassuring squeeze. It sounded like this whole situation had given him no choice and he clearly hated every second of it.

He looks into my eyes and his soften for one moment before he looks down at his lap, his voice turning into a sad whisper. 'What I saw... it was one of the worst moments of my life.' He gulps, and I wonder if he's holding back tears. 'She had raced off to meet up with some other guy. I saw them kissing from a distance. I couldn't catch their faces, but I knew it was her. I didn't think I knew who it was but I could only assume that I had been an absolute fool all along.' He shakes his head in disbelief – as though it still surprises him that he didn't see the signs. 'She didn't ever care about me one bit. I'd been such an easy target – all she'd wanted from me was some quick money, and moving into our large family home to steal had been perfect. She'd obviously been planning her escape route through stealing and selling jewellery right under my nose – probably giving all the cash to this guy! I was so embarrassed and angry. I'd never felt that betrayed in my whole life. I should have confronted them then and there – found out who the guy was too – but I was too shocked and couldn't face it. I came back here and fell apart. I just felt so used!

'But then, Maya came back home, and everything went from bad to worse when I confronted her about what I'd seen. I said some things that I'm not proud of, even though she'd hurt me so badly. It's all a blur... I was so angry. She tried to get me to listen but I didn't want to hear what lies and excuses she could come up with. I'd given her a chance already and she'd lied to my face. So I told her to get out.' He buries his face in his hands and I just want to hug him but I'm spellbound and can't interrupt.

'Mum had found us fighting and heard everything. I'd never seen her so angry. And honestly, it felt kind of good to see how much she cared about me too when she'd heard Maya had been cheating on me, as well as stealing from us. I was so shattered and ashamed, and I didn't know how to process it all. It seemed like my only option was to run away and pretend like the last year of my life never happened. That she didn't exist anymore.

'And that's what I did. I just ran out of the house and stayed away for hours. Maybe it had even been days – who knows. I'd found some mates and got obliterated. Truthfully I think I didn't return until Dad told me that everything was taken care of. So when I got back here, Maya was gone. He told me that Mum had made sure that Maya would never bother me again, but the best way to thank her for what she'd done was to never mention it again. He'd told me I'd been a coward for not dealing with it myself. But I was only twenty-one – it was my first heartbreak. And then he just told me to make better choices next time.' Miles shakes his head in embarrassment. 'So we haven't spoken about it again, and I never heard from Maya after that day.'

He slumps back, relieved to have finished his story. My head is spinning at this whole revelation, but I still have questions. 'What, you and your mum haven't spoken about it *ever*?'

'Well, no,' he admits in a quiet voice. 'I'm still so embarrassed about running away and I figured it was for Mum to bring it up if she wanted. She'd already done enough for me according to Dad, especially after I'd brought a thief into the house too. So really I just didn't want to burden her even more.'

'And what, all William did was give you a lecture then?'

Miles gives me a weak smile. 'Yes, typical William – and the old school British upper lip. But trust me, that was one of his more tender moments.' He doesn't elaborate. 'Dad did give me an address to send her stuff to. I was still too upset to touch it though, so the housekeeper sorted everything out.' Ahh – that explains how the lady from the party heard that gossip from her housekeeper. 'I know that sounds completely pathetic but I just didn't want to talk about it, or think about it. I deleted and blocked her number – all ways of contacting her actually. Like I said, I just wanted to pretend like she'd never existed. And Mum wanted the same. So no, we've never spoken about it. I respected her boundaries.'

He runs his hand through his hair as he exhales with a low huff. 'Honestly, I hope you can see that the whole thing was such a nightmare, so I just avoid thinking about it most of the time.' Then he takes my hand and searches my gaze with his clear blue eyes. 'But that's why I never told you before Iz, not because I meant to keep anything from you – please believe that – but because I try to pretend like it never happened at all. I'm sorry though, I should have known that they'd all still be gossiping. But you have to know that since I first met you, I haven't thought about this whole sorry business a single time.' His eyes twinkle. 'You're my future, and I trust you completely.' I smile back, and try to make it reach my eyes.

His disappears into an expression of complete seriousness when he adds, 'But one thing I will always remember was Mum being there for me that day. And then by not mentioning it or guilt-tripping me, she never made me feel like any of it had been my fault. She could see that I just wanted to forget. So I know it can take her a while to trust now, and she can seem a bit cold to new people. But I won't forget what she did for me – I can't,' he says fiercely.

And my stomach sinks at his loyalty to Cassandra. This is not good for me, not good at all.

Because if he's so loyal to her, how could he ever believe me? Will my proof when I find it even be enough?

Chapter Eleven

I'm going to have to attempt not to worry about what happened with Maya, and what Miles said about his mother. It just makes it all the more important to find what I need. I have to prove to him that she's not the woman he thinks she is. Show him that his seemingly perfect mother is actually the most evil liar of them all.

So his fierce loyalty is a little concerning, but all I can do is hope that if I can get my hands on this proof it will be enough to turn even Miles against her. I have to try.

At least thanks to what Miles has just told me I know now without a shadow of a doubt that the proof I need will definitely be in that locked study – where Cassandra keeps all her most precious things.

It makes it more important than ever that to Miles, I am perfect. I can't give him any reason at all to doubt me. He needs to trust me completely. As does his father, because I need him to grant me access to that room.

So I give Miles a tight hug as I whisper into his ear, 'I'm so sorry for what you had to go through.'

He nuzzles into my shoulder. 'Thank you for being so understanding, Iz. It feels so good to tell you, because I know you would never do anything like that to me.'

It's a good thing he can't see my face right now: my guilt is written all over it.

But this is entirely different. Maya stole and cheated on him. I'm not doing that. I'm trying to *save* him. Unfortunately I just have to lie a little in the process.

'Of course,' I murmur into his ear. We stay there for a while, in this place of peace. He must feel like a weight has been lifted off his shoulders from sharing his story with me. If only I could feel the same. Soon, I tell myself, soon.

Eventually he pulls back, glancing down at his watch. 'Right, I think it's time I start getting ready for the big first day back.'

After his relative autonomy in the Australian office, I know he's nervous about being under the shadow of his father's exacting gaze again. But he shouldn't be: he'd managed to land some huge new deals for King & Co. in the Asia–Pacific region, so he should return to the London office with his head held high.

'They're lucky to have you back. After everything you did back in Sydney – you turned the whole market around. So you go in there and show them who the real boss is!' I give him a big hug.

He laughs. 'You dork!'

I might have overdone the enthusiasm but at least it's made Miles smile again.

'And seriously, thank you for listening.' He gives me a deep and lingering kiss before rising up and heading towards the bathroom.

I can still feel the tingle on my lips where he'd brushed them, but I lie back onto the bed to try and digest everything I've just heard.

Thankfully, it doesn't change much. I feel so sad for Miles that he had to go through all that with his ex, and that people are still gossiping about it even now. But at least it wasn't anything too disastrous. If anything it explains why Cassandra would have an automatic dislike towards all Miles's new girlfriends. The one problem is that Miles feels like he owes Cassandra for what she did for him.

But will Miles still be as devoted to his mother when he finally knows the truth? I hope that he won't.

I still need to try and get Cassandra to accept me though, because I'm sure that if she suspects me at all, she'll do anything to drive him away from me.

I can't allow that to happen. I have to be beyond reproach.

And today, I have to get access to the library – the room that's the gateway to Cassandra's private study. When Miles returns from the shower, I'll ask him to help me arrange it.

But when he wanders back into the bedroom with a towel wrapped around his waist and his toned muscles visible, I'm not only distracted from asking by the sight in front of me. I'm floored by the next words that come from his lips.

'Oh, and Mum asked if you wanted to go shopping with her today while I'm in the office. She's leaving at nine thirty.' He says it casually as he pads across the room to open the curtains.

'Oh really?' I sit up in a flash. This should be music to my ears that Cassandra wants to spend some time with me, but I can't help but be worried. After how she was with me last night, trying to warn me away from Miles and her family, I thought I'd have to work a lot harder to get into her good books.

'Yeah, of course – it'll be nice for you to spend some time together, get to know your future mother-in-law a little... before we tell them the big news tonight.' He finishes firmly as he starts towards the walk-in wardrobe.

'What, tonight?' I say, jumping off the bed to follow him, now fully distracted by this declaration.

'Tonight,' he responds as he rummages through his drawers. 'Come on, why not? Let's not wait any longer. Let's get them excited and start planning.' He turns back to face me. 'And besides, telling you about *that woman*,' he clearly doesn't want to say her name again, 'makes me even more certain I want everyone to see how perfect you are.'

All I can do is nod. 'Alright,' I say, a note of hesitation still creeping into my voice. 'If you think they'll be ready for it.' I wasn't so sure his parents would take kindly to the news this quickly. But then again, at least if the announcement is made, they might be eager to get closer to me... I hope.

'Brilliant,' he replies, a broad grin spreading across his face. 'And I'm sure you'll have a great day with Mum.'

Rushing towards the shower, I just give him a thumbs up in return. In my haste I forget completely about asking for fingerprint access, and by the time I emerge back into the room Miles is already gone.

I sigh as I slip back into the bathroom and stare into the mirror at my tired expression. My brown eyes look opaque with weariness and I have deep circles under my eyes from a combination of lack of sleep, jetlag and constant anxiety about being found out. It'll all be worth it, I tell my reflection.

Turning away, I pull myself together, readying for what's to come. I just really hope Miles is right. It will make things so much easier for me. But I have a terrible feeling that Cassandra doesn't want to hang out with me today for simply innocent reasons.

It feels like I'm walking into a trap.

Chapter Twelve

I take care getting ready, hoping that today I might finally impress Cassandra with my appearance at least. At nine thirty I'm standing in the sweeping entrance hall, wearing the best 'daytime' outfit I own: black jeans, black ankle boots and a knee-length red overcoat that I managed to get in the sale before we flew over here. I twist my scarf in my hand round and round as I wait.

I'd texted Miles good luck when I'd realised he'd gone and asked about the fingerprint access. He said that we'd be able to ask his dad properly tonight – and after the announcement there was no way he'd not hand it over. I'd exhaled in relief. If Miles was so certain that this was the time and place to tell his parents, why should I slow him down? It would solidify our relationship to them, and that could only be a good thing.

He'd sent me some love heart emojis and told me to 'have fun'. I'd sent an over-the-top happy face emoji in return.

I hope he will be right. I'm trying to be optimistic. I can do this. Plan A is to win his mother over naturally.

I twist my scarf in my hand and glance down at my watch as the minutes tick by. I begin to wonder if I should go off in search of her in this vast expanse of a house.

Just as I am about to try, I hear a 'Good morning, dear' call out at me from the top of the stairs. I wave back awkwardly as Cassandra makes her way down towards me. She's wearing an elegant, navy blue coat paired with a creamy white scarf and knee-length black suede boots. Her hair is shiny and sleek, and her make-up gives her a natural glow. In comparison, I feel like a traffic cone in my bright red coat.

Her lips curl into a lazy smile as she assesses me up and down with her piercing blue eyes. Just like she did last night. How can a smile feel sarcastic? It's a talent, I'll give her that. 'So, shall we take you on your first day out and about?'

'That would be great,' I respond with too much enthusiasm. But she doesn't flinch like she did yesterday, so I take that as a good sign. She seems to be in a friendly mood. Maybe this will be our fresh start – and I'll be able to run with Plan A after all.

But the story Miles just shared with me echoes in my mind. After what happened with his last girlfriend, I doubt Cassandra will trust me easily. I'm certain this little excursion must be about sussing me out. I'm going to make sure she has absolutely nothing to criticise me for. Nothing she can report back to Miles.

If all else fails, I do have a Plan B. Which is to turn Miles against her. But that will be a much harder challenge, I think.

'Perfect,' she says, opening the door to me as she swings her black Mulberry bag onto her shoulder. 'I just have a few errands to get done, and then perhaps we'll even have some time for some clothes shopping for you,' she chirps at me in her brightest voice as I walk past her and onto the front steps. I flinch at the undisguised criticism of my clothes.

I remain calm though. Because Cassandra might think she has her son wrapped around her little finger – that much has become obvious to me over the past day – but she's never come across the likes of me.

I know what it's like to lose everything.

And I'm going to make sure she understands exactly how it feels when I take away her son.

So I follow her out the door.

Because two can play at this game.

And she has no idea what's coming her way.

Chapter Thirteen

We spend a good few hours flitting from appointment to appointment around Kensington and Chelsea. I try to stop myself from yawning through a furniture appointment for Cassandra to examine some new pieces, an appointment at a jewellery shop for her to find some new earrings for an upcoming soiree and a consultation about the flower arrangement for the next charity event.

I force an interested expression on my face the whole time. She's probably trying to tire me out, make me snap. I will not give her the satisfaction or the ammunition.

Cassandra keeps up a steady stream of chatter as we go from store to store. Everything is pretty pleasant. She must be lulling me into a false sense of security. It almost seems like I'm with an entirely different Cassandra today to the one I met yesterday.

As we now make our way towards the cheesemongers – honestly, I had no idea such a store even existed, what's wrong with a simple grocery store? – Cassandra tells me that 'perhaps after this, we can drop past Peter Jones, there must be a few additional things you need to get for your winter wardrobe.'

I bite my tongue to stop a sassy remark coming out and just smile graciously.

To distract myself and ensure my face remains completely serene, I gaze around the little pedestrianised street of this small corner of Chelsea. It's undeniably beautiful with delicate lights strung up, and little table and chairs dotted along outside various chocolate-box cafés and restaurants. Elegant people sit outside in the late autumn day, catching up over coffee and croissants. There's not a cloud in the sky and I could almost think we were on an idyllic little Parisian street, rather than reputationally rainy London.

If only I didn't have to keep up this façade and I could just sit down and enjoy it. I feel a pang as I think of the one person who I know would love this spot more than anyone else: my grandma. But she'll never get the chance to enjoy a peaceful moment on these pristine streets.

I keep up with my future mother-in-law, who expertly weaves her way through the crowds. Then, I hear a cry of 'Cassandra, Cassandra' ring out from somewhere in the midst of the busy little street. Cassandra must have heard it too, as she pauses and glances around. We both spot a woman laden with a couple of weighty White Company bags attempting a wave in our direction. Cassandra waits while she makes her way over to us.

'Oh hello, Amanda,' Cassandra says in her plummy accent, giving the woman two air kisses in the usual greeting.

'Hello, darling, how are you?' Amanda responds in an even more rounded English accent. 'It's been an aaage.'

'I know,' Cassandra says, her mouth pouting down as though she's terribly disappointed by this revelation. 'We *must* do something soon.'

I wonder if she really means it or if she's just pretending. She's good at it after all.

Amanda nods in total agreement. I guess she takes, or seems to take, Cassandra's word for it. Then she spots me hovering next to them both, and I see her thoughts make the connection that we're together. 'Oh and who is this?' Amanda asks in a feigned casual tone.

She needs to discover what my connection is to Cassandra, whether I am important or not, before she decides how to officially greet me.

'This is Isabel,' Cassandra says before I have a chance to speak for myself. 'She's helping me out today.'

'Is that so,' Amanda says in a flat tone, bored by this revelation as she turns her back to me now and continues to rabbit on to Cassandra about someone or other.

My cheeks flush as I realise that Cassandra has just dismissed me as absolutely no one to her. She has refused to introduce me as Miles's girlfriend – soon to be fiancée, thank you very much – to a friend of hers.

I can't help but remain rooted to the spot in embarrassment. If I told Miles about this, would he believe me? Or would he just think I'm trying to drive a wedge between him and his mum?

I'm sure Cassandra is trying to make me feel like this on purpose, knowing that if I told Miles I would look petty and weak.

I can't give her that satisfaction.

Around my whirling thoughts, the conversation continues and Amanda finally says, 'I must dash, but lovely to see you, Cassandra, we'll catch up soon.' And with a last wave she's off into the crowd, ignoring me again as she rushes past.

Cassandra turns to me with a condescending smile. 'Always running into people around here, and most of them are awful gossips. You'll have to remember that.' Without another word about what just happened, she strides off and into the boutique florist that I can see just a few doors down.

I stand there, my eyes narrowing after her.

Everything about this woman is an act. And it's so obvious to everyone – except Miles.

I want to scream but I can't let her see that I'm ruffled. I know that once Miles announces our engagement later tonight she can't just ignore me anymore. I will have the advantage.

But one thing is clear.

Cassandra doesn't want me to become a permanent part of the King family. I'm sure that once she finds out about our engagement it will make her only more determined to split us apart.

I have to be on my guard, because she is more cunning than anyone would ever think. Plan B is becoming more attractive by the minute.

Resolute, I follow after her. But before I even go two steps I feel my phone buzz in my pocket. I bring it up to my face as I continue walking, but what I read stops me dead in my tracks:

WHO DO U THINK U ARE? GET OUT NOW.

It feels like a bucket of ice has been poured over me and my stomach hollows out.

Because a message like this could only mean one thing: someone has found out what I'm doing here. Is everything over before it's even really begun?

Chapter Fourteen

I need to get out of here. If I stay with Cassandra any longer she will see that something is up, and I have no doubt she'll report back to Miles that I was acting strange. I can't allow that to happen.

After Cassandra emerges from the florist, I tell her that I have a terrible headache and think it would be best if I made my way back to the house to lie down. I wrap my scarf around my throat even tighter.

She seems unsurprised. She must think that she's succeeded in upsetting me. If only she knew the real reason.

Cassandra tells me that the housekeeper will let me in if I ring the bell. Tonight, I tell myself, tonight I *will* get direct access through William.

I muddle a goodbye and I don't miss the smirk on her face. I try not to hyperventilate until I'm far around the corner and out of sight.

As she walks away a niggling thought runs through my mind – could she have sent the message? But surely she couldn't have sent it – we've been together the whole time. Although... she had just been walking ahead of me.

I force myself to slow down and read the message again.

WHO DO U THINK U ARE? GET OUT NOW.

I frown at my screen as I message back, holding my breath.

Who is this? Why are you messaging me?

I exhale as I press send. The message was sent on Facebook Messenger. So I click on the sender's profile, but it's totally private. Except for the name, which reads: *Truth S.* That's surely a message in itself that whoever sent this must know the truth about me... And if that person *is* Cassandra, then I'm toast. I pray that it's not.

As I wait for a response, I begin to wander through the pretty Chelsea streets. I struggle to admire the view, lost in my thoughts, terrified that I've been found out.

I don't have to wait too long before there's another ping, and I rush to read the message.

Just someone that knows this family. You should stay away.

I breathe a small sigh of relief. It can't be Cassandra – this person doesn't know my secret, but appears to be *warning* me about the Kings. A family with a lot of skeletons in their closet.

Why? What do you know?

I impatiently wait for a response, pacing around the streets before realising I've gone too far towards the river. Grey clouds hover in the sky and I keep moving, wrapping my scarf tighter and tighter.

Finally, another notification:

If you don't get out, you'll be next.

I freeze. My throat tightens.

I frantically type back.

The next what?

I try to slow my breathing. My whole world is shifting as I wait for another response.

Another buzz.

The next one C & W will take care of. The next girl to disappear.

Chapter Fifteen

A cold sweat starts down my spine.

All the while I've thought I was one step ahead of William and Cassandra King.

But unknowingly, maybe I have stepped into their biggest trap of all…

What do you mean? Tell me more.

I type back, my fingers fumbling over the letters. But there's no response this time, and so I pace for another ten minutes along the river. My phone remains deadly silent.

I try to hold my panic at bay and read through the messages over and over to take in every bit of detail. I sit down heavily on a bench facing towards the Thames and run my fingers through my hair in frustration. If this person thinks they're being helpful, all they've done is succeed in making me feel even more paranoid and on edge.

But the good news is that they must not know what I'm really doing here. They just think I'm an innocent new girlfriend if they're trying to warn me about Cassandra and William and what they might be capable of. I already *knew* that, I remind myself.

Right now, I just can't tell what *exactly* this anonymous person is referring to. As they've mentioned another girl, I can only assume it has something to do with Maya. I need to have a chat with Miles, as much as I really don't want to bring up his ex-girlfriend again.

He values honesty. I can't be honest about my own connection to his family, but perhaps sharing these strange anonymous messages would serve to bring us closer together.

Maybe this person had done me a massive favour by providing me with some new seeds of doubt that I could share with Miles. Helping to slowly build my case against his parents...

I decide to give him a call and muster up my panic of just moments before. He has to believe how shocked and scared I am.

He picks up on the third ring.

'Hey,' he says in hushed tones. 'Having a nice shopping day with Mum?' I almost forgot that had even happened since the mysterious messages.

'I'm sorry,' I wail. 'I had to leave – I freaked out when I received some awful anonymous messages! I got so scared. I didn't want her to see me like that, so I just made my excuses and left.'

'Whoa,' he says, his voice flooding with concern, 'slow down. Tell me what happened?'

Briefly, I outline the messages and what they said. I tell him how scared they made me feel, and why I wanted to let him know right away.

He doesn't say anything for a minute; I just hear his breath crackle down the line. I begin to worry that maybe it wasn't the best idea to tell him. I wish I could see his expression, but I know that if I'd waited until I was with him I would have lost the element of urgency.

He finally speaks. 'I think I know who sent them. Because I just received a message too, telling me to stay away from you.'

My mouth drops open.

There is only one person that would want to warn Miles away from me.

His mother.

Chapter Sixteen

I feel like I've just plummeted beneath the icy water of the river in front of me.

I've played this all wrong. How could Cassandra have figured it out so easily? I thought I'd been so careful...

It's too late to back out from this conversation now though, I've already told him what happened. So I proceed carefully, trying to buy myself time. 'What?' I stammer down the line. 'What do you mean?'

I pace back and forth in front of the bench before he says, 'Oh they just said something ridiculous about how you're only in it for the money...'

He trails off as I collapse onto the seat again. I should be outraged at what I've just heard but all I feel is relief. I haven't been found out. They haven't told Miles who I really am. It's just a 'normal' horrible message trying to put him off me by casting me as a gold-digger. It's not ideal, but it's much better than the alternative.

Of course I have to still *pretend* to be angry, so I say, 'That's disgusting.'

'I know,' he agrees. 'But like I said,' and his voice drops to a weary whisper, 'I think I know who has sent these. Can I come meet you? I have a bit of time before my next meeting.'

I tell him yes, of course. He can find my location thanks to Find My Friends. I'm quite relaxed with him knowing my location.

After all, it shows I have nothing to hide.

And I don't, when it comes to *that* sort of thing. The only secrets I'm going to be uncovering are in his parents' home.

I gaze up towards the ornate bridge in front of me. There is a hub of activity even though it is late afternoon. Everyone going about their daily business, oblivious to the hidden dramas going on all around.

I chew on my cheek and twirl my grandmother's necklace as I think through who might be sending both Miles and me messages like this to scare us off each other. There is still only one person that pops into my mind: Cassandra.

It would be a perfect way for her to anonymously seed doubt in both our minds about each other.

And especially clever for her to accuse me of just being with Miles for his money, after what happened with his last girlfriend.

I doubt Miles will think that it could be his darling mother, though.

After about fifteen minutes I notice a black cab pull up nearby. Miles jumps out and runs towards me. I'm struck by how strong and powerful he looks with his height and speed. He sweeps me up into a hug as soon as he reaches me.

'Hey – you okay?'

'Yes,' I whisper, squeezing him tight.

As I look up into his deep blue eyes, the only emotion I can read in them is worry. Worry for me. I haven't lost him. All is well.

He takes my hand as we sit back down on the bench and I turn to face him. 'So who do you think sent these messages?'

He looks away from me, towards the dark mass of the river. 'I think it's Maya.'

Genuine shock flashes through me. That is not the person I thought Miles was going to say.

'What? Why do you think that? I thought you said it was all a sad and ancient history?'

'Because,' he begins, and a dark look crosses his face, 'this isn't the first time I've received messages like this when I've started seeing someone.' He looks across at me almost apologetically.

I don't respond, letting that sink in. How many women *had* Miles dated before me? But does it really matter? It's me he's going to marry. What worries me more is why he didn't mention it.

'Okay, but why do you think it's her?'

'Well, this sort of thing only started after everything ended with her. Like I said this morning, I blocked all ways of contacting her. I just wanted her out of my life. But, when I started to casually date someone like six months or so after we ended, I received a very similar message. I tried to message the sender back, find out who it was. But total silence. They just kept sending me freaky things that suggested they knew where I'd been with her. Honestly, it was so weird that I ended things with the other girl. Though it was running its course anyway.'

'But it happened again after that?' I prompt.

'Yeah, but only one other time, maybe three years ago. And at first, I didn't receive anything, so I thought maybe the messages weren't going to happen again. But then suddenly they did. I guess it could have been when things became a bit more than just casual. I don't know...' He shakes his head, still confused about the whole thing.

'What did you do?' I ask urgently.

'At first, I just ignored it. But they became more and more specific – not about what we were up to, but just about her really. Potential red flags, I guess...' He trails off, lost in thought.

'Why didn't you go to the police? Surely they could have done something about it?'

He shakes his head. 'I really don't think they could do much. They were from different accounts each time but had a similar feel. And they weren't exactly threatening either. In a way, it was almost like strange advice. About the other woman, almost warning me off her. Like what I received today about you.' He looks at me for a response but I remain silent, pursing my lips.

I have to keep a neutral expression, but all the warning bells in my mind are going off. What would Maya have to gain by doing this? I can't believe it could be her. Because there's surely only one person that would want to keep him from dating or trusting someone again.

However, I nod in understanding. I want him to get to the end of his story, and I don't think suggesting the idea that it could be his mother would do me any favours right now. Not when he worships the ground she walks on.

As far as his assessment about the police, I think he's probably right. Yes, something like that is extremely weird, but what could the police do? Maybe Facebook could block these people, but I doubt these messages were troubling enough for them to warrant it.

'So why do you think it's Maya then?' I ask. I have to understand *why*.

'Weeelll,' he begins, ticking reasons off on his fingers. 'First off, it only started after everything had ended with her. And as you heard this morning, it's not like it ended *well* exactly. Second, each time there are always incredibly specific references that only someone really close to me, or,' he coughs, 'someone who *had* been really close to me would know.'

'Like what?' I prompt, interrupting his counting. His fingers hover in the air.

'Some of the first messages specifically reference some of the date spots I took the first girl to – which Maya knew were my favourite places. But,' he admits reluctantly, 'there wasn't so much of that with the last one, and I guess nothing like that so far with you.' He looks apologetic. 'They all had a similar tone though, and I don't know, thirdly and mainly, it's just very *her*. When we were together, she didn't want to actually have any public social profiles but had disguise accounts to still stay up to date with things.'

'Wasn't that a bit of a red flag?' I ask, frowning.

'I sort of mentioned this morning, but Maya wasn't close to her family. To the extent that she didn't want them to be able to find her. So I understood that – plus a lot of people don't want to be on socials personally, but still like to follow brands. I dunno, I didn't think anything of it at the time. Then,' I see his knuckles clench as he says, 'when I saw her with that other guy, I assumed that she had other accounts, maybe even other phones, to contact him with.' He finishes through gritted teeth. 'To me, this whole thing just feels like Maya all over.'

I nod, and look out at the mass of grey clouds looming overhead. They look exactly how I feel.

Everything that happened with Maya was almost ten years ago now... Plus, she basically got kicked out for stealing and cheating – why would she still be haunting his dating life? What did she have to gain from that?

Cassandra, on the other hand, definitely had something to gain.

And these specific things that Miles thinks only a person close to him would know – like his favourite date spots – Cassandra would have known as well, if her loving son was open with her. She definitely didn't want her darling boy with anyone else again – she'd made that abundantly clear to me last night when, away from his innocent eyes, she tried to scare me off the family.

And now these messages. It seems like more than a coincidence.

'Why didn't you tell me about this earlier when you told me about what happened between you and Maya?' I gently ask.

'I just really hoped it wouldn't happen again, Iz, and I didn't want to worry you.' He runs his hands through his hair and rubs his temple. 'God I'm such an idiot, I keep messing things up. I'm so sorry if I did the wrong thing. But seriously, that is *everything* now.'

I take his hand in mine. 'I understand.' And I do. He didn't want to worry me unnecessarily. But once again, I feel a small twinge of guilt. He is being honest with me, whereas I'm keeping so much back from him. To distract myself I ask, 'But what are we going to do now?'

'I don't think we *can* do anything about it.' When I wince at his words, he adds, 'Yes, it's horrible. But the best thing is if we just block the user and carry on with our lives. She can't do anything to us and is just continuing to play some bizarre game. And we don't want to be part of that, do we?'

How can I say anything but okay? The last thing I want is for him to suspect anything about me, or think the messages he received about me might actually have some truth in them.

So as he envelops me in his arms, I mentally cross my fingers behind my back. No way would I leave this alone. I *have* to find out who these anonymous messages are really from.

It's too much of a risk to me to have an unknown like this breathing down my neck. Watching my every move.

Because if this person is half as observant as it sounds like they are, then none of my secrets are safe. After all, they aren't only mine to keep.

I'm here for someone else too. And everything I'm doing is for them.

Chapter Seventeen

'Thank you, I knew you would understand,' he whispers in my ear, planting a kiss on my cheek.

Then he pulls back suddenly, a wide grin forming on his face. 'Now, to cheer you up, and show how you mean the world to me, I want to give you something…' He slides his hand into his pocket to bring out a large box.

My eyes open wide. He had promised that he had a ring for me back home, but I didn't think it would be produced this quickly.

'What's this?' I ask, my mouth dry.

He opens the box to reveal the largest diamond ring I have ever seen. Its sparkle is blinding, completely contrasting the misty day around us. There is one large and shiny central diamond, surrounded by two smaller diamonds on either side, which make the middle diamond look even larger. I can't help it when my mouth drops open.

I have never seen anything so spectacular.

And it's for me.

My throat tightens.

'I told you I had a ring back here. This was my great-grandmother's – on my mum's side. Mum has the ancestry, William is all "new money" as they say. Let's put it on!' He's almost trembling with excitement as he reaches for my hand.

I almost want to say no. Guilt runs through every fibre of my being.

I know I had said yes to this, before, in Australia. But we had been in our own world then. And I was *so sure* that my plan would work.

Now that I'm here, I'm scared. There are so many more factors at play and people out of my control than I thought.

I'm terrified of being found out.

And the more I gain here, the more I have to lose.

He takes my hand and slides it onto my ring finger.

'Look at that,' he says, and for a moment I glance down to see my finger consumed by the humungous diamond.

It's a perfect fit.

But it feels all wrong – happening like this. When there's so much that he doesn't know yet. My stomach twists as this physical gesture makes everything feel real. I hate that it feels like I'm tricking him.

'What do you think?' he adds, realising that I haven't said anything.

'It's...' I try to find the words, 'just so incredible,' I eventually manage through the growing block in my throat.

'Isn't it! I'm so happy that it fits! Shall we prepare for the family dinner and the big announcement tonight then?' He looks so excited. 'Keep it a big surprise for the parents.' He sounds thrilled at the prospect.

'Wait,' I say, panic rising. 'I just assumed that you had asked your mum for the ring? She still doesn't know anything?'

'No, not at all. I always knew this was meant for me. So I did some sneaking of my own. This jewel has your name on it though.' But his brow furrows as he realises the unwitting reminder of what happened with Maya.

I take his hand to change the direction of his thoughts and say, 'I love it… I just hope your parents will too…'

'Oh, they will. Especially because…' and he lowers his voice to whisper to me in a conspiratorial way, 'we can also give them the biggest announcement of all! Don't you think?'

I don't respond for a moment as a tight smile crosses my face and an even greater sense of unease hits me.

Oh no. Not the other announcement.

I don't think I'm ready *quite* yet.

But it was the thing that kicked this all off, so how can I say no?

'Maybe… we could wait to tell them a bit later? After the engagement has settled in a bit. We don't want to overwhelm them, do we?'

He considers my words and then he nods. 'Maybe you're right,' he admits with reluctance. 'But we'll tell them our plans soon?' he asks with an undeniable gleam of hope in his eyes.

'Yes, of course,' I say as brightly as I can muster and distract him with a kiss.

'Okay, great.' He pulls away slowly. 'I'm so sorry Iz, but I'm going to have to get back to the office. Will you be okay now for the rest of the afternoon? I'll try to get back as soon as I can.'

'Absolutely.' I manage another smile back. I have this beautiful ring and incredible man. I should feel happy.

My wonderful, sweet and trusting Miles stands up with a whoosh as he spots the bright yellow light of a taxi coming down the road.

'See you later, I love you!' he cries as he dashes out, and with a final wave hops inside.

I try to whisper the words back as I wave goodbye.

There's a huge part of me that really does mean it.

But somehow, those words have begun to feel a little empty.

The little pieces of myself that I've had to hide are weighing down on me.

And now with the added threat of these anonymous messages I'm starting to feel out of my depth.

I whip out my phone and send a message to the one person that I think can help me.

The person who helped me set this whole plan in motion.

Chapter Eighteen

We sit in the Kings' ornate dining room. It glows with tapered candles and ethereal light as monochrome tapestries and sombre portraits cover the walls.

Soft.

Delicate.

Totally eerie.

After Miles had left me and I sent my message for help, I had made my way slowly back to the house.

My phone had remained silent as I'd walked, even as I'd wished for a reply.

It had even made me forget about the stupid fingerprint-activated home entry system. I was extremely embarrassed when the housekeeper – Maria, I think, though we'd never been officially introduced – had to answer the door for me. I'd thanked her profusely and sworn I'd get access tonight.

Because I wouldn't be leaving the house again until I did.

By the time the dinner hour rolled around, I still hadn't heard anything at all from the person that I so desperately needed to talk to.

Why are they ignoring me?

I gaze across the table, trying to distract myself.

Cassandra is in yet another expertly tailored, creamy white suit. Her hair is styled in a smooth and sleek bob and in this soft light, I can't see a single wrinkle on her flawless face. She could be mistaken as being in her late thirties, not the mid-fifties that she is.

The more I think about it, the more I notice that we perhaps look alike – if I also had a perfect haircut, designer clothes and glowing skin, of course. But instead my long, naturally wavy blonde hair is a bit more dishevelled and sun-bleached. My skin is definitely not flawless, covered in freckles from the sun. And even if she didn't wear heels all the time, she'd still tower over my petite build.

Cassandra is whispering to the housekeeper and William is glued to his phone, intently typing a message.

'So,' Miles ventures, breaking the silence. 'Mum, how was your day? Did you and Iz have a nice time out?'

Cassandra whips her head up away from her discussion like she's been stung. She looks put out, and glances over at me, trying to read if it's a trick question. It's as though she is trying to figure out whether I have told Miles anything that might suggest it had *not* been a nice day. Or maybe she's trying to assess how we've been affected by the horrible messages that she most likely sent...

She nods Maria away with an imperious wave, and I feel deeply uncomfortable as she scurries from the room. This silent and integral part of the day-to-day running of the King life just appears and disappears as if on command. It's a world I don't think I'll ever understand.

When she closes the door behind her, Cassandra smiles over at Miles and responds in a silky voice. 'Why of course we did, darling. Isabel was a delightful helper to me, but she did seem to suffer a bit from that horrible jetlag and had to head home. I just hope I didn't wear you out too much, dear?' she asks in her sweetest voice as she turns towards me to showcase her 'concern'. And no doubt flip the discussion so I will have to answer and admit my exhaustion.

After such a response in front of the whole family, I have to play her game.

'Not at all.' I try to grin back, though it probably comes out as more of a grimace.

'Wonderful,' she responds. 'Now William,' she snaps, flicking her laser gaze towards him. 'Will you put down that phone so we can enjoy our first proper dinner together with our son and Isabel?'

William is still absorbed by whatever is happening on his screen. It sounds as though she's telling off a teenager, not her own husband, and I cringe. Both at that and also the fact that she's avoided yet again saying that I am Miles's girlfriend.

William snaps his head up and, obviously used to this, responds in his most cheery, singsong tone. 'Of course, dear.' He waves the phone in her face with an accompanying eye roll before replacing it in his pocket. 'You have my *full* attention.' I watch as he turns the force of his electric blue eyes on to Cassandra. She looks ruffled.

'So Isabel,' Cassandra chirps out a little too loudly, turning back towards me as she searches for a change of subject. 'Tell us a bit more about yourself and your family. I feel we hardly *know* you.' She exaggerates the 'know', as though to suggest that she does not know me at all.

She brings her hands up to cup her chin as her intense stare bores into mine. Her bracelet jangles down her arm and I barely register her words as I stare at the charms more closely: a star… and a heart… and is that a…? But before I can be sure of what I just saw, she throws her arms down again.

'Oh, Mum, please,' Miles interrupts, glancing sideways at me. 'Please don't put Izzy on the spot like that. And you know about her family.' He almost stage whispers towards her.

'Yes, darling,' Cassandra says through gritted teeth. 'But I still think that's a perfectly normal question to ask, don't you think so, dear?' She turns to face me. 'We're all just getting to know each other here, aren't we?' she tries to make it sound sweet but I can sense a warning in her tone.

'Yes, we all just want to get to know *each other*,' I echo, emphasising the last bit so she understands that I also mean that should be reciprocal. Hinting at the fact that there must be *lots* they've never told me.

Of course I'm certain I've already uncovered their biggest secret. And after these messages today, I'm sure there are more to uncover. I just wish I could catch another glance of that bracelet.

'There's not that much to tell really,' I say with a shrug. 'I grew up with my grandparents in Australia, up the coast of New South Wales in a small town, and then went to university in the big city when I got the chance. Then I've been working in Sydney ever since. And, well, the rest is history,' I finish, smiling up at Miles.

Cassandra nods thoughtfully in response as she takes a sip of her blood-red wine. I manage to get another close glance at her wrist. And it's just what I thought: a small charm in the shape of a key.

I'm so lost in my thoughts that I almost miss Cassandra's next words. 'I was so sad to hear that your parents died when you were so young.' She surprises me with the sensitivity in her voice. But then she continues, 'It must have been so hard on you not having a *normal* family...'

Clearly I do not fit into the 'correct' mould for Cassandra King: I come from somewhere too different, too *abnormal* for her. My childhood might be irregular for her, but I was so lucky in comparison to many others.

Neither Miles nor William seem to pick up on the slight, but I take it for what it is and pocket it away for later. I'm not going to give her the satisfaction of proving her point that I suffered because of what happened to me. And besides, I'll play my trump card soon enough.

Then William jumps into the conversation. 'Ah Cass, what even is a "normal family"? Your father died when you were young too. And then it was just you and your mother left.'

Cassandra whips her head to her left with such force I'm surprised it hasn't rolled right off. And if looks could kill, then William King should be dead right now.

William just shrugs and takes a sip of his wine before continuing, 'Don't look at me like that, when you know it's true. And it sure seems like you and Isabel could have a lot more in common than might meet the eye... I thought this was a time for sharing, after all?' Then he gives me a wink.

I'm frozen in shock. I had no idea that Cassandra also lost her father so young. Miles had just said his grandparents had passed away – and I'd assumed from old age. Serves me right for not caring to ask anything more. Maybe Cassandra and I could find some common ground... I try to catch her gaze but she stubbornly refuses to look my way. I guess some people just don't like to remember. I can understand that more than most.

As the awkward silence continues to grow in the room, Miles decides now is the time to say, 'So yes, that's why it's so special that we can finally provide Iz with a close family of her own.'

'What do you mean?' Cassandra shoots across to Miles. William remains seated on my right-hand side, looking down at his wine glass as he swirls it around, a smile playing on his lips.

His relaxed and amused expression distracts me as tension continues to build in the room. I haven't had the chance to spend much time with him yet, but every inch of him appears to be calm and collected. It's intoxicating, and I can see how he's become so successful. It's a sign to be even more careful around him.

'We have some exciting news.' Miles announces as he tries to reach across for my hand. This table is far too large for that, so instead he jumps up to rush over to me, grabbing my hand to wave it in the air for all to see. There, dangling on my finger, is the large King family diamond ring. 'Izzy and I are engaged!'

The small hint that had just been revealed about Cassandra's childhood is now forgotten entirely as mayhem descends on the room.

'Wha—' Cassandra begins, her mouth falling open in shock. This is the first time I've seen her lose her composure and I have to admit, after how she's been treating me, it feels glorious.

But then I glance over to William and I see his smile has vanished. It's like a wall of ice has surrounded us. This silent rage scares me.

Miles doesn't seem to notice his father's expression and ploughs on regardless. 'And that's not all...!' He stands to move behind me and rest his strong hands on my shoulders, as though to signify our unified front.

'We're going to be starting a family of our own. Izzy is pregnant!'

Chapter Nineteen

For a moment I panic before letting my shoulders relax in relief. Everything is finally out in the open. Even though this is what I'd wanted Miles to hold off revealing until a better time, he must have been too excited to wait. I swivel round to glance up at him and he is beaming from ear to ear.

Maybe that's just how it needed to be. He's ecstatic about the reveal. And that's a good thing for his parents to see.

Even so, I itch to check my phone for the message I've been waiting for. A message that might help me handle what will come next.

Because with that final blow, the stakes have become higher than they ever were. A baby – now that changes everything.

My stomach clenches as I take in the thunderous expressions on Cassandra and William's faces.

'What...' Cassandra manages to stammer, her eyes wide. Her face has gone as white as the jacket she's wearing. William, on the other hand, looks like he's turning redder and redder. I can practically see the steam about to explode from his ears.

The door to the dining room opens with a deafening click and Maria appears with an immaculate tray laden with steaming white porcelain bowls.

'Maria,' William barks, though it comes out almost like a growl. She jumps back in fright, almost dropping all the beautiful food on the ground. 'Leave us for a minute,' he says more calmly. 'I'll call you when we're ready.' She nods and scurries out of the room. I wish I could go with her. I thought I'd be able to handle it, but I have to admit I'm starting to feel a little terrified of their wrath – I know what they're truly capable of.

I thought that maybe they'd be at least a bit supportive of their son's happiness. But their stony faces say otherwise.

'What do you mean you're engaged?' William is the first to speak, firing the question straight at Miles, who has begun to squeeze my shoulders even tighter. At least he's sticking by me under his parents' scrutiny. And that's not a small achievement.

'Exactly that,' Miles says in an ironic tone. He must be disappointed by their response.

'And a baby?' William shoots back. 'What about King & Co.? I thought you'd come back to London to pull up your socks and start properly working for the business. Not disappear back off to Australia the first chance you get.'

William is purposefully avoiding my eyes, but his accusation is not lost on me. He thinks we will want to go back to Australia, disappear into our own family life there. But we've got a different plan. And he doesn't know there's no chance I'm joining *his* toxic definition of 'family'.

Miles sighs in exasperation, his voice tight as he says, 'Don't worry Dad; we're not going anywhere. I will be here for the business. I've already started looking at homes for us nearby. This is what I meant when I said Izzy would be able to join *our* family.'

I try to ignore these words. By the time I'm done, this will absolutely not be what happens. I keep my face neutral. I don't want to give anything away, not when some of my plans are starting to click into place.

I'm certain that's the direction things are going in when I see William's expression change from a storm cloud to a sunny day. 'Oh I see,' he begins. 'In that case, my dear girl,' he looks straight at me, his frozen blue eyes boring into mine, 'welcome to the *family*.'

I clench my napkin under the table.

Stay calm. This is what I'd wanted: for him to accept me. Then why does an involuntary shiver go down my spine? Convincing him has been too easy.

He raises his glass first towards Miles and me, and then across at Cassandra. I can't shake my next feeling that this gesture towards her is in mockery. As though he's won somehow out of this. And she's lost.

I frown but I finally turn to face her: my now official future mother-in-law. Her face is utterly frozen, as though she'd had far too much Botox at her last session. But the colour has started to return, leaving two pink spots high up on her cheeks.

'Mum, are you okay?' Miles asks in a calm voice. He's now moved to the left-hand side of my chair, still towering above us all. I glance at him out of the corner of my eye and I see that his brow has furrowed in concern.

I dig my nails into my palms. Oh come *on* – this is such an act from her.

'Yes, yes.' She waves a hand as if to pretend like it's nothing. She wants to still seem calm and in control. Even though this is one thing she completely cannot control. 'I'm just surprised... It all seems very...' She pauses, flustered and trying to find the right word. 'Sudden.'

'Not to us,' Miles continues confidently. 'When we found out Izzy was pregnant, it just seemed like the right thing to do.' He beams down at me and I try to smile back.

'Well,' Cassandra says, trying to fix one of her own onto her face, 'it's the start of a new chapter in our family then.'

I'm stunned by her calm. I really thought this would get more of a reaction from her, from both of them really. And that might have had the benefit of showing Miles exactly the conniving and shallow monsters his parents really are. No such luck though.

They are both being extremely understanding. It unnerves me.

Maybe I'm not 'winning' as easily as I thought.

Miles, as always, is oblivious. 'Exactly,' he says, exhaling in relief.

'And I'm to be a grandmother... goodness!' Cassandra exclaims, this time with what seems like more of a genuine smile. I want to wipe it straight off. There's no way she's getting her hands on any child of mine.

'Now then,' William chips in. 'Let's celebrate with some champagne.'

He rises up to call for Maria, and Miles walks over to resume his seat. Cassandra takes the opportunity to stand up and walk around the table to say to me, in a tone dripping with warning, 'Congratulations, *dear...*'

I stand up and she takes my hand in a seeming show of affection. She pulls me in to give me a kiss on either cheek. But I don't miss the hard squeeze she gives me as she whispers, 'Remember, *I'm* his mother. Always.'

She hasn't changed her tune at all then. She just doesn't want Miles to overhear. And even though we might have one tiny thing in common, both having had losses in our childhoods, she obviously does not care about that fact at all. So neither will I.

I keep a pleasant smile plastered on my face – the lines have now been officially drawn. And as I stare into that unflinching gaze, I see a hunger in there. One I know well. I know deep down what it's driven by. A total all-consuming love that you would do anything for.

I have to stay one step ahead.

Or otherwise, if Cassandra finds out my real plan, she will leave no stone unturned to destroy me.

Chapter Twenty

Cassandra and William insisted that we celebrate and so we all continued with the meal. In the great British way, all our differences appeared to be pushed to one side as we at last toasted the news and finally ate.

Dinner was a delicious truffle risotto, but I didn't have much of an appetite as I kept catching Cassandra staring at me every time I looked up from my plate. She had an unreadable expression, which only made me feel more uneasy. She wasn't staring daggers at me, but she'd made her feelings abundantly clear.

Miles and William seemed to have moved on from the announcement, as they noisily discussed work over the top of our silent stare-off. It confuses me how one moment Miles was at his father's throat, and the next he was desperately trying to impress him. I guess that was the nature of some father–son relationships that I would never understand.

'So,' Cassandra begins once we have moved on to a dessert course of a delicate chocolate praline torte. Miles and William are momentarily distracted from their work conversation by their haste to finish their food first. Even eating is a competition between them.

Cassandra has not touched hers, but sips on the fresh mint tea she requested from Maria. I look up from the small bite I had been taking. It is delicious but I am struggling to find any sort of appetite.

'Do you think you'll have the wedding here or back in Australia?' Cassandra asks.

I freeze, feeling like a deer caught in the headlights. Miles is chewing on a large piece of his torte, so I have no choice but to answer for us. 'We haven't really discussed anything in too much detail yet…' I trail off.

'Oh,' Cassandra replies without missing a beat, 'so you have no set plans?' She arches an eyebrow.

'No,' I shake my head, blushing at how little I have to work with. 'But probably the UK, something low key and simple. It's not like I have a large family to bring along…' I let the end of my sentence hang open in the air.

'It's all happened so recently, Mum,' Miles now mumbles through a large mouthful of chocolate, trying to rescue me. 'We don't really want a big fuss.' I'm relieved at Miles saying so as I see Cassandra's triumphant expression fall. The first time he's disagreed with her for me. That's definitely a win.

'Why don't I help you out?' she offers as a compromise. 'I know everyone and everything over here. You'll be in *very* safe hands.'

'Oh no,' I begin, 'I don't want you to go to any trouble.' And I wouldn't trust her help.

'None at all, my dear. I *insist*.'

'Mum, that would be amazing!' Miles jumps in. He turns to me, a slight speck of chocolate on his cheek. 'Go on, Iz, Mum does know everybody and loves organising events. I know you don't enjoy this sort of thing. Plus, you shouldn't put yourself under too much strain right now. She will be a lifesaver.'

Miles looks across the table at me, his eyes huge and earnest. They're practically begging me to let his mum be involved.

If I say no that would be suspicious. So all I can do is nod back. Slowly, slowly. I must be patient.

'Brilliant, my two girls sorting things out.'

I shudder at his grouping of us together. He doesn't notice.

'It's settled then,' Cassandra exclaims. 'I shall begin making arrangements tomorrow.' She says it at me, not to Miles. I begin to wonder what sort of plans she has for me and why she's suddenly so happy about this after what she said to me before. It certainly didn't sound like she'd want to help with planning a wedding.

She and Miles fall into excited conversation, thick as thieves still. William and I remain silent, letting them babble on. I'm deeply suspicious of Cassandra's act in front of her son.

William has barely said a word. Just stared across at me and listened to the conversation going on around intently. At last

I force myself to meet his eye. And I'm shocked by what I see there.

Because it's not anger, or disappointment, or even curiosity.

No, it's total delight.

And then he *winks* at me.

Like he has a secret and he's letting me in on it. Alarm bells start to ring in my head.

I'm surprised by what comes out of his mouth next. 'Isabel,' he drawls. 'Miles mentioned getting you access to our systems. Now that you're going to be part of the family, why don't we get you set up?'

I'm about to reply when I see Cassandra's head flick up yet again at William's words. She is *always* listening.

'Oh,' she says, in a hurry to get her thoughts in first. 'You don't need to do that right this second do you, darling?' She shoots a look at her husband. A silent warning.

I immediately say brightly to William, 'If you have time to set me up now, that would be great!'

Cassandra's eyes narrow. 'But we don't want to break up the party, do we?' She gestures around the ornate room. Our plates are empty on the table, just the last drops of wine in the glasses.

'Don't worry, Mum,' Miles says with a shrug. 'It would be good for Izzy to get set up. Why don't we have a drink in the sitting room and they can join us after?'

Cassandra frowns once more. This is working out fantastically.

'Buuut,' she says through gritted teeth, 'the master system is in the library now.'

'Oh Cassandra, come on,' William says, pushing his chair back and getting to his feet regardless of his wife's protests. 'We'll be there for a few minutes and I *promise* we won't venture through the secret bookshelf in the library to your private study. Goodness, someone will think that you're hiding something in there!'

I don't miss her eyes narrow behind him. This must be some sort of game they're playing.

Cassandra breezes past it, tucking a glossy lock of hair behind one ear and rising to her feet too. 'Fine, we'll see you shortly then. Let's go, Miles.'

Miles shoots an apologetic look across at me, as though to say sorry about their bickering.

William strides towards the door faster than his wife, as if he's racing her. It could almost be comical – but instead of barging through as I thought he was going to do, he says in a strong, gallant voice as he pulls open the door, 'After you, darling.'

She rolls her eyes at him as she walks through, but a small smile escapes her. And I realise that as well as how to rile her, William knows just the sort of thing to appease her too.

William turns to me next. 'And you, Isabel – ladies first, after all!'

I walk through slowly and spy Cassandra disappearing somewhere around the corner, likely back round to the grand staircase. I hover until William walks through the door and gestures for me to follow.

'I'll see you soon, Iz,' Miles says, pecking me on the cheek before striding ahead to catch his mum.

He must sense she's in a mood after this, and like a good son, he is going to comfort her. I wish he was staying with me. I haven't been on my own with William since this morning in the kitchen and I feel uneasy at the thought after how Miles had reacted. But perhaps he's okay with me being alone with his father now after our announcement.

William beckons me into the next room, which takes us back through the sitting room and straight across to the door I spied this morning. The one that was locked.

We don't speak. There is only the sound of our footsteps as they reverberate along the polished wooden floor – it's so shiny I have to be careful not to fall over.

He places his index finger on the keypad for a fraction of a second. In the silence I hear a soft click, and then he slides open the panelled door.

'Here we are then, Isabel,' his voice booms out as he waves an outstretched arm towards the open gap. 'The room I'm sure you've been *dying* to see.'

My mouth goes dry at his choice of words. Just a coincidence, or a threat?

I keep my cool and walk in briskly. I decide to take control of the conversation. This is just to get me access, nothing more. Then I'll be able to get away from this man.

Even if I didn't already know that he was dangerous, I would have picked it up from his body language. As he swaggers into the room, confidence drips off him, and there's a disarming ease that makes me almost want to trust him. *Almost.*

I say calmly back, 'Thank you for doing this.'

'No trouble at all, and it's nice to spend a bit of time together, the two of us.' He moves closer towards me and a spider-like sensation crawls up my back.

I turn around, pretending to admire the room but really to escape his intense gaze for just a moment.

Three walls of unending mahogany bookshelves meet me. The room could have had a cosy feel, but instead the intensity of the rich wood and dark spines cloaks the room in a more ominous shadow.

My eyes take a second to adjust, as it's so much darker than the rooms outside. And when I turn around I understand why. William has closed the door.

He grins at me now, as though I'm a rabbit that's just been successfully lured into his lair.

Chapter Twenty-One

'Now,' he says, cocking to his head to one side. His voice is as thick and slow as dripping honey. 'Before we get you set up, I think we should have a chat, and you tell me exactly why you want to marry my son.' His face is serious, and I can't think of anything to say to this announcement.

'Don't be worried,' he adds with a glimmer in his eye as he takes another step towards me. 'It's just, and it's nothing against *you*, but sometimes I find it a bit hard to trust.'

I nod slowly, telling myself that it's likely something to do with everything that went on with Maya. I must pretend like I am just a normal, love-struck girl with nothing to hide. If I slip up, it will be the end of Miles and me, the end of everything I've built.

'Of course, I understand. Our news must have been a bit of a shock to you both. But,' I step towards him, ignoring my urge to run, 'I love your son very much. And I will do *anything* to make him happy.' That at least is true.

He crosses his arms and if at all possible, his blue eyes focus even more intently onto mine, as though he is a human lie detector and he's trying to read the truth.

It seems to have pleased him enough because he relaxes his arms away from his chest.

'Yes, I can see that,' he muses, 'which is good. Miles needs that, someone fierce, someone to show him the way. And,' he adds with an actual twinkle in his eye, 'this will keep Cassandra quite busy.'

'What do you mean by that?'

He raises his brows at my question and lowers his voice as though to bring me in on a secret. 'Oh, only that I think sometimes she doesn't have *quite* enough to do. You see, sometimes she can get a tiny bit paranoid. *But* planning your wedding and a baby on the way – now that's just wonderful news,' he says with a wink, as though we're now co-conspirators. It makes me uncomfortable to realise that our announcements must suit a hidden agenda of William's – that somehow, it helps keep Cassandra busy, which he appears to want.

I push my discomfort away. At least this means he doesn't see the true danger in me; I'm only a useful distraction for the rest of his family. And that suits me just fine.

'I think we'll have a lot to keep us occupied,' I agree.

'And that is perfect,' he almost purrs. 'Now, let's get you set up.' He reaches the back corner of the room in a few steps, and then pulls on a book that opens up a shelf to reveal a control panel. Too quick for me to catch which book though. Is each wall hiding something?

He turns around to catch my expression of amazement. 'Pretty cool, hey,' he says, a note of pride in his tone. People like William can never resist a boast.

But I have to agree. It is a cool set up.

'Are all of these bookshelves secret panels or doors?' I ask.

He chuckles to himself as he wakes up the system. 'Ha, you must think this is like something out of James Bond. But no, it's just this one, hiding the master control panel – and there's another one that goes into Cassandra's study. She came up with it; she just loved the idea of having her own private space hidden behind a bookshelf. And then this main library space would be mine.' He shrugs. 'I was fine to go along with it if it made her happy, but it's a little much if you ask me.' For a second, I almost think that he's said something sensible. But then he winks at me again and the moment is ruined.

'It is quite elaborate,' I manage.

'Happy wife, happy life, which Miles will soon learn!' It's in moments like these that I see the charmer in him come to light. 'Right, come on over and let's get you set up.'

I walk towards him, around the deep red sofas that face each other in the centre of the room, so plush that I think if I sat in them, I'd never be able to get up.

I brace myself. I'll have to stand right next to William. I feel tiny and insignificant as his bulk looms over me. The room seems to press even closer, the shadows wrapping around, as he leans towards me to whisper in my ear, 'Your finger please, Isabel.'

It feels like someone has run their nail down a chalkboard and I hold in my automatic reflex to flee.

Standing my ground, I offer him my right index finger. I can sense that he's looking down at me, daring me to look up into his eyes. He's so close I can smell his aftershave, a pure, unadulterated tobacco and leather scent. It leaves a bitter taste in my mouth.

I refuse to do as he's trying to silently demand. Instead I focus on moving my finger towards the control panel.

He sighs into my ear. As though he knows I've refused to engage in his little power game. *How boring*, I can almost hear his mind whirring.

He grabs my finger, just as I'm about to reach the pad. And the suddenness makes me blanch and look up. At this he grins, finally winning some little bet he had with himself.

'Don't worry, Isabel, dear, it won't hurt.' He chuckles and it's all I can do to stop from hurling myself across to the other side of the room.

I let him push my finger forward, forcefully onto the pad. I see it register, glow almost, as it takes in my details. And then it stops. I remove my finger, trying not to rip it from William's grasp.

He lets go reluctantly, and I take a slow step back, trying not to show that I am bothered in the slightest.

If only that were true. I rub my hands down the side of my jeans, trying to cool some of the clamminess in my palms.

'Great, thank you, William,' I say. 'So is that me all set up on the system now then?' I add without skipping a beat.

He presses a few buttons. 'Yes, indeed.' He turns to face me, a Cheshire cat smile creeping across his lips. 'We're all set, lovely Isabel, and *thank you*.'

'For what?' I shake my head confused. He's done me the favour, not the other way around. Right?

'For your trust, of course.' He waggles his eyebrows. 'After all, I have your fingerprints now.'

Chapter Twenty-Two

I let out a tinkling laugh and fan my hair over my shoulder. 'Oh William, you're so funny.' My stomach has plummeted at his words, but I have to make him think I don't have anything to hide.

He smirks back. He just enjoys the feeling of being in control. And yes, he's extremely successful, but he's no codebreaker. He wouldn't have any need of my fingerprints and he surely couldn't use them to find out who I really am. I hope.

'And so clever,' I go on in my sweetest voice, 'to figure this system all out. I'm so terrible at anything technical... how does it all work?'

'Oh well,' he puffs his chest out at my compliment, 'if you know what you're doing it's not that hard.'

'I suppose so, but it still seems very complicated. How did Cassandra do it?' I ask all innocence.

'Oh dear.' He guffaws as though I've made some sort of joke. 'Cassandra could never figure out something like this.'

'But doesn't she have her own access to her separate study?' I wonder out loud, trying to stop my voice from sounding too curious.

'Oh yes, but that's just by pulling the spine on her favourite book.' He points towards the other untapped bookshelf with its rows and rows of identical tomes. 'She insisted on that. I guess she was being whimsical. But which one that is – I couldn't even tell you myself, dear Isabel.

Is that awful?' he asks, looping an arm casually over my shoulder. I try hard not to cringe at his touch. 'But I like to let her have a bit of peace. Now, let's go and find your fiancé or he'll think I've kidnapped you.'

I laugh at his words but I'm certain it sounds more like a strangled choke. As William leads me out of the room, I risk a glance back at the voluminous shelves, my eyes trained on the one that apparently hides Cassandra's study. Her secrets are waiting behind those walls.

My mind flashes to the little key I saw on her charm bracelet.

I'm so close to my goal I can almost touch it. And I have to soon – because my time is running out.

William and I find Miles and Cassandra upstairs talking in hushed tones over another glass of wine. They look so cosy huddled in front of the roaring fireplace as we enter what the Kings call the 'upstairs drawing room'.

I wonder what Cassandra has been whispering to Miles about me: it feels like we are intruding as I take in their silhouettes framing yet another opulent room. It must be the largest and most ornate I've been in so far. Everything is perfectly placed, from the elegant sofas in front of the fire to the heavy curtains that shut out the streetlights beyond. A large marble chess table stands in the very centre of the room with two plush chairs on either side of its clawed feet.

William coughs and they both turn, two deer caught in the headlights of an incoming collision.

Miles jumps up and rushes over to me, as the expression on Cassandra's face turns glacial. Instead of inviting us in for a drink, Miles says that we are both exhausted from the jetlag.

Thank goodness. She hasn't been able to snatch my Miles away. In fact, right now, it seems like he even wants to escape.

It might just be the light but I swear Cassandra has a tinge of pink to her high cheekbones and William's expression transforms into a frown. This isn't what he had in mind either.

Before I have a chance to speak, Miles has grabbed my hand and pulled me from the room, closing the door behind us with a snap.

Low voices begin to murmur from within, and I swear I hear one get louder the further we walk away.

'Are you okay?' Even though we've got this entire palace to ourselves, his voice still comes out in a whisper, as though the walls have ears.

I glance around, paranoid.

'Yes, fine,' I respond, matching his hushed tone.

His shoulders sag next to me as we walk. 'Good...'

I open my mouth to ask him why he thought I might *not* have been okay, when he stops and opens the door next to us.

This house is so huge that I hadn't realised we were already back at our bedroom.

I step inside, worry etched in the corner of my mind. He's acting strangely, like he is on edge after spending so much time with his mother. Maybe she actually had said something to put him off me?

But as soon as he closes the door he sweeps me into the biggest hug and kisses me on the forehead. Back to being *my* Miles.

'I missed you,' he whispers into my ear.

I twist my head up to look him in the eyes as our arms wrap around each other tighter. 'But I didn't go anywhere,' I say with a laugh.

'I didn't like not being by your side. But I felt like I had to do some damage control with Mother.' He winces, as though at the memory.

'Why? I thought she was happy for us?' Maybe she had made her true feelings known to Miles.

'Well...' He weighs up his words. 'I know what she's like. She wants the best for me,' he adds hastily, seeing the frown that's crept across my face. 'But she's just protective is all.'

He doesn't elaborate, so I just nod, keeping my thoughts quiet for now.

'But Dad was all fine, he gave you access?' he asks, seemingly keen to change the subject. He releases me to play with a strand of hair that's escaped over my shoulder.

'Oh yes,' I say, and hold up my index finger. 'This now has all the access.'

Miles grins, but I see a shadow of something pass across his eyes. I want to know what it is. 'Why?' I ask, trying to read his expression.

'Sometimes he can be a bit... protective too. Maybe even aggressive, is all.' His frown deepens further, likely at some memory.

'What do you mea—'

He plants a kiss on my lips, silencing whatever words I was about to speak.

'Let's not talk about them.' His voice sounds weary.

I see the look on his face. This isn't the time to press him. He's deep in thought, like he has the weight of the world on his shoulders.

Something tonight has brought back some bad memories. Memories that he doesn't want to share with me just yet.

Patience. I must be patient. For him to open up to me and trust me completely. I will scare him off if I question him too much. Any sign of weakness or hesitancy from him and I know Cassandra will exploit it.

'Of course, thank you for telling them.' And I mean it.

The shadows in his eyes evaporate at those words. I've said the right thing.

'You're my world, Iz. We'll get through everything together. No one can tear us and our new family apart.'

He begins to kiss me more passionately, pulling me close to him. And so I let myself fall in deep, trying not to think, at least for now, about ever being torn apart. Even though I know that's exactly what I'm up against.

Chapter Twenty-Three

That night, I barely sleep. I toss and turn, continually waking Miles up. By the third time, I am entangled in the sheets, almost suffocating. So when I see that it's six in the morning, I cannot take this sense of dread anymore. I have to get out of bed and clear my head.

Plus, at last I'd seen on my phone screen the message I'd been waiting all night to receive. I get out of bed as quietly as I can. I have to read this alone.

I don't want to accidentally run into William in the kitchen again, so I need to get out of the house with the utmost stealth. I try not to wake Miles, who is happily sleeping away, and change without making a sound in the enormous en-suite bathroom. I splash my face with cold water a few times to chase the remnants of any nightmares away.

Slipping out and down the corridors, I'm thankful that I'll be able to get in and out easily. But when I reach the bottom of the stairs, with the front door facing me, I realise I have no idea where the exit pad is.

I try the handle, remembering that Miles had said that the lock on the inside of the door normally wasn't enabled. But nothing happens. The door remains frozen shut. My stomach sinks. Why have William and Cassandra locked us all in? Is it just because I'm here?

I frantically begin peering around in the gloomy light of the rising dawn, fumbling along the wall next to the door for the finger pad, or even a light switch.

Then I hear a small cough from the corner of the room. I jump back and swivel to see the quiet housekeeper from last night, Maria. At least it's not William or worse, Cassandra.

She nods as she walks over to me, barely making a sound as she treads across the tiles. She must be able to sense my palpable relief.

'Maria, right?' I whisper. Everyone else is spread far and wide throughout the house, but I wouldn't put it past Cassandra to have supersonic hearing as well. 'It's nice to meet you. How are you?' I ask. 'I was just trying to get out for a walk…' I gesture at the still shut door. 'But I'm not sure how to leave?' I finish, aware of how pathetic it sounds.

'I'm fine thank you, Miss Isabel.' She bows respectfully towards me as she comes to a stop.

'Oh there's no need for that, I'm just Izzy.'

'You're going to be part of the King family now, no?'

I nod slowly in response.

'So, you will be Miss Isabel to me then. Mrs King insists,' she adds curtly. I can't tell if there's a hint of resentment in her voice, or if I am being hyper-sensitive because I feel uncomfortable.

'Okay,' I say uncertainly. 'So, umm, do you think you could tell me where the opening is please?'

'Of course, Miss Isabel.' She walks purposefully to a small shelf I hadn't noticed further along the wall. She crouches over and as if by magic I hear a click sound coming from the door in front of me.

'You may leave now.' I raise an eyebrow at her words. It appears that all my comings and goings in this house are being closely monitored. I can't help but wonder whose side is she on.

When I push on the handle, the door opens and the hazy light of the streetlamps filter through. With the fresh air on my face, it feels like I can finally breathe again.

'Where is the access panel on the other side of the door?' I ask, but when I turn back I see that Maria has already disappeared. I shake my head. She is as much a part of this house and family as anyone else – maybe even more so as she is in control of all the little details. I would have to get to know her better.

I wrap my oversized scarf around my neck as I step outside at last. I'm more than ready to leave the oppressive atmosphere of the King family home behind. At least for a little while.

And, to make an important phone call.

I clutch my phone in my hand, thinking back to the message I received only a short while ago.

Call me.

This was my one shot of getting some much-needed help and I couldn't risk anyone in the King family home overhearing me. Because if anyone found out who I was talking to, then it would be all over before I've really begun.

The sun is about to rise as I set off at a brisk pace through the crisp morning air. Hopefully the promise of a new day will bring me luck as I manoeuvre into the next step of my – *our* – plan.

Squeezing my phone even tighter, I take a moment to think about the person who I'll finally get to speak to. I wish I could call right this second. But not yet. I'm still too close to the house.

Instead, I take in the idyllic tree-lined street as I walk. Every inch of exposed lawn or shrub is manicured to perfection and each one of these white mansions glistens in the half-light of the dawn. To me, it's all just too clean, and too quiet. It's strange not to see a single soul considering we're in the middle of one of the biggest cities in the world. But it seems at this time in the morning, everyone who has the fortune to live in one of these giant homes in one of the most expensive streets in London is still shuttered inside, far away from the bustle of the normal world.

As I near the busier Fulham Road, more people and buses appear. And with them come the familiar everyday sounds of people living. I breathe easier. Having other people around me just going about their own business reminds me that my whole world is not just a bubble inside the Kings' orbit.

I continue my walk towards the Thames, past the never-ending rows of beautiful houses and secluded gated gardens that line the squares. Just a few months ago I could never have imagined how someone in a home like that could live. Now I am inside the best in the area. I still don't feel free though. If anything, it's made me feel more trapped.

Finally, I reach the river. This glimpse of the water, though so different to the Australian beaches I grew up with, still reminds me of home. I feel a sharp pang for the wide-open spaces and blue skies. London is beautiful too, but right now the tightly packed buildings and dark sky is not doing anything to help this impending sense of claustrophobia.

Rain clouds are definitely starting to roll in off the hazy horizon, and I'm starting to doubt my ability to pull off what I came here for.

I shake off my nerves as I look around me. No one in particular in sight and I think I'm far enough away from the Kings' house now to make the call I've been itching to since I landed. My one tether back home. To the one person I trust implicitly, who knows everything about me. All my secrets. And my lies. My cousin, Gemma.

If the Kings knew who I was in touch with, everything would be over. Because they know Gemma – they know her far too well.

I hold my phone close to my ear, and at last I hear an achingly recognisable voice.

'Molly! You okay?'

My legs almost buckle as I hear Gem's confident, concerned voice down the line. And at the use of my name, my *real* name, the one that only those who know everything about me know to use.

Deep down, I'm wracked with guilt that Miles doesn't know my entire identity. But I can't let him, not yet. I tell myself again that he'll understand when it all comes out. And besides, it isn't entirely a lie... Isabel is my middle name. And what I've gone by for years in Australia.

I'd just needed a different surname when I joined King & Co.; using the one I share with Gemma would have been too much of a giveaway. It had been easy enough to do, because Atkinson is my official surname in Australia...

Technically I wasn't lying to anyone, not even Miles. I just wasn't telling the *whole* truth.

'Gem,' I whisper, hardly daring to say her name. 'It's so good to hear your voice.' And I let a smile creep over my face. This is the first time I haven't felt on high alert in days. Maybe even weeks. The first time I've been able to be totally myself.

'Good,' she says. 'What's up? Surely you haven't wrapped everything up already? I haven't seen anything online...'

'No,' I say. 'Not yet. That's what I have to talk to you about.' We both knew that communicating in close proximity to the Kings' is a risk. We've been so careful since starting this plan to make sure it looked like there was no connection between us. But this risk had to be taken. 'There have been a lot of surprises,' I start, and fill Gemma in on everything that's happened, particularly the ex-girlfriend that I had never heard about before.

'I'm sorry,' she says. 'I didn't know. No one in the office talked about it. *He* never mentioned it.'

I know who she means by that. But she can barely stand to say his name.

'I know it hurts to think back on that time, but I thought you found out everything.' I try to stop an accusation seeping into my words. That was what the original plan had been of course, for Gemma to expose Cassandra and William. She'd got close... but neither of us could have predicted how badly she'd fail.

What the Kings did to Gemma had been terrible, but it wasn't the reason why this had all started. No, there was something even worse that they were hiding, and it's what had led Gemma and I down this path in the first place. For the truth, and for justice at last.

Gemma working with William and then trying to get the proof for us had been our plan at first, but she had been burnt.

Now it meant that what we came up with next, with me at the heart of it this time, absolutely could not fail.

The problem is, neither of us ever expected me to fall for Miles, an innocent party in all this. It raised the stakes even higher – and made it even more important for me that we succeeded in exposing what his parents had done to the world.

Gemma sighs down the phone. 'I thought I *had* found out anything important about the family that there was to know. I guess I didn't have time for everything... But I'm certain that everything else I told you still stands. You know about the key, and you know about the diaries. The plan we have *will* still work.'

'Yes, but I just don't know that I can keep doing this much longer.' I drop my voice even lower. 'I feel so awful not telling Miles the whole truth... and now he's announced the engagement and the baby...' I feel nauseous as I admit those terrible words out loud.

Because the fact is, I'm not pregnant.

Chapter Twenty-Four

'I'm sorry, Mol,' Gemma says. 'I'm so sorry that you had to lie. But I thought we needed something big to distract attention.'

I wasn't sure she'd been right about that. William had seemed to accept me as soon as we said we'd start the family in London. Cassandra on the other hand... 'It definitely doesn't seem to have worked on *her*.' I retort. 'She seems *more* suspicious if anything.'

I hear Gemma humph down the line defensively. 'At least you've got William on board now. We always knew that she was going to be the most difficult nut to crack.'

I let her finish her justification, which I've heard so many times before, but I'm still annoyed at Gemma about this. The pregnancy was the one thing she did behind my back and that we didn't see eye to eye on. She had felt Miles and I needed something more concrete to prove our commitment to his parents; I hadn't.

She'd ignored me though. When Miles got the elaborate note from 'me' that announced I was pregnant just last week, right before we flew over here, I couldn't exactly deny it. It would have made me look delusional and Gemma had known that too.

Whether the fake pregnancy had helped or not with giving me some family points, at least now I had access to the security system. Which meant I'd be able to get into the library undiscovered.

But I worry about what Miles will do when he finds out. I'm certain he can forgive me the rest when I can at last explain it to him. This though, lying about a pregnancy, would it be one step too far for him?

What was I going to do? I gulp and wrap my arm that isn't grasping the phone around my body. I can't think about that now. What's done is done, and I'll have to face it at the end with everything else. There's no point wasting this precious conversation arguing with Gemma.

'I have access to the system,' I say, changing the subject.

She pauses for a second taking it in. 'Great! Well done, Mol. Now all you need is to find that extra key.'

'Yes,' I echo down the line. 'And I think I may have figured out where she's been keeping it...'

'That's so good. I know this isn't easy and I'm so proud of you, Mol – she would be too... Remember, you're almost there. I love you.'

My throat tightens at her words. I've been keeping all my emotion in check since I arrived here – I haven't allowed myself a moment of weakness. But hearing Gemma's words, the one person who knows everything about me in the world, has caused me to crack. I have to go before I shatter.

'I love you too,' I croak down the phone.

'We'll speak soon, okay. And remember, I'm here if you need me. But you can do it – for all of us.'

Then she rings off, and it's only when I taste salt that I notice some tears have escaped.

I turn my back towards the river. I have to start moving. And get back under control before I return to the Kings'.

That's when I spot her. A woman turning around at the same time as me. She's too far away for me to see her face properly and she's wearing a cap low over her head. As I step towards her, she reacts and moves away, speeding into a jog and disappearing before I can even think about calling after her.

In that split second of seeing the blurry face a little more clearly though, I feel my stomach sink.

Because I swear there's something familiar about it.

Chapter Twenty-Five

The elevator door in the immaculate entrance swooshes open and Miles ushers me inside. So far everything about King & Co.'s head offices radiates sleek.

The outside is a beautiful and grand old building, but the inside is modern. Shiny black marble floors reflect the gold light fittings glittering overhead. Even the elevators are stylish and over the top: polished bronze and stretching along a dark mahogany wall. It's the same dark mahogany of the library at the Kings'.

I glance up at Miles's handsome dark features as we wait for the elevator to arrive, forcing myself not to think about this morning. I'd tried to put my suspicions of being followed out of my mind once I got back to the house, as Miles had taken me out for a much more enjoyable tour of Chelsea, and to some of his favourite pubs. For a few hours today, I'd almost forgotten my worries and felt normal. It had likely just been my paranoia talking, right?

But now as I step into the elevator, I feel self-conscious as I tug my new red dress around my body. I'd been extremely surprised, and a little insulted, when Miles had told me when we got back from our afternoon out that his mother had bought me a dress for tonight. I'd seen the designer label and my eyes had watered. Miles seemed to think it was a nice gesture; I wasn't so sure.

Obviously, Cassandra didn't think any of my wardrobe was good enough after judging it the last two days. I'd managed to speak to her for one moment to thank her, and also asked to pay her back. But she'd just given me a look of disgust and walked away like I'd offended her. And so here I am, feeling uncomfortable in the dress as a result. She 100 per cent wanted this to happen – this time, her power play has worked and I can't believe I let her win this round. I try to take comfort in the fact that very soon, if all goes to plan, I will have the upper hand again.

Miles is looking suave in a shirt and black velvet jacket. We must look like a perfect couple. I wish that were true.

'Here we are,' Miles declares as the elevator slows and the doors open to reveal a room of people celebrating the acquisition of a new company, toasting success with much champagne. I can't help but think of all the people that are likely to lose their jobs as a result of this latest venture. No one else seems to care.

Miles sweeps me through the crowd and towards the floor-to-ceiling glass windows that run along an entire side of the building. All I can see as we get closer are other dazzling rooftops surrounding us on all sides.

'It's better in the daytime,' Miles says, nodding towards the windows as he takes a champagne glass from a waitress. Just as he's about to take another, he stops. 'Oh wait, Iz, shall I find you something else?'

God, I wish I could take a sip. But to Miles, I am pregnant and I should behave accordingly in front of him.

'Yes, please.'

The waitress has already disappeared into the crowd when he turns back to her. 'Stay right here.' Miles murmurs as he brushes a kiss onto the top of my head.

I sigh as he disappears into the crowd. I really could have done with that drink. It was one thing going to a family event with Miles, quite another to come to a company one, considering that up until a month ago I was still working at the Australian arm of King & Co. There doesn't appear to be anyone that I recognise, but it's possible that word had still got over here.

I edge further into the shadows to avoid being too visible. Which is when I spot William in a dark corner of the room. And I see something I probably shouldn't.

He helps a beautiful woman off her chair, kissing her hand flirtatiously as she giggles, flipping her hair behind her shoulders. She leans in to whisper in his ear and I turn around, not wanting to see any more. I start to hastily retreat but then I spot a tall woman with an iconic blonde bob. This is the opportunity I've been waiting for.

'Oh excuse me,' I say as I bump into the back of the woman at the very edge of the crowd.

The woman exclaims, almost dropping her drink.

'Ah, I'm sorry, Cassandra,' I add as I look up at her ruffled expression. I take in her outfit; tonight she looks soft for once in a flowing dress. It is a dark forest green, the material a rich velvet. She appears more vulnerable somehow. But that feeling swiftly evaporates as her eyes narrow on me. *And the usual Cassandra is back.*

'Hello, Isabel, enjoying the party?' She motions around with her hand in a bit of a show at the now bustling party. We're on the far fringes and no one is paying us any attention. Perfect.

'We just arrived,' I respond, ignoring her sarcastic manner. 'But it seems like it's going well. Quite busy, and I think William is having a good time.' I say on purpose under my breath.

'What do you mean?' she snaps.

'Oh, I just saw him back there celebrating with someone... from the new company perhaps?'

'A woman?' Cassandra asks quickly.

'Ugh yes, she was a woman and they looked very cosy...' I begin as I see a figure beeline straight towards us through the crowd.

Cassandra lashes back. 'I am sure he is suitably enjoying his success, as he should. But I think you should know, Isabel,' and her eyes narrow in on me as she folds her arms across her chest, 'that William is only ever respectably friendly, and no one appreciates a gossip attempting to spread rumours at a party. So I would keep out of other people's business and your little mouth *shut*.' She emphasises the word and it feels like a slap across the face.

But when I hear an astonished voice from behind her I try not to smile.

'Mum?!' Miles emerges from behind his mother. He caught the end of her sentence just as she was delivering the final blow. I'd planned this flawlessly, saying the right thing at the right time to hit a nerve. Gemma had said she'd only found two real weaknesses when it came to Cassandra: her son, and her husband. And after speaking to Gemma,

I knew that I had to speed things up here and try escalating her one of these things to make her snap.

Of course, I'd had no idea that I could pull it off right when Miles returned, but I had. I'm ecstatic that Miles has now finally seen a glimpse of the *real* Cassandra.

'Why are you speaking to Izzy like that? You sounded like you were having a total go at her.'

He walks around her to put a comforting arm around my shoulder. He's choosing to be on my side, over hers. Just as I'd hoped.

'Miles,' Cassandra snaps at him, letting her act totally drop in a moment of exasperation. 'Can't you see what she's doing?' Her voice rises in a squeak at the end.

'What do you mean what she's doing?' Miles tightens his grip on me even more as he raises his voice in response.

'I don't think this is the right place for this conversation,' she says, attempting to regain her composure and change the subject.

'Oh, but I think it is,' Miles stubbornly insists. 'We need to sort this out now.' I look up at him with a frown, but he continues. 'Mum, it's been clear from the first moment Izzy walked in our door that you've been acting a bit off with her. I thought that you were just being a bit reserved at first, but now I think there must be something else on your mind. So, we need to get everything out in the open – stop being so British and hiding things away. Izzy is going to be part of our family soon. God, I'm going to be a dad, you're going to be a grandmother! We *have* to all get along.' I blink – I was sure he hadn't really noticed how off his beloved mum had been with me. I guess he'd been more observant than I'd given him credit for.

'But – but, that will be impossible,' Cassandra responds, trying hard to hide her emotions.

'What? Why?' Miles asks, exasperated. 'You can't dislike Izzy just because of what happened with Maya.'

Cassandra takes a step back, shaking her head in shock. 'No, no,' she says, 'it's nothing to do with that.'

'Then what is it?' I hear myself say. Her eyebrows shoot up in surprise at my interruption. I feel the exact same way. What was I thinking directing her attention straight at me? Everything was going so perfectly to plan...

And now it's as though me demanding the explanation has pushed her over the edge because she says, 'Fine! Just remember *you* asked for it.' There's an undeniable threat in her eyes. I gulp. All I wanted was for Miles to get a glimpse of the real Cassandra. Instead, it suddenly feels as though I've opened a can of worms that I desperately want to slam shut again.

'Oh Mum, come on. Just spit it out already.' Miles snaps.

Cassandra's face flushes bright red at her son's tone, and she looks around to make sure that no one is listening. The party is so busy now that it would be impossible for anyone to hear. As she turns back to face us, I see the moment the decision is made in her eyes. She launches right into it, and all at once, everything starts tumbling out. 'She's trying to trick you, to trap you into this marriage of course! Do you really think it was a coincidence that she was working with you in Australia? No of course not, she must have been planning this for years! Do you think I didn't know about the two of you getting together over there? Of course I did, and so, like any responsible mother, especially when their child is on the other side of the world, I got some people to look into her background.'

She pauses and glares daggers at me as Miles steps back in confusion and says, 'What?!'

My heart beats faster as my mind whips through the possibilities. I'd suspected she'd try and encourage Miles against me, but I didn't think she'd run a whole investigation on me.

I try hard to keep my face neutral – like I have nothing to hide. But on the inside I'm starting to panic. What has she discovered about me? We'd been so careful. But what if...

'I was *not* taking another risk after last time. You should be thanking me, Miles.' Her eyes glint as she waves her finger at him, and her champagne sloshes in the glass. She frowns down at it in distaste. She'd had a few drinks before she came here. I'd made sure Miles had taken her out first while I'd been getting ready. Gemma had told me Cassandra had a short fuse when she drank. And an even shorter fuse if you suggested any sort of infidelity from William. Turns out, she was right.

'Because you know what I found out,' hisses Cassandra under her breath, trying to avoid the attention of the rest of the party, 'when I heard a full report of Isabel's work history? That she knew of us *before* her job at King & Co. That she lived in London after university and worked as a waitress, of all things. Probably on purpose to gain access to events like this and meet rich young men like you, Miles. And in fact, I discovered that she'd worked in this very building before, been in our actual house before... as one of *them*.' She points at a waitress bustling by. 'But did she ever mention that to us?! No!'

I glance at Miles and his mouth is open in shock at his mother's accusations. She goes on in an exasperated voice, 'I knew all this when she arrived two days ago. I was suspicious, of course I was. But I *tried* to give her the benefit of the doubt. I asked and asked about her.' She nods at me in withering acknowledgement. 'I tried to give Isabel plenty of opportunities to tell us the truth about her background – and *nothing*. She was not going to tell us by herself, Miles. So I'm telling you now – just like you asked, remember.'

She looks imploring now, her anger fading fast. She grabs his hand but he lets it lie limp. She takes her hand back and adds in a softer voice, 'I had to do this digging and now I've told you before it's too late. Don't you see? I'm just trying to protect you – Isabel knew all about our family, and when she returned to Australia, she must have seen an opportunity to join the company, and eventually to get into your good graces. She's been planning this all along!'

The colour in her face continues to rise, but she rolls her shoulders back as though she's now about to make the biggest announcement of all. 'Because you know what else, darling...' she says in a soft voice to Miles, but looks directly at me with unmistakable triumph in her eyes. 'Isabel isn't even her *real* name.'

Chapter Twenty-Six

I feel like I've been punched in the stomach. And oh, Cassandra knows it. She can't help but let a small smile play in the corners of her lips.

They both must be able to hear the thumping in my chest, and I think this is it. It's all over before it's even really begun.

But then she adds, 'It's actually *Molly* Isabel Atkinson.' And I almost fall to my knees in relief. Because that means she doesn't know the whole truth. She doesn't know my connection to Gemma.

'Oh my god, Mum,' Miles says, trying to keep from raising his voice in anger. He puts an arm around my shoulders again and gives them an even tighter squeeze. He's showing his support. He's still on my side – maybe more than ever before. 'You seriously thought I didn't already know this?!'

Now it's Cassandra's turn to look taken aback.

'It's an extremely normal thing to be called by your middle name, Mum. People do that all the time.' Condescension drips from every note of Miles's words and I have to try hard to keep a controlled mask of calm. All I want to do is laugh in her face. 'And of course Izzy told me she'd worked in London as a waitress before – I didn't know about this very building, sure, but Iz, how many events do you think you worked as a waitress? Hundreds, if not thousands?' I nod mutely in response as Cassandra's face turns whiter and whiter. 'And you said to me just yesterday you thought there was something familiar about our house, right?' I nod again in relief.

I'm so glad I'd thrown out that casual comment last night as we were falling asleep. I'd been in so many incredible locations when I'd worked as a waitress in London so it's perfectly plausible that I'd get them all muddled up. Of course, this building and the Kings' home were fully etched into my mind. But the Kings didn't need to know just how much of an impact they'd actually had. Yet.

I see the sheer disgust in Cassandra's eyes and her nostrils flare as she stares straight at me before she turns to face her son, her eyes desperate now as she tries to hiss a final shot. 'But, how can you even be sure that she really is pregnant? Where is the proof?'

Miles shakes his head in exasperation and takes a deep breath. It's costing him everything to stay under control. He is just as aware as I am that he is in a room surrounded by colleagues and clients, who miraculously seem to have missed Cassandra's outburst. But if he were to start shouting, I don't think anyone could miss that.

'Mum, you're being ridiculous. You had no right to vet Izzy. To stalk her!' He can't help shout the last words. A few people turn to glance towards the sudden angry outburst, but we all pause and they turn back to their conversations. 'And as for if she's pregnant or not...' he hisses, shaking his head as though he can hardly believe he even has to say this. 'If she tells me she is then of course I believe her. It's called *trust*. Something you evidently don't understand. It's not only Izzy you've insulted and hurt with all this, it's me. You don't trust *me*.' His voice sounds dangerous, rumbling as low as thunder.

'No... what... of course I trust you,' squeaks Cassandra. 'I have just been trying to *protect* you... don't you see?'

'No, I don't,' he snaps. 'All I see is that you've been working against us from the start. You don't want us to be together. Really it sounds like you're doing everything possible to stop this...' He bears down on her and she shrinks away. 'And you must have been the one following Izzy this morning...'

I'd told him this little piece of information earlier, and made it sound like I felt that I'd been followed. I didn't think he'd mention it to Cassandra though.

'Pardon?!' Cassandra bursts out, and she looks genuinely shocked, unless she's a brilliant actor.

'Oh, don't pretend now, Mum. It's the most obvious thing in the world that you'd try and follow her yourself next. You have already admitted that you've dug into Izzy's past to try and break us up. How far are you going to go to ensure this marriage won't happen? No matter what you do, it absolutely *is* happening.'

'That wasn't me!' Cassandra protests again.

Miles rolls his eyes and says nothing, folding his arms. 'I think it's time Isabel and I stay somewhere else. I don't think we're welcome at home.'

'Honestly, Miles, please, I was just trying to help you...' Her words come out whiny and desperate.

'Save it, Mum. It's too late.' He holds up a hand to silence her. 'Iz, let's go. We'll find ourselves a nice hotel for the night, and go from there. Pass on my congratulations to Father, *Mother*.'

And with that, Miles grabs my hand and practically pulls my arm off with his strength and speed. I look back one last time to see Cassandra standing there. Utterly crestfallen. A shadow of herself in the softly luminescent light.

I try to stop the smile sliding across my lips as I let myself be led away.

Phase One is complete.

Part Two

Chapter Twenty-Seven

Cassandra

I rush out of that godforsaken room, trying to ignore the whispers circulating behind me. Honestly, I'm used to them – sometimes I even welcome them. Normally it is just trifling gossip born out of jealousy. But today I fear I may have lost control, and my carefully curated narrative has spun out of my reach.

It's all because of *that girl*. I press down hard onto the elevator button and notice a chip in my manicure. I stifle a groan of frustration. Everything was perfect until she strolled into our lives.

I step into the elevator and hurriedly press the ground floor button. *I will say that I had a headache*. The elevator whooshes down. No one need know the truth of what happened here tonight. I'm good at covering things up.

As I slip into a waiting cab and direct them back home, I allow myself to think back to the hideous argument. I have never seen Miles look so angry. Not since... I don't need to think about that. I shake my head to ward off the thoughts. And *that girl*, just standing there entirely mute the whole time. Though she had tried to look confused and demure, I saw the gleam of triumph in her eyes, that's for sure. I've perfected that look myself, after all.

I sigh. I'd been so sure that she... *Isabel*... has been hiding something from us all. That she has been planning something.

That's why I had to do what I did. We didn't know her at all, so she needed to be vetted. And after the last one... I certainly wasn't taking that risk again. I thought Miles would understand that. But now it seems like everything I uncovered he'd known already. And he doesn't seem to understand at all why I needed to try and protect him again.

Was it a coincidence that she had waitressed for us at a party in London and then ended up working for our company in Australia? It's possible, I begrudgingly admit as I stare intently out of the dark taxi window at the mass of people swirling around London. But then why not mention that she had lived here previously, or been in this very building before, when I asked about her history?

Ever since she arrived, Isabel has seemed purposefully coy to me, keeping her cards close to her chest. I'm certain I saw momentary panic in her eyes when I mentioned that Isabel wasn't her real name. But maybe I am just imagining everything...

I am fairly certain of one thing though: there's *no way* she is pregnant. Miles still seems convinced that she is. But the look on her face when he announced the news and her face just now spoke volumes: there's just something about this 'pregnancy' that doesn't seem right to me.

I can't believe they thought I'd stoop to following her though – what an outrageous insinuation. But who was it then? Or maybe Isabel was just making the whole thing up. I wouldn't put it past her.

I scowl into my lap as I press my nails into the palm of my hand until I feel an ache develop. I shut my eyes to ease the pounding headache that is starting to grow. Since when did I become so paranoid? I think back for a moment to the young woman I used to be: proud and stubborn, yes, but also painfully shy. It was William who had helped draw me out of my shell all those years ago.

William. I squeeze my hands even tighter to try and stop myself from biting my nails. An old, distasteful habit, but one I always struggle to control in my weakest moments.

Ah *William*. How did he turn me into this nervous creature who mistrusts anyone that comes across my path? I exude confidence and control on the outside, but on the inside I am always a push away from crumbling. I swear I didn't used to be like this – it was William who taught me to constantly second-guess myself. And now I can't do without him.

I crave his approval, his desire, even now. It is like a curse. I've become absurdly jealous too over the years, constantly thinking he is having affairs, but I can never find one shred of proof. In the end, he always convinces me that it is in my head. And of course, I don't want it to be true. But he keeps things so hidden sometimes that I *have* to wonder occasionally. On my good days though, I try to believe him.

I always wonder what Miles really knows. He must see things when they work together that he doesn't tell me about. But I would never ask him. He already has a difficult enough relationship with his father, and I don't want to make it worse.

I feel a distracting pain start to spread across my hand as I keep squeezing it tight. For the millionth time, I think that maybe if I left him I'd be better. But even if I was brave enough to leave, I never really could. We share too many secrets.

So here we are, no matter what, irrevocably tied by the shadows of our past. Of the things we have both done and can never let get out – or we'd both be utterly ruined.

I can't think about that now. I need to figure out how I can fix this situation with Miles. He's my everything.

I stare at my dim reflection in the windowpane of the taxi, distorted by the dazzle of this heartless city, and wonder who this bitter, suspicious woman looking back at me is. Because that's what I have become, according to my own son. But I also see my strong, defiant jaw and the steel of my eyes, and I know deep down that I am not entirely imagining things with Isabel.

There's a reason this girl made me suspicious in the first place. And it's not just that she hadn't told us about her past. Ever since Isabel arrived, she's been like a shadow, following me everywhere I go, even on my most boring errands. Watching me closely. And when she wasn't like a *faithless* dog following me around, I'm certain she would have been snooping around the house, in rooms she shouldn't be venturing into. I'd seen her with those terrible gossips at the charity party too. Trying to dig up anything she could, no doubt, and add more fuel to the gossip mill. And she had been obsessed with getting access to the house security systems. Which William had willingly granted at the promise of a grandchild. An heir to his empire. I couldn't believe it had been so simple to dupe him.

But, I wonder now as I stare back at my fierce reflection, perhaps there is a grain of truth in what Miles said. I had not been the most welcoming to Isabel either. Again, I can't help but remember the less confident woman of my youth, as well as my own mother and her barbed comments. It was a wonder I endured the thousand cuts of her sharp tongue. I hate to admit it, but perhaps my words and actions of the last few months, perhaps even years, have become more like those of my mother's than of someone I would be proud to be.

But what I'd done for Miles, or tried to do, had all come from a good place – unlike my mother's spiteful words, which always radiated hatred. All I wanted to do was protect my only child. I would do anything for him.

Because I haven't always been there for him. There's a time in my past that I'm not proud of. But since then I've tried to make up for it and do everything I can for him. To give him everything. And I don't want to see him throw everything away on someone that doesn't deserve him, or be locked into a marriage he can't escape from, with secrets left unsaid. I know too well what that's like.

Lately he seems to have forgiven me for being a terrible mother during his childhood. I thought he understood how deep my love went. But maybe not. I hear Miles's words echo once more in my ears. *Save it, Mum. It's too late.*

It can't be too late. If I want to keep my son in my life, my suspicions of Isabel will have to stop here. Or at least, I'll have to be smarter about it. What I need to do now is gain his trust once more, whatever it takes.

I will apologise and convince them *both* to return. *No matter what, I will not lose my son*, I tell my murky reflection in the window. It's streaked with London rain, reminding me of the tears that I could never publicly shed.

I won't give up. I will get to know this Isabel, my apparent future daughter-in-law. And, rather than relying on second-hand information, I'm going to discover the truth of her motivations myself. What was that saying again? Keep your friends close and your enemies closer.

Chapter Twenty-Eight

The blustery day throws me off course and I catch my hat as a gust of wind tugs it from my reach. The clouds are as grey as the tarmacked pavement I march along. They bear down on me as I try to prepare for a conversation I do not want to have.

I'm going to make my amends with my tail between my legs. Somehow, I will beg Isabel and Miles to come back home.

After a sleepless night, I finally reached Miles this morning. He was frosty but he took my call. Deep down, I knew he always would. A son can never say no to his mother.

Apparently, he and Isabel had taken themselves off to The Goring to get away from our house. *Very nice* for that girl. I'd scoffed when he'd told me. It is my favourite hotel in the whole borough – and she probably knew that.

Miles was wrapped around her little finger. I exhale the chill air; I have to stop thinking like this. I had managed to convince Miles to meet with me this morning so I could apologise. It would be a terrible blow to my pride, but I will do anything for him.

So here I am, my cap literally in hand, going to plead my son's forgiveness. I hope I will not have to beg. How embarrassing.

As I reach the front steps I hesitate for a moment. Am I doing the right thing? Perhaps it would be better for us all if I left them alone. But I can't leave Miles to this fate without at least trying to make amends with him. And then I'll be able to find out what this girl is really up to. So I press on.

The doorman doffs his hat to me as I pass and welcomes me inside. Alan, the general manager, greets me at the door with a kind smile.

'Ah, Mrs King, I saw your lunchtime reservation and I wanted to come down and welcome you myself. How are you?'

I nod politely back at Alan. I'm a long-term patron of The Goring, having my monthly ladies' luncheon club here, as well as having hosted a number of intimate dinners in the restaurant. I am a *very* good client. Which is why it irks me even more that Miles chose to stay here *with her*. The Goring is *my* place.

'Good thanks, Alan,' I say. 'And yourself?'

'Oh, wonderful thank you, Mrs King. Now let me take you through; your guests are already here. Your son of course, and a charming young lady accompanying him.' I narrow my eyes. He takes in my expression and professionally averts his gaze. He can tell I am unimpressed and so will say no more on the matter. This was his way of letting me know that he knew they had stayed here last night. Of course he knew. But he was discreet and wouldn't pass anything on, that I was sure of.

He guides me through from the entrance towards the restaurant. We pass through the beautiful hotel, but I barely take it in. I'm so focused on getting through this meal. Gold glitters in my periphery, as everything else becomes a blur. We finally enter the dining room where, laughing with a ring like a tinkling bell, I see her. Is it just me, or is there derision in the laugh that only started as soon as I entered the room? I'm being paranoid again.

Alan escorts me to the table, nestled in my favourite spot looking out through the window. Miles's back is to me so he can't have seen me yet. But we are coming from a direction where Isabel could have spotted me.

Instead, she ignores me and continues to cackle even louder. It is only when we are practically on top of them and Alan interrupts in that easy way he has that they look up to see me. The mirth is still in Isabel's eyes, though thankfully she has stopped that hideous laugh now. Miles's eyes look hollow, shadows under them from a sleepless night too, I imagine. I am glad I'm not the only one. He stands stiffly to greet me, kissing me formally on one cheek.

'Mother,' he says in a cautious tone.

'Hello, darling,' I respond, as Alan pulls out my chair to help me into my seat.

'Here we are,' Alan says, pushing me back in. 'Welcome all of you to The Goring. So wonderful to have you back again, Mrs King,' he adds to me with a purposeful look. 'Xavier will be over in a moment to see you, and I hope you have a lovely lunch. Call if you need anything *at all*,' he stresses, directing his address to me. He has seen me in enough moods and situations to know when I might need saving. Bless him. I think on some level he can sense that my outward projection is not the real me inside. Or I like to think so, unless I have become just *that* good at pretending over the years.

'So... you asked to meet me as a favour. Isabel is here too, of course, because she's part of my future now.' Miles nods unnecessarily towards her. I know where she is for goodness' sake, right next to me, lapping up every second of my misery, no doubt. I risk a glance towards her and sure enough her expression is sombre but there is mockery in her eyes. How can Miles not see this?

'Of course, I see that now. And…' *Here it goes*, I dig my fingernails into my palm. I have to get through the little speech I had been planning all night. 'I am extremely,' I pause for effect and then let it out in a rush, 'sorry for doubting you both. I was just trying to protect you Miles, and I did what any mother would do for their child. I think I just got carried away, but it's only because of how much I love you.'

I see his eyes soften as I knew they would. Or I think I do. Because the next instant,

I see them harden. He had just turned back to face me after looking at Isabel. I glance in her direction and I see her eyes are full of tears. *Tears!* Does she cry on demand too? What an actress.

'That's all very well, but you have really hurt us – hurt Isabel especially. I think you owe her an apology too.'

I try not to scream. Of course she was going to get her way on this. So I swivel to face her and try with all my might to un-grit my teeth. 'Isabel, I am so very sorry that we appear to have got off on the wrong foot. I would really like us to start again.'

There – not quite an apology for what I did, because truthfully, I am not sorry for it. I would do it again, just better. As I said, anything to protect Miles. But I had crafted this apology perfectly. I was sorry *now* that we had got off on the wrong foot: if I had become closer to her, perhaps I could have uncovered her weaknesses and secrets much more easily. Now, I hoped that I would get another chance.

Isabel nods, and seems to consider my words for what feels like an eternity. 'Thank you, Cassandra,' she finally says, her eyes still looking tearful. 'I understand now, and it's beautiful you care so much about your only son.' She wipes away the stray tear that has fallen down her face.

I resist the urge to roll my eyes.

'Sorry, it's just lovely to see, is all,' she adds as Miles look at her with a concerned expression. It makes me nauseous to see him so besotted. These are obviously crocodile tears. She can't genuinely think what I did was 'lovely' – I tried to expose her for a fraud!

'Now there we are,' says Miles with a note of triumph in his voice. 'My two best girls getting along, and starting again.'

I smile in response, wanting him to think that on the surface I agree.

'Cheers to that,' he adds.

My wine glass had already been filled up, so I obediently raise it. As they clink, I don't fail to notice Isabel's now dry eyes.

She might have won this round. But I'd come up against worse than *Molly* Isabel Atkinson before. She has no idea how far I'll go to protect my son. And this is just the beginning.

Chapter Twenty-Nine

Over the course of our elaborate lunch, I successfully convince Miles and Isabel to return back to the house.

'It just makes sense,' I coo at Isabel, realising I need to direct all my energies to making us 'the best of friends' – or 'BFFs' as *she* would probably say. 'You will be so much more comfortable with us, and we can all spend some proper time together,' I reason. 'Now that you will be *family*.' I was proud that I managed to add this without spitting. I had rationalised that I could freely say these things to her for now – because it would not last long if I had anything to do with it.

Isabel had looked smug throughout the rest of the meal. I had wanted to shove her pretty little face into the lobster bisque she was enjoying at my great expense. *Goodness Cassandra!* If only people knew what I actually thought sometimes. Of course none of my thoughts had showed, and I'd put on my perfect charm offensive, honed after what has felt like millions of hours at society functions. Honestly, sometimes I am just so *bored* of it.

All the same, I did take some small pleasure during lunch at how happy Miles had looked now his 'two best girls' seemed to be getting along.

But secretly I was filled with even more joy at the thought of how happy he would be when I proved she wasn't pregnant and could free him from her grasp.

He will just be *so* much happier with someone I choose for him. I cannot take any more chances after that first girl and now this one. But I'm getting ahead of myself. I need to deal with the problem in hand.

We finish up lunch, a three courses and coffee affair, and agree to meet back at the house in an hour or so once they have checked out of their room. We part ways and I finally can breathe again. The 'apology' is complete.

As I step outside onto the tree-lined street, I notice that the wind has calmed down and the sky is looking bright for a November day. A walk back through Chelsea will do me good. Give me some time to clear my head.

I am surrounded by the noise of other people and for once, I don't resist the tide of humanity. It gives me some anonymity, which is a true release from constantly keeping everything together. Some might say I'm extremely fortunate, and I suppose that's true in a lot of ways, but if people knew about the secrets that haunt me, I think few people would *actually* want to be me.

As I walk through Eaton Square my mind wanders back to when Miles first started school, and I would insist on taking him myself to his little prep school on the square. He was my pride and joy – still is – but our relationship was so much less complicated then. I miss those days.

I was his 'Mummy', the person he would come to with any thought, no matter how big or small, and I would listen and take care of anything. Perhaps I had spoilt him sometimes, but I had been a good mother back then, that I was certain of. I like to only think back to that part of his childhood. I try to never think about what came next, those years I'm so ashamed of.

I continue to walk along the charming streets of the part of London we call home. But my thoughts are far from charming: walking down memory lane of Miles as a little boy makes me think of Isabel now and the apparent child she has growing.

Maybe I should just believe her – but her being suddenly pregnant is too convenient. I know my Miles and how I raised him; he would want to do the right thing, the chivalrous thing. I have heard some ghastly stories in the news about women getting pregnant on purpose to entrap their partners. That's what I need to find out before I can allow myself to feel anything towards this possible child. And if I'm right, all I need to do is try and prove it to Miles and their relationship will be over. I hope. I think this all through on the journey, barely registering the streets as I pass them.

Back at home, I instruct Maria to prepare Miles's room once more. As per William's instructions, when Miles went off to boarding school, it had been cleared out. I was devastated when all traces of my little boy had been removed, but William was so insistent that we needed to help Miles create an adult space. 'He needs to learn how to be a responsible grown-up, Cassandra, this is a small start.'

Miles had been upset when he came back from school but didn't want to let it show. Oh how it had broken my heart, but in those days I was so weak, I went along with everything William said. Now Miles has become a man in his own right, and sometimes I barely recognise my sweet little boy. That must happen to all parents – it is part of them growing up.

At least I always have my study. My safe space, full of my most prized possessions and memories. The one place I can be myself and write down all my thoughts and feelings without anyone seeing. I can't bear to let anyone go in there without my knowledge. Especially not since *her*. I can't trust that someone won't steal from there again. I take comfort that I'm the only one who knows which book grants entry. Well, Miles does too – but of course I trust him.

As I enter my bedroom, I glance at William's side of the bed and sigh. There's a pull that man has over me that I'm powerless to. To everyone else, I seem indestructible. But it's not true; he knows all my weaknesses, all my secrets. And I *think* I hold all of his. They tie us together more than anything else. But sometimes, the cost of it has become suffocating.

Secrets are like a noose around the neck. What a dramatic thought. I have been too fraught the past few days; it's making my negative side come out. I must shake these thoughts away before they set in too strongly. Before they cause me to break apart once more. Because, of course, that's the other thing no one knows about me. How close to breaking I always am.

I walk to the window and sit down on the soft cream chaise that I have placed in front of the large bay windows and take deep breaths. I need to slow my heart rate and control myself. Before my dark thoughts take control of me. *In and out, in and out.*

I hum and try to still my breathing in the way I've been taught. When a lighter feeling settles over me I open my eyes to take in my lovely street. This view always calms me, as I look out over the elegant square and magnificent buildings facing our own. The church catches my eye and I gaze down on the stained-glass window that glistens in the light, creating an ethereal glow.

I need to freshen up and make sure everything is in order before everyone returns. I enter my walk-in wardrobe – it's something I had insisted upon having built when we first moved in. It was not that I had always adored fashion, but I knew that I needed to be good at it to achieve what I wanted. Excellent style will always be a power move, whatever anyone says. And over the years I have collected many carefully curated pieces to complete my wardrobe, ensuring it's suitable for every occasion. When I was younger, it was more for vanity and to project a confidence I didn't have. Nowadays, it's to feel stronger and more in control. Something I always fear losing.

Today, it was no accident that I wore a hat to complete my 'cap in hand' look, which had also consisted of a softer, more voluminous dress and jacket combination. I hadn't wanted to look fierce or intimidating. Instead, I wanted to appear gentle and more fragile – a rare look for me. Miles and Isabel seemed to have bought it, so fashion has paid off once again.

But as I change into another relaxed look of a soft white cashmere sweater and corduroy slacks, I can't shake off the feeling of unease that has continued to grow on my walk home. Looking back, it had all been just too *easy* to convince them to return – hadn't it? And now, the more I think about it, the more anxious I am beginning to feel. What if Isabel had *wanted* to come back here all along? If that is the case, it just proves that she definitely has some unfinished business. And with her here right under my nose, I *will* find out what it is.

I need some time in my study to think things through and write out my feelings. So I take the familiar route all the way down the stairs to my own little haven. I unlock the entry with my fingerprint and slip into the library, glancing up and around the array of shelves. I have always loved the ability of books to transport me into another world. Which is why I made the secret entrance to my private space literally *behind* a bookshelf. I get a thrill every time I pull the correct book that opens the room.

The door swings open to reveal my sanctuary. I breathe in the acrid but wonderfully calming aroma. It smells like the inside of a good book, and I love it. It is a decently sized room, though the books and half-finished paintings haphazardly strewn over every surface always makes it appear much smaller.

This is the one room in the house where I allow clutter. It is *my* space after all. What feels like thousands of prints and pictures mark the walls. There are all sorts of collections and recreated moments from my life over the years, which is why it feels too intimate for anyone else to be allowed down here. They would uncover the real me in a heartbeat. Not to mention my diaries that I keep hidden away. My diaries that no one knows about. I touch the little key on my charm bracelet as though to remind myself that they're safely locked away. And I'm the only one with access.

But before I have a chance to settle in and write an entry, I hear a commotion echoing back through the library from the upstairs entrance hall. A loud door slams, and then raised voices. Could that be Miles and Isabel already? What are they fighting about?

Hurrying, I scurry around the desk and back through my secret door, but do so as quietly as a mouse. Hopefully I will overhear some of what they are fighting about.

'HAPPENED AGAIN!' I hear Isabel shriek in her strong Australian accent as I peek my head out through the library door – when she speaks, you can never miss her.

I don't catch Miles's reply as his voice is soft and low, and I am too far away to hear. I take a chance and step out into the sitting room, tiptoeing through it and over towards the alcove that separates this room and the entrance hall.

They must have just stepped inside, their voices travelling across the otherwise silent house. I continue to creep closer.

'Look,' I hear him say, in the voice I recognise as his 'be reasonable' tone. 'I told you before, this happens sometimes. But there's nothing we can do about it.'

I continue to slip silently along the walls, ever closer to the alcove gap. I feel like an intruder in my own home.

I catch Isabel's response: 'What am I supposed to think when I receive another message saying, "*I warned you. Watch your back*"?! How could she even know that we're coming back to the house?!' Isabel asks.

My mind is racing. What on earth are they talking about – who is sending Isabel such threatening messages?

My breath catches as I hear Miles respond, 'I told you, I've been receiving these for years. And it might sound like she knows we've returned but she could have sent that very same message just because she can tell that we haven't split up yet. If you read it again, it sounds like it could be referring to anything.'

Miles has been receiving messages like this for *years*? My mind is spiralling. It couldn't be...

'Are you even sure that it's Maya?!' Isabel exclaims.

There's a roaring in my ears. My blood runs cold. They *are* talking about that other girl – but that's impossible.

I hear a thump on the tile. It sounds like Isabel's stamped her foot on the ground in frustration. 'Come on,' she says in a tone of complete exasperation. 'What if it *is*... someone else?'

'Someone else?' Miles asks. 'But who else would want you to stay away?'

'Do I really have to spell it out?' Isabel cries. 'It could be your—'

Just at that moment, Miles speaks over her in a loud voice. 'Oh hi, Maria! We didn't think anyone was home!'

I should move now before I am discovered, but I am frozen to the spot, my thoughts firing in a million directions.

Somewhere far in the distance, Maria replies, 'Oh I am always here, Mister Miles, and your room is all sorted again. Can I help with your bags?'

Sounds of murmurs and footsteps walking away reach me through the fog but I am entirely lost. I sink to the floor and try not to shake.

They seem to think that... I can't even *think* her name... that girl, *that first girl*, is back. Or rather she never went away. She's apparently been sending Miles threatening text messages for years and now Isabel is receiving them too.

But I know that can't be true.

When I close my eyes, I'm taken back there, to many years before, and all I can see is her frozen body lying on the ground.

I know she can't be sending Miles or Isabel any sort of texts.

That would be absolutely impossible.

I know that she's dead.

Because I killed her.

Chapter Thirty

I have tried for so long to keep from returning to that day. But their words have sent me spiralling back in time and I can't see a way out now. As I curl into the smallest ball I can manage in my large sitting room, everything starts to return to me in the strangest flashes.

The moment when Maya had first arrived on our doorstep, a waif of a girl but with bright sparkling eyes and an easy laugh. It had been a surprise to all of us; we weren't expecting Miles to return from travelling with a girl in tow. But she'd seemed so innocent and sweet. Maybe a touch too confident and bright, but I'd thought that might be good for Miles.

I hadn't known much about her or her family, but Miles had seemed thrilled and after all we'd put him through, I wanted him to be happy.

Maya seemed to take a genuine interest in becoming part of our family too. I even hoped she might help us fully heal. With her around, there were times when we almost seemed to be a normal family.

I wanted to get to know her, and so we spent more and more time together. We had a lot in common: she loved my books, my jewellery, my art collection. And I even showed her willingly.

Then, after a few months or so, she seemed to change. I didn't noticed at first. I guess I had been so busy with some charity or another that I didn't dwell on it.

But in hindsight I appreciate that maybe the girl that had first arrived on our doorstep had become quiet and withdrawn. And I should have noticed sooner. Thinking back, I'd caught her skulking around the house and being in places she shouldn't. If I'd spotted the signs earlier, maybe things would be very different.

Now, huddled on the floor of the sitting room, I shut my eyes tighter; I don't want to remember the rest but the flashes continue to come unbidden. I don't want to remember the day I heard screams and raised voices racing along the corridor. But the visions come back to me.

I'd thought everyone was out, even the help. And I'd been trying to take a nap. I hadn't been sleeping well. My 'dark cloud' as I thought of it had been trying to descend on me again. William had been terse and distant. Miles had seemed constantly on edge, snapping and rolling his eyes in an awfully teenage way at everything I said. And Maya had been avoiding me. I should have known that something was coming.

As I had groggily opened my bedroom door, I heard them. Miles and... Maya – her name flashes across my mind and I feel sick – in the middle of the greatest fight I had ever heard. What I witnessed today between Miles and Isabel has terrible parallels.

But I'd rushed towards the fight that time, listening in snatches until I got close enough. There were such wild accusations on both sides, and I heard Miles use terrible language. I was appalled. I had not raised my son to speak to women this way. What had chilled me to the bone though was how much he reminded me of William in that moment.

But then he said, 'It wasn't enough to just cheat on me, no you had to steal my family's jewellery too!'

Both of those revelations shocked me and I ran down the last few steps of the hall away from my bedroom and around the corner. They were standing at the top of the stairs, as Maya grabbed onto his shirt and Miles tried to pull away. But her grip looked vice-like.

'WHAT?' I screamed as I came to a standstill a few feet away.

They both turned to face me, their own expressions red with exertion. Seeing me momentarily silenced them.

Miles spoke first, pain and anger contorted across his entire face. 'Mum, I'm sorry you had to hear that,' he choked out. 'But she,' he took this moment to wriggle out of her grasp, 'she's been cheating on me for God knows how long.' He gulped. '*And* has been stealing your jewellery.'

'Let me just ex—' Maya tried to pipe up, reaching back towards him.

But Miles jumped away from her. 'I can't believe a single word you say!' he shouted, and a great rasping sob had escaped him. It was guttural and animal-like. My heart broke to see my beautiful son torn in two.

Maya took another step towards him, but Miles flinched further away from her grasp like he'd been stung, and leapt down the stairs two by two. 'Just get away from me!'

I saw his shadow disappear at the bottom of the stairs as he opened and slammed shut the great front door. He was gone.

And I was left with Maya, this girl that had so completely shattered my boy's heart. My blood was on fire.

'Cassandra,' she tried to start, walking over to me, her hand outstretched. 'Please let me explain...' But at the expression on my face she faltered, and stood stock-still.

An icy, dangerous voice that I barely recognised as my own dripped from me.

'Explain what? My son is in pieces, all because of you. How can you really explain *any* of what I've just heard? You're pathetic,' I spat, and I couldn't stop the poisonous words that continued to fall out of my mouth. My vision was full of the devastated look on Miles's face. 'He was far too good for the likes of you anyway. You're just a pretty face and nothing else. Frauds always get found out in the end.'

Maya's mouth dropped open, her face flushing even redder. And then she threw her head back and laughed, actually *laughed*. Right in my face.

'You're seriously calling *me* just a pretty face and a fraud? How about you look in the mirror, Cassandra? Ever since I came into this house it's been so *obvious* how fake and lost you are. Trying to follow Miles around like a puppy. Desperate for any love and attention. You know he laughs about you behind your back, right? And thinks it's pathetic how you're wrapped around William's little finger, with no thoughts or backbone of your own. Oh, you put on that perfect front alright. But everyone can see right through it. So don't you judge me for what's happened here. Not when you don't have the full story...'

In the blink of an eye I strode over, only an arm's length from her. 'How *dare* you speak to me like that?'

Close up, I saw her eyes were red-rimmed and bright with tears like she'd been crying for a long time. But she pulled her shoulders back, and even though she was still at least a few inches shorter than me, she seemed to grow, even as she tottered on her high heels.

She scoffed. 'I'll speak however I damn like. You're pathetic, the lot of you. All pretending like you're better than everyone else, but you're just the same. No you're *worse*! And your son... I thought he'd be different, that he wasn't like the rest of you, but he can't even stand up to his little posh friends when they look down their noses at me.'

I shook my head in disbelief. 'That's pretty rich coming from someone who's been cheating on him. And stealing from our house.'

Maya unfolded her arms and I didn't miss it as she clenched her hands into fists, a steely expression transforming her pretty face into an ugly snarl. 'That's not what happened. But he doesn't believe me. And I know none of you will. You're all in your own merry delusional club. He pushed *me* away. He didn't stand up for me. And when someone else did, what was I supposed to do? Your son is a *coward*, Cassandra.'

And it all happened so quickly. One second my hand was by my side, the next it was streaming across to close the distance between us, slapping her hard across the side of her face.

The sound reverberated, as did her sharp intake of breath. She staggered back a couple of steps, tottering on those ridiculous shoes. The first step was just inches behind her. Any further back and she would have tumbled down the stairs.

Maya grabbed onto the banister and regained her balance, shaking her head to turn and face me. Her eyes went wide and a bright red mark glowed on her cheek. But again she just laughed. Her eyes had a manic tinge to them as she said, 'Oh Cassandra, maybe you do have a bit of backbone in you after all. William said you didn't. That's why he gave these jewels to me.'

My mouth dropped open at Maya's words. And then she had the audacity to lift her arm and jangle a familiar ruby-studded tennis bracelet in my face.

'Recognise this?' she taunted. 'Yes, I think it suits me much better too. It's what William said. It's remarkable what that husband of yours will give people to try and keep them quiet.' Maya's eyes glinted dangerously.

My mind screamed at me to say something, anything. But I just stood there frozen as I stammered out, 'Whaa...?'

'Oh your husband's a bad boy, but you already know that, don't you, Cassandra? Or are you really that delusional that he would still be attracted to an old hag like you? That you'd really be *enough* for a man like that?'

It was the mirthless, derisive laugh that broke me. Maya's words struck a cracked part of me, deep in my core. That feeling that had *always* been below the surface, that I just wasn't good enough. Wasn't good enough for the life I lived, wasn't good enough for my successful and clever husband. It was what my mother had told me again and again. That I just wasn't *enough*. Never enough.

And so, the look in Maya's eyes and the venom in those words finally tipped me over the edge. Her words hit home. They hit right to the centre of my being, to the broken little girl I somehow still was deep down.

I screamed at her to 'SHUT UP!' and at the same time tears sprung to my eyes. I *never* cried, but something had snapped in me.

Maya's eyes widened in delight, or maybe just surprise. 'Or what, Cassandra?' she replied, raising one eyebrow as she kept her arms tightly crossed. When I gave no response, she added, 'That's what I thought.' She smugly flipped her hair over her shoulder as she turned towards the stairs. 'Pathetic and *weak*, just like your son.'

Those words, that last withering look, sent me lunging towards her. It wasn't just me that Maya had been smearing, it was Miles too. I would not be the same sort of mother that mine had been to me. I would defend my child when it counted.

'Don't you walk away from me,' I shouted as I closed the gap between us and grabbed at her wrist, at that glinting tennis bracelet. 'And give me back that damn bracelet!'

I pulled hard on the clasp, and the bracelet clanged against her wrist, stuck tight on. But the push and pull caused Maya to stumble again on those silly shoes. This time she started to trip properly and spun face first towards the stairs.

I panicked. As much as I hated her for all that she'd said and done, I hadn't wanted her to fall. So I pulled harder on the tennis bracelet, the only part of her that I still had a grip on. The shock flashed in her eyes as she continued to lose her balance. I thought that if I grasped with all my might, I'd be able to bring her flying back towards me.

But then it happened.

I heard the tiny snap and suddenly I was tumbling backwards. I fell to the floor of the landing with a loud thud. My back whacked hard into the ground and I gasped for breath as the wind knocked out of me.

And like some mocking echo, I heard another crash. And another. And another. As Maya fell and fell backwards down the stairs.

Then total silence.

My mind screamed at me to get up, get up. But my breathing continued to come out in a rasp.

Finally, I'd hobbled up and reached the edge of the stairs.

Her pretty, perfect body was lying crumpled at an awkward angle at the bottom of the stairs.

Fragments of ruby and diamond had created a glittering trail all the way down the stairs.

And interspersed between them, I'd been sure I could see blood.

Chapter Thirty-One

There was a scream, and for a second, I thought someone else had seen everything that had just happened.

Then I realised that the scream ringing through the air was mine.

Raw and terrified. An out of body experience.

I' ran down the stairs, skipping over what remained of the shattered bracelet. A reminder of what had caused all this.

When I reached Maya, she looked like a broken doll. All that confidence and youth knocked out of her as easily as a feather floating away in the wind. Her legs and arms were at strange angles, a trickle of blood coming from a gash on the side of her head.

Surely she wasn't dead. She couldn't be.

I got down on my hands and knees and tried to feel for a pulse. Something, anything. But all I could hear was a roaring in my ears and wrenching sobbing starting to break out from my chest.

So I did the only thing I could think of. I called my husband. He was the only person that could help me in a situation like this.

After all, it wouldn't be the first time. And he owed me after what I'd done for our family. But I *never* let myself think about that other time.

I brought my phone out of my pocket with shaking hands.

Miles could never know about this.

Once, twice, three times I called and William did not answer. Bile rose in my throat and panic had coursed through my veins. When I got through, I pleaded for him to come home, citing an emergency. He agreed, reluctantly, noticing the fear in my voice.

As I waited, all I could see over and over again was that moment she'd tumbled. I refused to look behind me at where she still lay. So I had paced at the entry, becoming a sentry at our front door. Every so often, I'd run to the window to see if anyone was coming, praying it would be William first.

When his dark blue Porsche drove onto the street, I stumbled to the door in relief. I rushed to open it and usher him in. The door closed with a deafening bang behind him.

And then, William saw her. Maya's too-still body at the bottom of the stairs.

'Oh my god, Cassandra!' He threw himself back towards me and grabbed me roughly by the arms. 'What the hell happened?!' he screamed in my face.

It felt like I had been running a marathon, my heart was beating so fast, and at that moment my knees collapsed in on themselves. It was only William's strength that kept me upright.

Somehow I started to babble out a disjointed retelling. 'Okay, okay,' he said more gently. But the horror of my words at last hit me, and bile rose up and out onto my shiny marble floor.

William let go of me in shock and I collapsed onto the ground.

The next thing I knew I was being carried upstairs.

I made it to the bathroom just in time before all the bile that I'd swallowed came back up a second time.

After I was done, scraped raw from the inside out, I just lay on the cool marble tiles. Trying to float myself away somewhere else.

That was how William found me.

How much time had passed? Who knew?

I only knew he was there when a shadow passed across my blurry vision and a hand reached out to gently stroke my hair.

I flinched at the caressing touch.

And then he whispered in my ear, 'It's done, Cassandra, I've sorted everything.'

I managed to tilt my head up from the icy floor to face him.

And saw that cool glint in his eyes.

I wasn't able to speak the question that was etched into my mind. But William seemed to sense what I'd been trying to ask.

'She won't be troubling us again, Cassandra. And what's done is done. I've buried the problem and now you just have not to think about it and move on.'

Sobs broke out from my chest as his words had sunk in. William continued to stroke my hair as I lay there helplessly.

'Shh... you did what any mother would do. You protected your son. And thankfully you have me. I will always clean up your messes. I promise.' A kiss brushed the top of my forehead. I didn't want to be touched. I just wanted to be left alone. But I had no energy to move away.

'It's things like this that are why we'll be together forever,' he continued in a thoughtful tone. 'For better or worse, our secrets bind us.'

Then he turned my head forcefully to look straight into his piercing blue eyes. 'So don't forget that. Okay? Don't ever forget what I've done for you today. Will you, Cassandra? Whatever I might do, it has nothing on this.'

He held my gaze until I managed to blink out a response. *Yes*, my bloodshot eyes had said in response. *Yes, whatever you say.*

'Good,' he mused again. 'Now come on, let's get you cleaned up. You're a complete state.'

He pulled me to my feet before sitting me down on the edge of our oversized marble tub. Turning the faucet on, he faced me once more. 'All you need to do is tell yourself you did this for Miles, okay. But don't ever share with him what happened – he can't ever find out. Or it will completely destroy us. I'll make sure he doesn't ask you any questions and you need to focus on making peace with it. Or I'll have to take you back to the dear doctor.' He squeezed my knee but I flinched at his words.

The clinic, I thought with a shiver down my spine. I was never going back there.

No way.

Not after last time, when I'd almost never got out.

I can still hear the screams.

As I watched the bath fill up with swirling water inch by inch, I told myself that what had happened with Maya was completely different to what had sent me to Dr Smythe's all those years ago. Maya had been a nasty piece of work. A cheat, liar and a thief.

It was an accident.

I hadn't meant to kill her. Everything I did, I did to defend my son. And wasn't that a good thing?

There was going to be one way out of this. And that was by doing exactly what William wanted. Forever. Because now, after what I've done, I would always be trapped in this marriage. If I hadn't already been before.

So I'd told myself I couldn't give him any reason to lock me away from my son. Not again.

I'd gazed at my pallid reflection in the mirror as William had hummed and added a generous amount of bubble bath to the enormous tub.

No, I'd promised myself, I would make it through. Even if it meant trying to forget that this had ever happened.

But now, here I am on the floor of my beautiful sitting room, rocking myself through the terrible memories that race back into my mind. Memories that I thought I'd pushed away forever. All it took was hearing one fight between Miles and Isabel now to bring them all back.

My thoughts taunt me: *you should really know better, Cassandra. Because after all, you can hide the past from others, but you can never hide it forever from yourself.*

I try to gather myself as I think back to what had happened next.

After that night with Maya, the first time I faced Miles had been the greatest test; I'd been terrified that he would ask me about what had happened after he left. I'd been so scared of lying to him, that he might be able to see right through me. But he hadn't brought it up as William had said he wouldn't, so I happily never mentioned it either.

All William had said was that he'd told Miles that he'd sorted everything out with Maya, and that he would never have to see her again. He'd said Miles had just been so grateful that he wouldn't have to face her that he didn't ask any questions. I'd breathed a huge sigh of relief.

Since that day, I tried to be normal by busying myself with more charity organisations, luncheon clubs and household renovations. I'd wanted to change our whole space, to remove all traces of it and pretend that it had all been a terrible nightmare.

Miles and William had seemed to be getting on better than ever before too once Maya was gone, and Miles went straight in to training at King & Co. For such a long time, everything had seemed to be going so well.

But then Miles had wanted some freedom, to build the business on his own terms in a newer marketplace. And I hadn't realised it then, but now I could see it: that move to Australia had signalled the start of everything unravelling once again. Of everything I'd worked so hard to rebuild between our family just crumbling away.

Because of this new girl.

And now, it was bringing back the guilt and terror that I'd tried so hard to bury for so many years.

I have to get a grip.

So I force myself to stop rocking, and place my hands firmly on the ground, feeling the soft edges of the rug run through my fingertips. I breathe deeply and open my eyes. Everything around me is still the same. All is okay. I repeat this again and again as I shakily push myself into a crouching position and then on to my feet.

I smooth my jumper back down where it's creased and tuck my stray strands of hair behind my ears. Once I've erased all evidence of my momentary breakdown, I pull my shoulders back and stretch my neck to one side and then the other.

I have to become the steely Cassandra again. I can't afford another moment of weakness. I can't allow myself to be overwhelmed by the past. I have to figure out what on earth is going on.

If I could see my face, I would have my tell-tale glint of determination back in my eyes. I narrow my focus onto one question only: if Maya wasn't sending those messages to Miles and Isabel, who was?

Chapter Thirty-Two

We all settle into a kind of rhythm. I am cautious and observant. And I begin my work of getting to know Isabel properly this time, trying to put her more at ease around me. I invite her to my luncheons and actually introduce her. I resist the urge to scream when I see her smug face light up when she shares the news of her engagement. The women around us nod in surprise as they offer their congratulations. I remind myself this is only temporary.

Even she and William appear to be getting on, which makes me wary, and I try my best to warn him without irritating him. He rolls his eyes and kisses me on the forehead. We're tied together by our shared secrets, and I have learnt over the years that the only way for me to manage is to go along with things as best I can. I have to find a way of talking to him about Maya and what I overheard, without him thinking I'm becoming delusional or obsessive. Because that's what he'll say. He'll try and turn it around on me.

Despite outward appearances, the overheard conversation between Miles and Isabel continues to gnaw at me, and I wish they would confide in me so I can help them figure out who it actually could be that's sending the messages.

It's been almost a couple of weeks now since Isabel arrived and the weather is starting to turn sour. I'm sitting in my bedroom, looking out my beautiful windows into the square below. The leaves are beginning to fully drop from their branches, leading us further towards winter. Rain begins to lash against the window, almost out of the blue, and I flinch in shock at the sudden storm. The darkness is setting in, and streetlights begin to float on.

I have to keep my thoughts bright – I'm hosting tonight after all. I've concocted an intimate dinner party with some friends. Some friends that I hope will unwittingly help me get more information out of Isabel than I've been able to achieve so far. She is still deeply suspicious of me. But I can be patient; I have time on my side to get her to trust me. I hope.

I have slowly and carefully been building up a picture of Isabel. More than once, she has become flustered when I've interrupted her when she is sending a text message, and she is extremely private about her belongings. Who could she be talking to and what is she hiding?

I have gone into their room a couple of times too when she and Miles have been out and she appears to have some items locked in her suitcase. I rattled it to check. A simple key lock, but I need that key. I just need to find out where she keeps it.

Tonight, over dinner, I will attempt to eke more information out of her. For now though, I have time to reflect and plan.

A knock on the door interrupts my reverie.

'Yes?' I respond, annoyed by the disturbance.

The door opens a fraction and Maria peeks her head in. 'Mrs King, sorry to disturb you, but these just came in the post for you.' Wordlessly she places a collection of letters on the sideboard and disappears out of the room.

I roll my eyes at the mundane getting in the way of my thoughts. I rise and walk over to the sideboard, deciding to read them now before I have to get ready for dinner. I lean down to the bottom drawer and pull out my silver letter opener, careful not to accidentally prick myself on its sharp edge. It is the one thing I have left from my father.

The first I open is yet another thank you card, the second a routine invitation for another boring event. I stifle a yawn. There have been so many tedious invitations lately. Then the third envelope catches my attention. The address is written in a strange fashion. I look closer. The letters have been cut out carefully from a newspaper. They are arranged to spell *The Kings* and our address. It's so finely done that unless you looked extremely closely, you wouldn't notice at all.

Perhaps someone has finally thought of an interesting way to send an invitation.

But when I open it and scan the contents, my blood runs cold.

Inside is a simple scrap of paper, with words scrawled across it that I have always dreaded reading:

I KNOW WHAT YOU DID.

It drops from my hand like it has scalded me. The room feels like it's spinning, though I am still standing perfectly still.

My mind begins to race at a million miles an hour, one question following another: who sent this? Why would they send this? How could anyone have discovered my secret? And is *that* the secret they're referring to – or, and my stomach drops at the thought, is it something else?

My legs wobble and I have to sit down on the bed before they give way. I'm clutching the envelope in my hand. But the scrap of paper lies there in the middle of the rug – looking completely innocent, though it's anything but.

You have to get a grip, Cassandra. I have to think about this logically. It could be *anything*.

I un-scrunch the envelope that I had unwittingly squished into a tight fist in my shock, trying to see if I can discern anything from it. I pat it out into its original rectangle on my lap, though the lines from where it was squished remain.

The letters, sinisterly cut out with such care and attention to detail, don't yield any clues. I inspect the stamp, but it looks ordinary – just a regular first-class one. There are no international marks on it so it must have been sent from within this country.

What could have happened for something like this to be sent now? The only thing I can think of is that it might be linked to the messages that Miles and Isabel have received. But I can't ask them about it without admitting that I was eavesdropping the other day. And I can't show this note to Miles. He can't know I've been keeping a secret. Can't ask what it is.

I leap up off the bed, scooping the scrap of paper back up from the floor to study it more closely. The same carefully cut-out newspaper letters spell out the simple but terrifying message. But there is nothing else that I can see that could give me any helpful information.

I begin to pace up and down, up and down the room, trying to think what to do. I only have one option: William. He will know what to do; he always does in a crisis like this.

Unless it's because of him that we've received this in the first place.

Chapter Thirty-Three

When William arrives home, I am poised at the vanity in our dressing room. It's a vintage piece, the one thing of my mother's that I wished to have. Even though it's antique, it works in the space as a statement piece. Its three tier mirrors reflect back towards me and the rest of the room – which is my full floor-to-ceiling walk-in closet. Behind this dressing table is the window, which ensures that I always have my favourite view in front of me as I get ready.

Whenever I look in the mirror I hear my mother's voice echoing back at me. *You're too thin. Your face is so long. What colour do you call that hair, mousy brown?* And finally, *Always remember, beauty is pain.*

Some might think it would be a torture to be reminded of those words, but it always ensures I put my best foot forward. I am always ready to *be* Cassandra King. Whoever that is. And whenever I lose her, I come back here and remind myself.

This approach has saved me time and time again, especially after what happened with Maya.

I have been doing my make-up in my usual considered way, taking my time as I wait for William to return. I have always found the relaxing ritual therapeutic: the steps of putting on 'your face', the perfect mask to show to the outside world.

William arrives, blustering into the room with a bang. I stare in a slight daze at myself, lightly brushing my powder brush across my skin. I am in an almost trance-like state. His arrival sparks me into action and I swivel round to exclaim, 'William!'

'I know, I know, I'm late, don't shoot me!' he mutters. He doesn't pause to even look at me as he continues to tug at his tie to loosen it. He swings it up and around his neck in one swift motion and leaves it discarded on the ottoman in the middle of the room. The circle in the middle of the tie is still intact, but the tail dangles off the precipice. I shudder involuntarily. Seeing a tie like that always reminds me of a noose. And suddenly, I see my father, his feet dangling like they were in a dance.

I shut my eyes. *Stop it, Cassandra.* I scream at myself, *Do not go there.* I let the brush continue to glide across my face and take a couple of deep breaths. Once more I am in control.

William is changing his shirt now, completely oblivious to the dark slide my thoughts have taken. He would be very concerned if I told him about all these flashbacks. He would insist I go back to Dr Smythe to check on my medication. But I really don't want to; they diminish my faculties and I need every last shred of my wits about me if I am to get to the bottom of Isabel, and now this anonymous letter.

And of course, I always have to try and stay one step ahead of my *dear* husband. Because ever since Isabel arrived here, I've started to think that he's been keeping something from me too. It's not just what Isabel commented on at that terrible party – I've heard the gossip surrounding my husband on numerous occasions and I've always tried to shut it out.

But now with Maya being dredged up again, and the arrival of this threatening note, I am starting to wonder if I should be so readily believing of everything he tells me.

'William,' I say in my most beseeching voice. The one that he loves but I rarely use. He loves feeling like he's the one in control; I suppose in many ways he is. I'm still here after all. But equally, I don't really have a way out even if I wanted to.

'Yes?' His fresh, more casual shirt is halfway buttoned up, and I notice how he really is in good shape. Why – and for who?

I shake my head. That's not what I am here to discuss.

'William,' I begin again, trying to sound as calm as possible so he can't say I am being overdramatic and catastrophising. 'We received a very concerning letter in the post today.'

'Oh?' he says curiously, as he finishes buttoning up his dark blue shirt. It contrasts with his piercing blue eyes. Those eyes that I can never say no to.

I gulp and stand up to retrieve the envelope from where I had placed it next to me on the dressing table.

I hand it over, keeping a close eye on his face as he reads the intricately pasted address first.

He seems unperturbed but then his brow crinkles as he takes a closer look. 'They look like they've been stuck on,' he remarks in a puzzled tone.

I nod wordlessly, waiting for him to read what's inside.

He takes out the note so slowly that I feel the urge to scream at him to hurry up.

As he unfolds it, his eyes go wide in shock. Then, they crease in anger. I know that look well. 'What is this?' he manages to spit out, his expression turning dark as a thundercloud. 'Is this some kind of sick joke you're trying to play on me because I've been messing up the Cassandra show or something? Because you're obsessed with Isabel and can't bear to become second best in you darling boy's eyes?'

'What... no,' I begin, confused. Why would he think that I would do this?

'Because it is absolutely not funny or cute,' he says, tossing the envelope and paper to one side before crossing his arms to face me.

'William,' I say. 'It came in the post for us. It's a genuine threatening note,' I explain, trying not to sound hysterical. Why doesn't he believe me?

'Really?' he says, looking down at me, and his voice drips with derision. 'Because this wouldn't be the first time recently that there has been some sort of fabricated drama.'

'What are you talking about...?'

'Oh Cassandra, you know exactly what I'm talking about. Isabel. Ever since she's arrived you have been absolutely *convinced* that she's hiding something. She's *not*. She seems like a perfectly lovely girl. She's going to be our daughter-in-law for goodness' sake! And I know that you're terrified of your precious little boy being *stolen* away from you,' He rolls his eyes at that. 'But after the last time,' he says with unmistakable meaning, 'I would have thought that you would see that you have a tendency to let your anger out a bit too rashly where Miles's girlfriends are concerned. And we don't want another situation like *that*, do we?'

'William,' I try again. 'That... that... was completely different, and you know that.'

'Was it? Can't you see it even now? You drove that other girl away, you *caused* that situation – with your judgement and derision. She knew she'd never live up to your pedestal. No wonder she strayed away from your coddled boy as soon as she could see what you were like. How weak he was too.'

'That's your son you're talking about!'

He scoffs in response. 'Pfft... that boy is so weak. But you've never been able to see it.'

All I can do is shake my head in despair, wishing we weren't having this conversation anymore. But William continues anyway. 'But you *had* to lose control. And then I had to clean up your mess. As always. Remember, Cassandra,' he drops his voice low as he stares me down. 'We made a deal. I cleaned it up for you and you were going to be my perfect wife. Or you'd have to pay the clinic another little visit. Did I not make myself clear enough?'

He takes a step towards me and I hate myself as I take an involuntarily step back. Even though our dressing room is big, it's not that big, and my back bumps against the corner of my vanity cabinet. I stifle a cry as I rub the sore spot.

William always has a way of turning these things on me, but I try frantically to bring us back to the threat at hand. I point at the note tossed carelessly to the ground. 'Look, it's obviously a threat!' But my voice comes out high-pitched and shrill, and I regret my words when I see the look on William's face.

It's hard as stone. And he says in a low, dangerous tone, 'Have you fabricated this yourself, Cassandra? Do we need to go on another visit to Dr Smythe? Because we both know this isn't the first time something like this has happened...' His brows crease, looking at me intently, trying to discern what is going on in my mind.

'No, no!' I say quickly. 'William, this is real this time, I promise.'

Oh, how I now regret last year – when I was convinced William was having an affair. Back then I'd felt tired, so tired of just believing everything he said. So, I wrote a letter threatening to expose him. I'd hoped that it would panic him enough to tell me one way or the other.

Unfortunately, he found the stationery I had used in this very drawer of my dressing table. I don't like to think back to that moment. The look of anger on his face. I had grovelled to no end and accepted a higher dose of medication for a short while to avoid being taken back then and there.

And I would do *anything* to never go back to *that place*. Because if William could be controlling, that doctor was something else. The only way I got out of there the last time was by doing everything he said. My life with William was the only option.

After my time there, I knew more than ever before that there was no way out of this life for me. My only way through was to always be on William's side, no matter what. But when this letter I appeared, I *had* to tell him. Only he doesn't believe that I am telling the truth.

Desperate, I clutch onto the one thing that might convince him. 'This isn't the only threat our family has received!'

'What do you mean?'

'Miles and Isabel have been receiving threatening messages too,' I say with defiance.

'How do you know?' He raises an eyebrow.

Then my stomach drops – in my haste I had not thought about how I would explain that I had been eavesdropping.

'I... I...'

How is it possible that I appear as the strongest, most put together woman to the outside world but when it comes to William, I fall apart?

'I heard them talking about it, that's all,' I say, crossing my arms.

'You mean you were eavesdropping?'

'No! I was at home and they were talking so loudly I couldn't help but overhear.'

He frowns, and steps close again to grab my wrist. 'Cassandra,' he says, looking into my eyes. 'You remember what happened the last time you overheard part of a conversation. Come on.' He shakes my wrist and pulls me closer to make his point. 'You *can't* keep doing this.' He drops my wrist like it's burnt him and steps away from me.

'I haven't done anything!' I screech. All at once I'm losing it and my anger starts to bubble over. In the silence that's left from my outburst I hear a loud creak and we both turn to look at the door.

My eyes go wide. Has someone been snooping and overheard us?

I race back out through the walk-in wardrobe to the main door of our bedroom and fling it open fast. But no one is there.

My eyes dart left and right trying to spot any movement, and I swear I see a small shadow pass at the end of the corridor. But before I have a chance to fly out there and check, I am distracted by the sound of laughter behind me.

I spin around to see William hunched over and shaking his head as a derisive snort escapes his lips.

'See?' he says, gesturing his arms wide. 'There's nothing and no one there.' He walks over to me and grabs my hands again, pulling me firmly back into the room. 'It's all in your head, Cassandra. No one is trying to get at you or "uncover" you, least of all Isabel. You have to stop imagining things.'

'How are you so certain?' I'm still talking too loudly, feeling wild and out of control. This was not how this conversation was supposed to go.

'I've been getting to know her, Cassandra.' He leads me back across the room and through to the dressing room. He pushes me gently towards the ottoman, forcing me to sit as he goes on. 'She is different, I promise you. You have been so focused on trying to see things that aren't there that you haven't seen *her*. Honestly.'

My brow creases but I let him go on. Why has he been getting to know her so well? And when? 'And,' he continues in a magnanimous tone, '*if* this threatening note *is* from someone else...' He still sounds highly sceptical and is choosing to believe that I made the whole thing up to cause drama. 'Then, just think, we have so many people that are envious of us, that want to be us.' He sits down next to me and holds my hands tightly. 'It's probably just a note sent in jealousy. Remember, we have everything, and everyone wants to be us.' He finishes with a shrug.

When he looks at me like this, his powerful blue eyes drilling into my own, I can almost believe it. *Almost.*

And almost forget about his threats. *Almost.*

'Now,' he adds, 'can we put this behind us, or do I need to give Dr Smythe a call?'

I shake my head in response. This will always be the way that he wins any discussion. Because I do *not* want to go back there.

'No...' I begin shakily at first, then more confidently. 'No, you're right. It is probably someone sending a note in jealously. We are so lucky. *I* am so lucky.' I force out a smile even though my stomach twists and untwists.

'That's right,' he says, nodding, then stands up and kisses me on the forehead. 'Now, shall we have this dinner? I'm starving.' He turns and marches out of the room, ready to move on.

I sit there, dazed.

I glance down to where William had been sitting just a moment before. The tie has been crumpled, but the noose-like circle is still intact. I feel nauseous.

Why won't he believe me? Even with what happened last year, he normally always would. Again I can't help but think of the only thing that's changed between now and then: Isabel. And their apparent new friendship. When did that happen? Has she been whispering things about me, making jokes about me in his ear?

I glance down at the tie again. Perhaps I am just being paranoid, putting myself under too much strain and stress.

I am not sure. But I won't let this feeling get to me, like it got to my father. I won't be worn down. Not by William. And certainly not by Isabel.

Because I am not imagining things. I just need to prove it.

If I don't, my very sanity is on the line.

Chapter Thirty-Four

I am glad that we have a larger dinner party this evening, with our friends Edward and Allegra coming as well. It's a good distraction for me after my and William's disastrous conversation earlier.

And I can focus on the original goal I had with this dinner plan too: hopefully Isabel will feel she is being less closely watched with more people around.

As dinner progresses and everyone becomes more relaxed by the food and wine, I notice that Isabel and William are getting along famously. She's really come out of her shell, laughing and joking about all sorts of things. I hadn't noticed it before but Miles appears to sour when they are laughing too much, a frown forming across his brow.

At one point, she has a long conversation with Allegra, who is sitting next to her. I have always found Allegra quite an odious woman, constantly hunting for – and spreading – gossip. Which is why I'd wanted to invite her tonight – I thought she might be able to get more out of Isabel than I have managed. It looks like they're getting on famously. My plan is working.

As we near the end of dinner, William has to step out of the room to take an 'urgent call' – how unsurprising.

The conversation takes a natural lull at that point and we sip our wines in silence for a moment. I am about to announce that we should all move to the sitting room when Isabel turns to me out of the blue and asks if any post has come today. I almost spill my red wine glass all over the table. But her eyes are wide and innocent. Purposefully so?

'What, why?' I can't help but spit out, causing Miles to look at me sharply in rebuke. He's been watching my behaviour with Isabel extremely closely since they returned. Allegra and Edward also look a little surprised by my tone. I must keep it under control.

'Oh, I am just expecting a letter inviting me to a doctor's appointment, that's all,' she says.

I narrow my eyes but manage to respond in a calm voice.

'There was nothing for you today.' I take another sip of my wine.

She nods and looks away. She thinks I don't see but I continue to watch her. I don't miss the little smile she makes into her lap. Oh, I wasn't imagining things. Not imagining them at all.

'Really?' Allegra coos. 'I hope everything is alright?' She can't help herself, that woman. Always trying to dig up something new to spread.

'Oh definitely,' Isabel says.

The twelve-week mark in this supposed pregnancy hasn't passed yet, so that will be why she isn't saying anything more. I swear a knowing smile passes over Allegra's lips in return, as she files this information safely away. Maybe inviting her wasn't my best idea after all.

Soon, William returns and we finish up this tedious dinner. Even though it was my idea, I am tired of the whole thing now, and wish to just speak to Allegra and see if anything came from my little plan.

After what feels like forever, I decide it's an appropriate time to suggest we have a drink in the upstairs drawing room. Miles, always my polite boy, tactfully excuses himself and Isabel, citing an early start in the morning. He does not have one, but he probably wants to get away from the evening as much as I do. I don't blame him. I am glad that they will be out of the way: I can freely quiz Allegra.

We move into the drawing room, and William and Edward wander off in search of more drinks. I have instructed Maria to finish up after dinner and we would take care of ourselves.

Allegra and I take a seat in my carefully curated room. I wanted it to feel warm and welcoming: perfect for sharing secrets.

The lighting is low and the two matching sofas facing each other in the shade of the Victorian bay window and bookshelves enhance the cosy feeling. The curtains are rich, red and velvet. My favourite kind. I'd drawn them earlier to top off that feeling of an enclosed, safe and comfortable space. I even made sure that the fire would be roaring to complete the effect. Allegra has no chance of leaving this room without sharing everything she spoke about tonight.

She flops onto the sofa, her cheeks pink from all the wine and food.

'Ah Cassandra,' she remarks, 'you really have the most excellent taste in everything. Food, wine and this room. My, I haven't been in here before and it's just exquisite. So delightful. I feel like I could just hole away here all day.'

Exactly.

'Oh, you know me, Allegra, I can't stay still for long. And this room was my latest project. I wanted to get it just right in time for winter. This is its first proper use.'

'It's just wonderful. I wish I could create something just like this… I bet Miles's new young lady, Isabel, must love this space.'

'Why do you say that?' I ask, pleased that already Allegra was ready to share something she had found out that she thinks I won't know. Normally, this irks me, but not today.

'Oh,' her voice drops low in anticipation of a gossip. 'She was talking about how much she *loved* all the houses here. "So full of history and character", she said. Apparently, she has admired them for *years*, coming around here all the time when she stayed in London before. Did you know that?'

I pause, thinking for a minute how to answer. 'Yes, of course, I knew she was in London before.'

'Right,' Allegra adds, a disappointed edge to her voice that she hadn't managed to reveal anything new yet. 'But did you know she lived in one of those tiny little flats, over in East London? How peculiar to make her way over here just to wander around the streets and admire the houses.' I did have to admit it was a bit odd. I had not known where she was living before, so this was interesting new information.

'Why yes, of course I knew that. And I think it's quite normal to explore different parts of the city, don't you think?' I wasn't going to let Allegra think that I didn't know what she was talking about. Or that I thought Isabel's behaviour was strange. I certainly didn't want my real thoughts about her being flung around town.

Allegra presses on regardless of my words. 'Oooh yes. She just said that she thought her family might have lived around here once,' she adds.

'Really?' This is information is even better and I've even stopped caring about pretending to know everything. Isabel had continued to be so coy about her family, just saying that there weren't any of them left. I never knew that some of them had lived in the UK before, and I was impressed that Allegra had got this piece of information.

'I mean she didn't say that explicitly...' she hastens to clarify when she sees my excitement. I try not to audibly sigh. Allegra is basically making this up.

She continues on, 'But I got that general sense. I was asking her about Australia, and telling her about my second cousins that moved out there a long time ago.' I nod, wondering where she's going with this. 'I asked her if she thought her family was from the UK originally, and she responded with an "oh yes", and so I asked if her interest in this part of London came from that and she seemed to change the subject swiftly. So I don't know, but *to me* it seems like family connections could be part of the reason for her loving this area,' she finishes with a shrug.

Before I have a chance to ask another question, the door swings open and William and Edward enter with a tray of drinks.

'There you are, boys,' Allegra coos.

I get to my feet, ready to play the part of hostess once more.

'We were positively dying of thirst,' I say with a spring in my step.

Allegra's information might not be much, but it's definitely something.

Isabel has something to hide about her family, and I am determined to find out what.

Chapter Thirty-Five

All in all, the evening hadn't been a total waste – I learnt that Isabel doesn't want us to know about her family history. That would be the next thing I would look into.

But now, as I lie in bed, my mind tosses and turns over who could have sent that letter. Could it be a member of Maya's family? Come at last to uncover our dark secret? Or could it be someone closer to home… Isabel?

Deep down, I'm terrified. William's threat of forcing me to return to Dr Smythe scares me.

If I'm honest, as well as being scared, all of this has thrilled me too. I had been bored before; ever since Isabel had arrived, there has been so much more to focus my energies on. Just as long as my son doesn't get burnt in the process. That is my priority.

I can't sleep. Perhaps if I go down to my study, I could let off some steam at my easel. Distracting myself with drawing has always worked before. Or maybe I'll even write down a few thoughts in my diary.

Quietly, I creep out of bed. I can't wake William, he would be annoyed, and concerned to see me getting up in the middle of the night. I haven't done that in many years – not since what happened with Maya.

It would be yet another reason for him to think I need to return to the clinic. If he questions me, I will say I was getting some water. All this subterfuge exhausts me, but what else can I do?

I slip on my merino wool slippers and fumble in the darkness for my silk dressing gown that I left draped over my chaise. This was not the first time I have coordinated a middle-of-the-night escape without William's notice, and I ease myself soundlessly out of our room and into the corridor.

Smatterings of light from the streetlamps funnel through from the large windows above. London is a city that never sleeps.

I creep along the corridor. I cannot be caught – it would cost too much – but I could not stay in my bed for a moment longer either.

I reach the top of the landing and I'm struck by the brilliantly full moon that I can see shining through the skylight. Its glow helps illuminate my path. In my silk dressing gown, I can't help but feel ghostlike drifting through my home. As I make my way down the steps, I try not to think about the other ghost that haunts this house.

I descend silently, trying to discard all worries from my mind. When I reach the bottom of the staircase, I tread more purposefully. I am far enough away from our room that the sound won't carry. But as I walk under the floating chandelier and through to the sitting room, I am surprised to hear a scuffling noise and then the words, 'We'll catch up tomorrow – but I've got to go, bye.'

There is a tinge of urgency and panic to them, and I recognise it is Isabel.

It takes me a moment to spot her in the dim light of the room, but then I see her crouched in a corner, directly opposite the piano.

She leaps up, just as shocked, which helps me gain a moment to put together my mask of composure.

'Cassandra,' Isabel says, more flustered than I have ever seen her. 'I was just uh, making a call to... Australia.'

My instincts take over, eyes narrowing. She must be unsure about how much I overheard and is attempting to keep her explanation broad, hedging her bets that hopefully I won't have heard much.

I fold my arms, remembering this is my house and I can demand what I want. Who cares if William hears me now – I can say I heard movement downstairs and look, here I am finally proved right. He can't put it down to being in my imagination.

'Oh yes?' I ask slowly. 'Is everything alright? It sounded tense.'

Even though she is bathed in half-darkness herself, I swear as I take another step closer that I see her face go pale.

'Ah yes... just some family affairs to sort out.'

I remain still, unsmiling. I hope she'll say more. But the silence stretches out so I try again. 'Oh, but is everything alright with such a call in the middle of the night? I didn't think you had much family left...'

'It's to do with my grandparents affairs... lawyers...' she replies, regaining her composure.

I have not flown off the handle at her so perhaps she has realised that I didn't overhear anything of importance. Or she genuinely wasn't discussing anything that she needed to hide. But then why do the call so secretively?

'Oh I see, and they could only talk in the middle of the night here? That seems strange.' I cross my arms, leaving no mistake about the fact that I think she is withholding something.

Isabel shakes her head and I don't miss the note of condescension in her voice as she says, 'There's a time difference, Cassandra. And right now is the start of their working day, so the best time to get hold of them.' She begins to walk towards me and the exit. 'And of course I didn't want to wake anyone.' As she crosses in front of me, the moonlight illuminates her face fully. Her eyes look red and puffy, like she's been crying.

I stiffen; I haven't seen her in this state before. She is, like me, in pyjamas. But unlike me, in very plain ones with an oversized hoodie on top. Her face is devoid of even her usual small scrap of make-up, and without it she looks younger and more vulnerable. As she approaches me in the doorway, I can see that her face is tear-streaked and for a moment I soften, seeing her look so frail.

Automatically, I place a hand on her arm as she tries to pass me. She pauses in her tracks. She looks across at me, her eyes wide in shock, and I have another flashback to that moment many years ago with Maya. Anger flares in me, but also regret. Can I manage this better?

'Is everything really okay, dear?' I ask in the smoothest voice I can manage. And for a second, I think I see a softening in her eyes as she looks into my own. Her mouth opens like she is about to speak. But then I see it: the flash of some deep-rooted anger.

I have not been imagining it all this time.

There is something she is hiding. The look I have just seen in her eyes tells me that, without a doubt, it is something to do with *me*.

She shrugs me off with surprising force and I retract my hand like I've been burnt. I suppose I have, in a way. I don't give empathy out that frequently, and when it is rejected like this, I don't forget. The anger that's never too far away flares in me too.

'Absolutely fine,' she says with an unmistakable note of steel. 'Don't you worry about me, Cassandra... just look after *yourself*,' she adds with a slight threatening smirk, and her eyes blaze for a moment with undiluted hatred. Then, without a backwards glance, she slips out of the room and out of sight.

I'm reeling and my heart races much faster than it should. *See, Cassandra, this is what happens when you have a moment of weakness.*

But what I'd just realised shook me to my very core. She didn't just distrust me, she *despised* me. Her thinly veiled threat ran in my mind on a loop. *Look after yourself.*

I was now certain: Isabel had sent this letter; Isabel was trying to destroy my family from the inside out. I just wasn't sure *why* – yet. And still, only I seem to keep seeing this other side of her.

I bury my head in my hands, exhausted and frustrated. It would have to be me. Again. I have done it before with Maya after all.

It is the only way, and I will not fail. I will expose her before it is too late for William, for Miles and ultimately, for me.

Chapter Thirty-Six

After all that had gone on with Isabel, I didn't have the strength to go into my study. Instead, I'd crept back upstairs like a thief in the night. I'd lain wide awake next to William's carefree snores the rest of the night, until morning seeped into the horizon at last. Perhaps I'd dozed for a moment or two, but I couldn't get my mind to still. It had fizzed with a million different possibilities of who Isabel might really be, and what she really wants.

The inescapable thought had come into my mind that could she be linked with Maya somehow.

But Maya was from here, Isabel from Australia – they couldn't really be further apart. What Allegra had found out about some of Isabel's family possibly being from the UK could be important perhaps. And what *other* reason could Isabel have for such hatred of me?

There was, of course, that one other secret... the worst secret of all. But surely not. It was impossible. No one knew about that.

I'd shaken it out of my mind, not allowing myself to go there. Really, it doesn't matter why she hates me, all I know is that Isabel is not all she seems or who she says she is.

So after my sleepless night, I rise early, the beginnings of a plan formed in my mind. Isabel had mentioned on the call that she would be catching up with someone tomorrow. So all I need to do is follow and see who she might be meeting to help piece together the puzzle at last. I would have to be fast, quiet and unseen. Something I wasn't sure I was capable of, but I had to try.

And now as I finish getting dressed, William is already up and on his way out. 'Busy day today,' he says, brushing my cheek with the briefest of kisses. 'You'll be good?' he whispers in my ear. It takes all my self-control not to lash out in retaliation at his patronising tone. It would not end well for me.

'Perfectly,' I respond, trying to keep my tone neutral whilst at the same time balling my hand into a fist. I press my nails into my palm to stop myself from screaming. Losing control at William will not help anything. I have to prove myself beyond all doubt or I will end up back at Dr Smythe's. Or worse.

He leaves with his best smile plastered to his face, and not for the first time I wonder how he rationalises his behaviour to himself. Probably that he just knows best; he *always* knows best in his world. And there's no point dwelling on it. It's something that I can only work within, and never truly change.

Yes, perhaps our marriage is not really full of joy and happiness, but we have worked hard to create this image and build this life for Miles. I'm not going to let one measly girl snatch it all away.

I take a strange sense of comfort in this thought process. I work to transform into my curated exterior, taking care at the mirror to apply my make-up. I choose the exact right 'errands' outfit, before ensuring that there isn't a single hair out of line as I straighten my expertly cut blonde bob. By the time I emerge from the dressing room, I am ready to face it all.

Then I perch on my chaise longue and peer down upon my favourite view in London. The houses opposite mirror ours as usual, the square quiet and the day a bright one, with not a cloud in the sky. I open my phone and bring up the security system. I'll receive an alert when there is motion in the hallway, and so I'll be able to stage a run in, without anyone suspecting a thing.

It's time for me to take control of the situation. Enough is enough.

Chapter Thirty-Seven

My plan works a treat and I glide down the stairs coat on, bag in hand, as I spot Miles and Isabel in the hallway.

'Good morning,' I chirrup in my most positive tone.

'Morning, Mum,' Miles says shrugging on his coat.

Isabel forces a tight smile at me but doesn't say anything more. I can read the unspoken agreement between Isabel and me not to mention last night and that's fine by me. I have a longer game to play, and I don't want anyone to know that I was roaming the house at night again either.

'Are you both leaving now too?' I enquire as I reach the bottom of the stairs in the most casual way I can muster.

'Yes,' Miles responds for them, 'and I was just saying to Isabel that she should let me order a taxi for her. She has to go to a doctor's appointment, and I can't come with her I'm afraid. But you shouldn't have to walk or Tube all the way to Victoria.' He shakes his head at Isabel as though exasperated with her headstrong decision. And I see an opportunity.

'I could do with the journey and fresh air,' Isabel insists. She's affecting a carefree manner, but I can tell from the look in her eyes that this is quite important to her to go alone. She busies herself with wrapping a scarf around her neck.

'I'm walking down to Fulham Road and the King's Road for some errands. Perhaps I could come with you some of the way?' I ask.

I watch Isabel's nostrils flare and eyes widen with a sense of panic. This is not what she wants. I know now for certain, that wherever she is going right now, she doesn't want anyone to follow her.

'Would you, Mum?' asks Miles happily. 'That would work, don't you think Iz?' he tosses the question over to her as though it's not the grenade that Isabel and I know that it is.

Isabel responds in a small voice, 'Yes, why not.' She can't say no without giving an acceptable reason, so the only answer is a yes. Or so I think. She makes a show of looking at her watch.

'Oh god,' she says in a dramatic voice. 'I'm going to be late for the appointment, so I think I really ought to catch the Tube. And I don't want you to go out of your way for me, Cassandra.'

It's all I can do to stop my mouth from dropping open. I've already said I was planning on walking, so I can't change my mind and go with her now. It will look too obvious.

'Ah, never mind then,' Miles shrugs. 'My car is outside, let's go, I can drop you at the station at least, Iz.' She nods, the slip of a smile on her lips.

'Oh, but...' I stammer.

'Don't worry, Cassandra,' Isabel says with that infuriating grin, placing an icy hand on my arm as she walks past me. 'I'll be perfectly fine. We'll see you later.'

With that Miles clicks open the front door, holding it open for Isabel who all but runs out, and Miles turns one last time, throwing me a small wave over his shoulder on the way out. 'Thanks though, Mum, see you.'

As the door clicks shut, I stand there stunned. I shake with anger for a moment, unable to believe it. I want to scream; I want to throw every delicate item that I so carefully curated in this room at the wall in anger.

Instead I hurl my absurdly expensive Prada handbag straight at the front door. It makes a resounding thud and a slight cracking noise before it slides down to land on the floor, its contents spilling out.

The anger seeps out of my body, and instead I'm left with a feeling of listlessness and despair. What am I doing? Did I really think I would be able to follow Isabel like some sort of detective? I'm no spy. More than that, I'm letting my paranoia take over. But I don't know how to stop it. I don't know what I can do when I'm sure she's here to destroy us.

As I pick up my belongings, I notice that one long crack runs straight down the middle of my phone screen. That's just *great*. I shove it back in the bag.

I breathe deeply, trying to keep myself calm. Because if I couldn't follow Isabel to where she was going, I would have to seize the only other option left to me. And that is searching their room *properly* this time.

The time is over for being too careful. We are receiving threats, and after last night I know that Isabel is planning something.

So it's time to take a risk. And I'm breaking in to Isabel and Miles's room, whatever the consequences might be.

Chapter Thirty-Eight

As always when I enter Miles's room, I'm struck by how empty and soulless it looks. None of his personality remains and it looks like any of our other guest rooms. The one difference is the dark red curtains he insisted that he wanted during the refurbishment. He said he wanted the room to feel cosy. But when they're open like they are now, I can't help but think it looks like blood is seeping across the carpet.

I shudder as I glance around the room, looking for any sort of bag or drawer that might be holding more notes, cards or anything else that could give me a clue about who Isabel really is. And what she's really up to.

The room is spotless. Maria must have already come in to clean, which means she won't disturb me either. I start with the bedside drawers. I pull open each one but find nothing of interest in them. It's such an obvious place though. What a stupid starting point.

I feel anxious, like I'm already running out of time. I take a deep breath; I need to remain methodical. If it were me, where would I place something that I didn't want to be found?

I pace the room as I think. The bathroom? Possibly, but there's a likely chance that Maria would go through the drawers in there, and it's shared with Miles. Where to hide things when you're a guest in someone else's home?

I glance at the wardrobe and wonder. Where would a man or housekeeper never look? It's another walk-in, but smaller than ours, with the wardrobe on the left and the bathroom across to the right. Inside, I see an array of coats, blazers and dresses hanging up haphazardly. The one place someone may not look or accidentally come across when cleaning... inside the pocket of a jacket. It's what I would do, after all.

I rifle through the first couple of pockets and come up with nothing. Going through someone else's belongings feels a little desperate. *Needs must*, Mother used to say, and this is certainly one of those times – though my mother's words of advice ringing in my ears isn't particularly a comfort. I push her voice out of my thoughts as I strike on something with my fingertips that feels hard and rectangular. Something you wouldn't expect to feel inside a pocket. Success at last.

Pulling it out, I'm surprised to see that it is a dark blue passport. Australian passports are blue, so I assume it's Isabel's. But as I flip it over, I can't believe what I see. Because it's a blue *British* passport.

Why would Isabel be hiding a British passport? Why would she even have one?

I flip open the book and scan the page.

Two realisations hit me at once.

'Isabel' was actually born in London.

'Isabel' is not who she says she is.

My knees feel weak and I lean back against the drawer behind me, the passport still clutched in my hand. It feels like I've been punched in the chest. As I finally understand who Isabel *really* is.

Chapter Thirty-Nine

My heart thunders as I try to piece the puzzle together. It cannot be a coincidence that 'Isabel' has the same unique surname as the assistant I'd forced William to let go a year ago. The same assistant that had betrayed me.

And it especially can't be a coincidence when she didn't go willingly.

No, that girl disappeared under a cloud of smoke.

Because I'd caught her trying to steal something that didn't belong to her.

Gemma McKenna had been the best executive assistant William had ever had. She'd been responsive, organised, understanding and, above all, discreet. Crucially, she'd also always kept me in the loop. Some of William's previous assistants had been terrible at that. But no, Gemma knew that a happy wife would be a happy life for William. And I'd appreciated that about her.

She was with us for about two years, and in that time, I'd got so used to having her around that it had almost felt like she'd become a friend of sorts. At tedious events that I had to go to with William, it was always a relief to see her there and we'd share a drink or two. On a few occasions when she had to drop something round to the house, I'd invite her in for a drink. She'd seemed genuinely interested in my books and art that I'd even mentioned that I had a whole special room for them off the library, and shown it to her. I should have known better than to share anything that was special to me. I hadn't told her explicitly my favourite book, but I guess she'd studied me closely as I'd pulled the spine and had seen which one allowed entry.

But Gemma just had such an easy and relaxed way about her, with a mass of dark, curly hair and understanding eyes, that it felt like I didn't always have to put on the Cassandra show around her all the time. It had been refreshing.

So I guess it could be said that I'd let her become too close – I'd started to like and trust her too much. And that was my big mistake. Because one day, in a moment of weakness, I told her something I shouldn't.

It had been forty years since my father's death and even though that day is ancient history, it still surprises me how much it affects me. I guess I try not to think about it all the other days of the year, but that one day always gets me.

I'd been feeling anxious all day but William insisted that I had to accompany him to an awards ceremony for the charity King & Co. was sponsoring. 'It would look dreadful if my wife wasn't there, Cassandra!' he said. And I've never been able to deny him when he needs me.

Trying to sweep my emotions under the carpet, I'd shown up to the bustling event in my favourite Chanel evening gown. I'd thought it would help my mood. But I recognised no one – and William was busy schmoozing the room. I'd not had it in me to try to make small talk, and so I was relieved to see Gemma in the corner of the room, standing sentry in that assured way she had.

I'd made a beeline to her and she made me instantly feel more relaxed, even as she kept topping up my glass, I only realised later.

But one moment I'd been fine, and then the next I heard my father's favourite classical piece begin. Memories of me as a little girl on the edges of his toes, waltzing around the room, had flooded back to me and I had to rush from the room. I couldn't very well burst in to tears in front of everyone.

I'd managed to retreat to the large luxurious bathroom and tucked myself into one of the sofas that lined the powder room portion of the enormous suite. I'd retrieved my small journal and began writing my way into a state of calm again. If anyone saw me, I'd explain it away as writing down some ideas for my next charity event.

I wouldn't normally risk bringing one of my journals out with me at all, but I'd thought I might need a moment of relief at some point on a day like this. And I'd been right.

I've kept a diary ever since I can remember; it was something that my father had encouraged me to do. *'To keep track of all those big thoughts and feelings you have, my darling girl.'* Mother had scoffed of course.

But after his awful death, it had felt like a tiny tether still to him and a way to process it all.

It was something that William had asked me to stop doing when we'd married – he'd emphasised that it was important to him that we never had anything written down. At first, I'd tried to follow what he'd asked of me. It was just a diary after all. But I'd found myself becoming too anxious – writing my thoughts down had become a crutch. Sometimes, it felt like the only friend I had, and I couldn't give it up. So I simply hid it from him.

But I'd also started to appreciate over the years that my journals had become a record of everything I've ever done. And in the wrong hands, they could be lethal. And yet I couldn't bring myself to ever get rid of them either. It might sound silly, but even now I feel like they give me some sort of substance, a tether to reality and a way back to myself. When sometimes I can feel so lost. We're all allowed a vice, aren't we?

For the longest time, I'd been so careful about no one ever knowing about them. Until that night.

'Cassandra,' Gemma had approached cautiously. 'Are you okay?'

I looked up in shock. I hadn't heard her creep in, and I'd been so lost in my thoughts.

'Oh yes, yes.' I waved my hand in the air to be casual. 'I just needed a minute,' I finally managed.

'Anything I can help with?' Gemma asked, her eyes bright with concern.

I could have breezed off her question, just used the excuse I'd already pre-prepared. But somehow, seeing her there with such worry written on her face, I hadn't been able to help but tell her the truth. Or at least some of it.

'Today is just a difficult day – it reminds me of someone I used to know, is all.'

Gemma had nodded with understanding and moved closer. 'And so writing helps you process it all?' she guessed instantly. I'd looked up with a small frown, holding the book tightly in my lap. 'Oh I journal too,' she continued, 'so I'd just assumed. I find it helps me on tricky days.'

In that moment, it had felt so wonderful to actually be *seen* as me for once, not just the Cassandra I always had to appear to be to the outside world. And it also genuinely felt like she'd understood me too. So in a flood of relief after all the tension of the day I admitted in a rush, 'Yes, I've kept many diaries over the years too. Isn't it wonderful?'

'Yes,' she agreed eagerly, 'just have to be careful to hide them somewhere safe is all. I remember when my mum found my teenage journal and that was terribly embarrassing! I'd thought I'd found a great place, hiding them in my underwear drawer!'

I laughed and it felt like a long-held ache in my chest being released – so much so that I hadn't thought before saying, 'Absolutely, my father taught me both to journal *and* that the best place to hide them is always under the floorboards! Try that next time!'

But as soon as the words were out of my mouth, I wanted to stuff them back in. Because I'd spoken without thinking. Something I *never* did. But all the tension of the day and the champagne I'd drunk had got to my head. And unwittingly, I'd revealed exactly where my current hiding spot was. But, Gemma wouldn't care and wouldn't have noticed my slip – would she?

So I tried to just keep breezing past it. 'Anyway,' I said, 'I better get back to the party.' I placed the small book back inside my black clutch and strode over to the mirror to reapply my lipstick and put my mask back on.

'Sure,' Gemma said with a smile, 'I'll see you back out there then.'

I nodded into my glass reflection. But as she'd turned to leave, I called after her in the most casual way I could, 'Oh Gemma, if you could just not mention this whole thing to William, that would be great. He'd worry if he knew – both that I had a bit of a moment, but also about the diary. Okay?'

I hoped I'd made it sound as casual as possible. Like there was nothing strange about my request.

And Gemma raised her eyebrow a tiny bit but shrugged. 'Of course, Cassandra. It'll be our little secret.'

Chapter Forty

I really shouldn't have been shocked when I found Gemma on her hands and knees in my study. Now of course, everything seemed so obvious. She'd just been trying to get close to me to what, discover all my secrets? I had no idea what exactly she had against *me* but I knew it had to stop then and there.

Alice, our last housekeeper, had come into my room as I was just starting to get ready for the annual party that we always hosted at home to celebrate King & Co. She'd told me that Gemma had just arrived and had gone straight to the library, to gather some things for William and help tidy up. I'd found that strange, as normally during this party, we kept the library safely locked. William too had important documents and valuable pieces of art in there. But I'd gone down to say hello, and of course, found that she wasn't in the main part of the library.

When I'd entered my secret study, she hopped up from behind the desk where she'd been crouching and tried to brush it all off. Using that same excuse that she'd been sent over to help clear up. She'd gone bright red. I looked her up and down in distaste and told her to get out in my most commanding voice. She ran out with her tail between her legs. There had been no reason why she should be in this room, and she knew that. After what I'd accidentally let slip about the floorboards, I could only assume she'd tried to use the distraction of the party as an opportunity to search.

I checked my hiding place and everything was as it should have been – but I still didn't believe her story. How could I?

I had to carry on with the party as usual that night. At last, when all the guests had left, I had a chance to talk to William. I asked him about whether he'd sent Gemma over early to tidy up; he said he had, and had wanted her to get something from the library. I frowned – maybe I'd got this all wrong and she was telling the truth. I couldn't take the chance though. Even if he'd asked her to go into the library, there's no way she should have been in my separate wing.

So I took matters into my own hands.

'William,' I said softly as I sat across from him in the library. I'd decided to approach him carefully, when he was in a happy mood after a successful evening, lounging in the library with a glass of whisky in hand. 'I didn't want to tell you this earlier. But Alice believes she saw Gemma take some extra files from the house away with her.'

'What do you mean?' his head shot up.

'Oh, just I know that you'd asked her to retrieve a few files. But Alice just mentioned it looked like she'd had a stack of papers with her tonight when she left. It might be nothing at all. Just wanted to pass it on to you.' I said as sweetly as possible, taking a sip of my own red wine.

He frowned. 'I didn't ask her to take anything away from the house with her. She'd just been supposed to gather a document I had here so we could give it to Charles this evening when he was over.'

He had stood up and wandered over to his large walnut desk and retrieved the small key from its hiding spot in the nook under the table.

Opening the drawer, he swore when he saw that it was empty.

As I'd known would happen.

'Whaaat!' he slurred in his exclamation. 'She shouldn't have taken these!' He slammed the drawer shut in frustration.

'I'm sure it's just a misunderstanding,' I said, playing my innocence perfectly. 'If you ask her, I'm certain she will have just made a mistake.'

But of course I knew that would not be the case.

He'd called Gemma up immediately, in spite of the late hour, and in a predictable fashion she denied it.

But when David Archer at the *Telegraph* got in touch with William a few days later to tell him as a friend that some files had been sent to him that really should *not* see the light of day, Gemma was fired immediately without a reference. No matter her protestations.

It had been a risk sending some of William's sensitive files to a journalist, but I'd known that David would never expose William – barely any of the papers would dare. He'd worked hard over the years to have many of them in his pocket for just this sort of eventuality.

Of course, Gemma hadn't sent them. But I couldn't afford the risk of having her around any longer, the risk of exposing my secret diaries to William, but also her stealing them for herself. And that would be *way* more damaging than whatever sensitive work documents William kept in his desk. I'd had no choice. I simply had to get rid of her, and in such a way that she'd be completely discredited.

I was even a tiny bit proud. I'd thought I'd finally pulled something off all by myself. There was no way Gemma could have known that it was me that set her up.

But now, as I stare at Isabel's sickeningly familiar name, or should I say her *real* name of Molly Isabel McKenna, my blood goes cold. Without a doubt she must be related to Gemma.

I can't believe I missed this. But then again why would I have ever put two and two together without this passport? They look nothing alike, and I only ever knew Miles's new girlfriend as *Molly Isabel Atkinson* – which is on her Australian passport, the one she'd used for her work history. It was the information I'd been given to discover where she'd worked previously of course. I didn't think about the fact that she might be a dual national. With two different names – which for some strange reason is legally allowed.

She must have decided that 'McKenna' was too distinct a name and would have signposted a connection to Gemma.

So I stand frozen in the wardrobe, clutching the passport like a talisman. It's the one source of truth that I haven't been going crazy. That girl *has* been keeping something from me, from *Miles*, the whole time.

Because from what Miles has said, he also only knows her as Molly Isabel Atkinson. And now the look of terror in her eyes for that split second when I said that Isabel wasn't her real name makes complete sense. Because she thought I'd meant the one on this passport. McKenna. And she thought I'd found her out.

My head spins with all this new information as one thing above all else becomes clear to me: Isabel must be after what her cousin failed to achieve – she must be after my diaries. The question is, what do these McKenna girls want with them? They have *all* my secrets in there. But which one are they most desperate to find?

I'm frozen by what I should do next and how I can expose her. I know I can't simply tell William or Miles. Or at least, not yet.

If I told William, I'd have to tell him why Gemma McKenna might have such a vendetta against me, and I'd have to admit to him about my secret diaries. I'm already on the precipice of being sent to Dr Smythe's as it is; this could throw William over the edge if he learns what I've been doing behind his back all these years.

The only person that really matters in all this is Miles. If I can get him to accept that he's been lied to by Isabel, then perhaps William doesn't even need to be brought into it at all. Isabel can just disappear, and I'll have my darling son back.

I can't just tell Miles outright though. I can't admit that I've been snooping through all their things. Not after last time. He'll likely get all defensive and then just dismiss me in anger. I'm sure Isabel would find a way to turn it around on to me.

From what happened before, I've come to realise that the only way to get what I want is for him to find out for himself that he's been lied to.

I twirl this secret passport in my hand. I know exactly how to do it.

Chapter Forty-One

I'm back on my favourite perch overlooking the street, mentally preparing for the evening ahead.

Before this same party three years ago, I'd found Gemma rifling around on the floor. Now, I'm watching numerous glittering people traipse into our house. I suppose I should call them our guests, but I have been dreading this party all year. The night of our famous anniversary.

Of course it's not mine and William's *wedding* anniversary party. Who really cares about that? No, it's the anniversary of King & Co. and all William has achieved. It is his job to be celebrated and mine to look like the perfect bauble on his arm.

At least it won't be a wasted evening, because my plan is all set since discovering Isabel's *true* identity a few days ago.

'Isabel' will have no idea what's coming, I'll finally get my son back and everything will be played out in front of all our family and friends. It's perfect.

Two birds. One stone.

I don't normally like to make things public – but it's the only way to ensure Miles grasps the extent of Isabel's lies.

I stand up, a small flutter of excitement in my chest.

I am certain everything will work out this time, as it should.

Because there's a surprise in store.

And it's going to be a good one for me.

And a terrible one for her.

I glide back over to my walk-in wardrobe so I can take one last look in the floor-to-ceiling mirror, expertly placed just beyond the open arch.

I take in my statuesque appearance. My shining hair grazes the edge of my razor-sharp cheekbones. I spent hours at the hairdresser this morning ensuring they cut and coloured it to perfection. My make-up is equally flawless; I spent over an hour ensuring everything from my contouring to my delicately blended eye shadow is exactly right.

Now as I smooth my hands over the folds of my floor-length, midnight blue gown, I see it catch the soft lamplight, its luxurious silk shining like onyx. It stops short just above my ankle to ensure my favourite Manolo Blahniks are on display, their signature crystal buckle peeping out purposefully.

I take it all in and nod in approval.

My battle armour at the ready.

I try to smile at my reflection, my pearly white teeth glistening in contrast to my dark red lips.

Though I'm not happy, I *am* pleased that it's all going to finally be over after tonight.

At least after the drama I'm planning, we won't have to have another one of these silly parties again. Tonight will become too notorious.

There was a time when I loved it all. Adored being the centre of attention, the queen of our own little kingdom. The glamour was always a welcome distraction from everything I was trying to hide inside. Both William and my mother were alike in encouraging that in me. '*Always exhibit what you want people to see,*' she would say. '*Never admit to weakness.*'

But over the years, it's become harder for me to push away all the doubts. Harder for me to unwaveringly support my husband as I've started to suspect more and more that there are things he's hiding from me. Most of all, I don't like the person I've become.

A creak at the door has me turning around, away from my meandering thoughts.

The hum of the party starting downstairs hits me at the same time as I spy my husband.

I can't help it as my breath catches. To me, he's still handsome, still has that edge of dangerous excitement that first attracted me to him. And what I've been unable to tear myself away from since.

Honestly, William could have just stepped out of a James Bond movie as Daniel Craig's double. His eyes smoulder as he takes in every inch of me from top to toe, his gaze searching. Finally, his mouth quirks up into a small smirk and I know that I've met his approval. On a physical level anyway.

As much as I want to pretend that I don't care about that sort of thing, I do. Of course I still do.

He walks slowly over, each step feeling like an hour as he continues to scan my body. I let him. I've never been able to deny him anything. I know that. As does he.

He stops right in front of me, barely a breath away. In silence, he leans down to place a hand on the small of my back. I can't help it as

I feel a small tingle there. It's been so long since he's touched me like that.

He presses firmly, so I turn to face the mirror once more.

For a moment we stand side by side, and it's like we're back at our very first party.

Before everything went wrong, when I'd thought we shared a dream.

We're older now of course, but just as perfect to the outside world as we've always been. My still slim figure paired next to his tall and broad frame make us look like the golden couple that we try to pass off to the rest of the world.

If only they knew the truth of what it cost to get us here.

In the mirror William turns towards me and cradles his hand against my cheek. He lifts my head slowly to stare straight into his eyes. I can't help it, but as always I melt. His eyes can convince me of anything. And I let myself be mesmerised. Sometimes it's so nice and easy that way.

But then he opens his mouth.

'Cassandra darling, you'd tell me if you weren't feeling well, or if you were planning something, wouldn't you? We can't afford to have any more mishaps than we already have. If you're not feeling up to it, I'm sure Isabel can help out. She seems very willing.'

I look away from him, his hold on me disappearing into thin air as quickly as it came. Of course, all he wants to know is if I'm going to 'behave' and not ruin his precious evening.

He's got his new family backup now: his daughter-in-law. Someone he seems to believe so willingly. But that's only because she panders and agrees to everything he says.

William won't like what's going to happen tonight. But he'll have to see past himself for once in his life. I'm doing this for all of us.

So I turn back to face him, my scowl replaced by the brightest smile I can muster. 'I would never miss *our* anniversary party, darling.'

He looks pleased at that for a moment before I continue, 'I'm the principal executor of *our* trust after all, of course I want to celebrate that.' In many ways, King & Co. is just as much mine as it is his. If anything were to happen to William, *I* would have the right to decide what should happen next.

I think he forgets that sometimes. And he looks taken aback, shocked at my forthrightness.

But I don't wait for his response as I strut towards the doorway. 'Coming?' I ask curtly as I turn back to see him taking a deep breath.

I know it well. He's replacing his annoyance with a mask. We've become perfectly trained in this dance over the years, he and I. But how long can we keep it up? That is the answer I don't know.

After what I have planned for tonight, I'm going to find out.

Chapter Forty-Two

We emerge onto the landing at the top of the stairs in unison. There is a sudden pause in the music as someone announces, 'The Kings!'

I glance down the staircase at what feels like hundreds of pairs of eyes staring up at me. At us. This is our usual grand entrance and it feels a little like royalty peering down at our subjects.

William has always loved doing this, and though I now hate it I know how important it is to play my part. Especially tonight of all nights. No one can suspect me of being anything but the perfect wife and mother.

So we beam down at everyone magnanimously, welcoming them all. Making sure that it's seared into their memories that we are the one and only Kings. William trained me in that early on.

We've reached the top of the stairs and William takes my arm as we embark on our descent.

Everyone claps and roars in approval.

For a moment I freeze, as this clattering of applause brings me back into the past. To the sound Maya made as she tumbled down these stairs.

William stops beside me, and I feel him squeeze my arm tightly, but I can't seem to stop myself reliving that moment.

Her terrible scream.

Am I doing the right thing tonight?

Or have I overstepped the mark yet again?

I know my son, and once he finds out what she's been hiding, he'll show no forgiveness – but am I going too far to unravel Isabel in front of everyone?

'Cassandra, come on,' William hisses in my ear. 'Everyone is looking.'

The clapping has stopped, snapping me out of my confused reverie, and I smile automatically down at them all.

Even if my mind doesn't behave, my body always knows what to do.

I look out at the sea of faces staring up at me. A mixture of confusion and concern on their faces. Except for one.

Isabel's.

She smirks back up at me. A defiant look on her face as she latches onto my beautiful son. Miles looks concerned as he stares up at me. But she doesn't care at all. She's enjoying my fumbling entrance.

As she whispers something in his ear, Miles guffaws in response and completely ignores me to turn and kiss her on the cheek, whispering something back. Isabel never takes her glittering eyes off me.

A sharp clarity hits me.

Because she will do *anything* to take my son away from me.

So I am right in what I am about to do to her.

It's this surety that chases all doubt from my mind as I say loudly to everyone, 'Thank you so much to all of you for coming, as always. It means the world to us.'

Everyone's concerned faces turn back once more to smiles. A swell of British relief at avoiding an awkward moment is palpable. It radiates from William most especially, and I feel his eyes on me as he gives a small tug on my arm. He thinks this is over. It absolutely isn't.

'And I want to also take this moment,' I continue, 'to officially ask you to all welcome not one but two new members to our little family.'

A hum of whispering starts at my words as everyone looks up at me in anticipation. There's an ever so subtle frown on Isabel's face. The only sign that my words have affected her at all.

Miles breaks out into a broad grin. I do feel upset that he'll be hurt by my plan, but it's a necessary hurt. One day, he will thank me for saving him.

In the corner of my eye, William's momentary confusion is turning to panic. He opens his mouth to speak over me, but I won't let him.

'And so we're delighted to announce the engagement of our wonderful son to Isabel Atkinson.' I gesture towards the two of them with a flourish. The whole party moves as if attached to an invisible string to stare at them.

A string that I'm pulling.

'And the next generation of Kings, with the arrival of our first grandchild!' An audible gasp and murmur runs around the room.

'To the happy couple and their future family!' I cry, and beneath me everyone raises their glasses towards Miles and Isabel. Miles is smiling broadly. Isabel tries to match it, but she looks uncertain as all eyes fall on her.

She doesn't take her own eyes off me.

But I stop there. This is just the start of the night after all. The first of many breadcrumbs that I intend to lay. Breadcrumbs that by the end of the night will all lead away from me. Because all I will have done is welcome her in, *not* tear her down.

No, I intend to let her do that herself.

Chapter Forty-Three

As we continue our way down the stairs William murmurs into my ear. 'Nice little show, Cassie. Did you really mean it?'

I turn to face him, eyes as innocent as I can make them. 'Of course I did. It's time for us to all be aligned.'

He nods once in response, a sceptical smirk gracing his lips. 'Keep it up, old girl,' he says as he gives my arm a squeeze.

I want to lash out at his patronising words, but as we emerge at the bottom of the stairs, a mass of people swells to greet us and thank us for another brilliant party. All I can do is nod and take in their praise.

I respond as graciously as I can, and by the time the throng thins, I notice that William has disappeared from my side. He must have slipped away into the party. We weren't supposed to split up, so this annoys me. I need him by my side as a witness to the next part of my plan.

I excuse myself from the group and go off in search. My beautiful sitting room is full of more people than I've ever seen before in it. The atmosphere is oppressive and hurts my head. I need to get this show on the road.

'Champagne?' a voice asks behind my shoulder, and I turn to see a young girl offering me a sparkling glass on one of the silver trays I insisted be used for serving drinks.

I try to ignore the fact that I feel like I'm pressed in on all sides and nod, taking the proffered drink, downing it practically in one. The bubbles tickle my throat on the way. I need something to calm my nerves, and why not some champagne at my own party after all? The girl hasn't moved away yet and she smiles at me as I replace my glass and take another one, twirling away from her with an imperious wave. It's my party; I can do what I want.

I sip my second glass more slowly as I scan the packed room. Where is William, Miles, Isabel? As I take another gulp, I can't help but feel a slight tightening in my chest. Things are now not quite going as I planned, and I do not like it.

I'd planned for us all to be together – for everyone to be gathered around when Miles receives a message proving Isabel's deception. I can imagine it now: he will be upset, angry and distraught.

He'd cause a scene right in the middle of this party; accuse his beloved fiancée, the woman that I'd just welcomed to the family for all to see, of being liar.

It would all start to unravel in front of my eyes. And I would not be blamed for it at all. But I would be there to support my son, of course. Pick up the pieces after the betrayal.

Instead, people I barely recognise surround me.

I scan the party. There's a sea of faces, smiling and laughing, alongside the accompanying tinkle of glasses, the overpowering smells of expensive perfume and aftershave and the soft hum of music playing in the background. All are enjoying the Kings' party of the year. All are oblivious that there's not a single King milling around amongst them. A flash of anger rises in me.

I have worked so hard to curate the perfect image, the perfect husband, the perfect house, the perfect 'friends' over the years, and sometimes I just have to wonder what it's all for. None of these people even seem to notice me. We go around the social circuit, from one party to the next in a never-ending blur. I once thought our anniversary party was different. I thought these people came here for *us*, to celebrate our success each year. I've always been right in there, the centre of attention. But now that I'm removed from the scene, one of the crowd on the outside of the party, I see it all for what it really is: make-believe.

And then I see it. The door at the other end of the room – the wood-panelled sliding door that leads through to the library is ajar. It should be locked tight. But the light is on and I swear I can see shadows of movement through the crack.

I tilt my head in confusion. The only people that have access to that room are members of our family. Why would William or Miles be wandering round in there during the party?

But then my stomach drops.

Isabel now has access to the library as well.

If someone wanted to get in there, now would be the perfect opportunity. When we're all distracted.

I realise with a growing thump in my chest that if Gemma knew which book to pull, then Isabel would know too.

I try to calm down – even if she does get in, there's no way she'll know where to look. They're not hidden under the floorboards anymore.

There's no way she can get access to the drawer where they're all stored without my key. Which I keep on me at all times – as one of the 'charms' on the bracelet at my wrist. Hiding in plain sight – something I thought even William would never suspect actually *worked* as a key.

So I smile: maybe I could catch her in the act, going through my stuff like I did with her silly cousin. It would all help me.

Absentmindedly, I twirl the charm bracelet round on my wrist before bringing it up to the light to admire it and my developing plan.

But my stomach drops to my feet when I see what's missing.

I twirl around each charm one by one, staring at the silver star, the ruby-encrusted heart and the glistening moonstone. But the one I'm searching for isn't there. The tiny silver key.

My breathing shallows. How did I not notice this earlier? How long has it been missing?

I last locked up my diary drawer this afternoon. Right before my run and shower, before I got ready for tonight. I always take off all my jewellery for that, leaving it in the same place each time – I never thought anyone would take it right out of my room. How had I missed this earlier? I guess I'd been distracted by thinking about my plan and getting ready.

Only someone in this house could have snuck into our bedroom and slipped it off the nightstand.

And I know who it must be.

Isabel.

I begin to push my way through the crowd more frantically. I don't care if I cause a stir – a much worse one will happen if Isabel gets hold of my diaries.

How could I have been so stupid? Now it makes sense why Isabel wanted access to the security system. All along she had a plan of her own.

I thought I'd been so clever, hiding the key somewhere I thought I'd never lose it, and in a spot I'd always have access to. Now everything could fall apart in a matter of minutes.

After what seems like forever, I manage to squeeze my way through the crowd and slip into the library without anyone noticing. They're all too interested in themselves.

I pull the door fully closed behind me and rest my back against the door for a moment. Though I can still hear chatter from the room outside, it's more muffled in here. I gaze around the shelves of books and the dark mahogany furnishings. No one is here. The person might have left.

Or they're in my study.

I cross the room to the trick bookcase and run my finger down the mechanism, pulling the correct book until I hear a satisfying click. The sensor light switches on as I step inside.

I run my gaze around the space but all seems still. No one is hiding there. I rush over to the drawer that hides my diaries. It's also still shut and locked. Everything looks exactly as I left it, from my ornate paperweight to my neat pile of papers.

I can't be entirely sure though – what if they're already gone?

There is a second key though, hidden in the nook of the desk. I'd placed it there for emergencies – and hoped I'd never have to use it.

I open my Chanel clutch with a quiet click and fish out my phone.

On my hands and knees, not caring if my matching designer gown gets destroyed, I scrabble under the desk. Unless you knew, you'd never suspect it. It's so dark as I crane my neck and I hover my phone torch-light, searching for the small glint of silver amidst the darkness. I finally see it and grab the tiny little key.

My knees protest as I jump to my feet, and I wobble in these stupid heels. I want to throw them against the wall.

I shove the little key in the lock and turn it. I hold my breath as I pull open the all too familiar drawer.

And sag in relief. It looks *exactly* as I left it. Not a corner out of place.

Maybe I'd simply lost the small key. Or – whoever had stolen it was biding their time. In desperation, I draw out every diary one by one, and throw them into the dark hollow of the still-exposed gap under the floorboards. This will have to do for now, until I can find another hiding place. Maybe upstairs. I can't keep these in the floorboards much longer – not if Gemma had shared that with her cousin too.

Once everything is cleaned up, I lean against the wall. Dishevelled, exhausted and even more annoyed. This was a distraction and waste of my time. I have to get back out there and get my plan back on track.

Miles would be receiving the proof of Isabel's lies soon. And I have to make sure that I am by his side when he does.

But that's when I spot it. Under the shimmering glass of the paper-weight is a small booklet. The same shade as the desk, so similar it is almost camouflaged. *Almost.*

I lean over and remove the weight, gathering the file in my hand. Flipping it open, I freeze, my mouth dropping open in shock, unable to take in the images in front of me. A series of photos, one after the other.

All of William. All of him with different women.

Some he has his arms around, some he's kissing, some... I can't even begin to describe. But one in particular jumps out to me and I'm unable to look away as I feel bile rise in my throat.

One is with... *Maya*.

I blink in disbelief.

William had said that Maya had been lying when I'd been brave enough to tell him what she'd said on the stairs to me. That William had been the one to give her the jewellery, and that she'd heavily implied having an affair with him.

William had said she'd made everything up. And what other choice did I have at the time but to believe him? He'd cleaned up my mess after I'd accidentally killed the girl after all.

But now my whole world tilts and I grab onto the desk to stop my legs collapsing onto the floor.

My fear over my diaries being discovered flies out of my mind.

Rage consumes me.

Not only because of his betrayal with Maya. No, seeing these other pictures of his other affairs laid out in front of me makes me think back to all the times he's belittled me over the years, all the times he's said I've been making things up or imagining the worst. That it was 'all in my head'. How many times had he said those words to me over the years?

I throw the photos to the floor in disgust.

Chapter Forty-Four

All these years, I've made excuses for William, trusted him, allowed him to belittle me, to make me believe that I was crazy for even thinking he would betray me. And yet, here is the proof.

I could weep, with anger or relief, or perhaps a bit of both, I'm not sure. But one thing is for certain, I *am not* crazy. He has made me believe that everything that has gone wrong in our marriage is always my fault. But he has been lying to me this whole time.

While I am relieved to know I am not crazy, I'm also now sick to my stomach.

I am tied to this man forever by our shared secret. How can I ever get out?

And Maya... did Miles know that it had been his *father* that had been behind her affair?

My mind races around unending possibilities.

And then I see a scribble in the bottom right-hand corner of the page. I squint as I read a flourishing feminine hand:

I did warn you. xx

My anger at William is instantly replaced by a deep hatred for someone else. Of course, this hateful document could only have been left by *her*. By Isabel. Everything started going wrong as soon as she got her claws into Miles.

I don't know how or why, but discovering William's betrayals is all part of Isabel's plan. I want to scream in frustration. If these photographs are from Isabel, then has she already shown Miles the proof of William's betrayal?

Miles would never forgive William for lying about his affair with Maya for all these years. And maybe he'd even be angry at me for being so wilfully ignorant for so many years. More than anything else, Miles would never think that these pictures, designed to hurt me, were Isabel's doing either. How could I prove it?

He would choose her over all of us if he thought I was just trying to frame her. And she would have her way.

But before I have a chance to decide what to do next, I hear the sound of voices through the hidden bookshelf door. I'd lost track of where I was and what I was doing. The sound of the party has ebbed away to nothing and only now do the low sounds of talking rouse me to move.

In a rush, I slide open a drawer in the desk and shove the thin file inside.

I need to get a grip. I have my own plan in place, and I need to *not* be distracted by whatever game Isabel is trying to play. She's just trying to get into my head and tip me into losing my control again, like I did at the last party. I can't give her that satisfaction.

But then I hear a shrill laugh echo through the hidden door.

The secret door opens silently, as it always does. And I am back in the library blinking. I cannot believe my eyes. Because there is William, his hand sliding around another woman's waist as she reaches up on her tiptoes as though to kiss him. And I would recognise that woman and that scarlet red dress anywhere.

It's Isabel.

And despite my resolutions of just moments before, something primal breaks inside me. Something so raw and all-consuming that I feel myself losing control.

My insides burn liquid hot as she turns around, as though she's heard the screaming in my thoughts, and says in a tone of surprise, 'Oh Cassandra!'

It's that: the feigned innocence in her voice. A wild scream escapes my throat.

I can't help it when I lunge for the two of them, wanting to tear them apart.

And it's that moment when the perfect plan I thought I'd set in motion tonight finally slips from my grasp.

'You just wait until I'm through with you!' I scream. 'Both of you!'

I can't think straight. All I can hear is a roaring in my ears and the sound of my heavy breathing. After all of these years, I have snapped. Seeing them together is the last straw, and I can't keep control of this deep anger and pain coursing through every vein.

'Liars!' I shout. 'You're both liars!'

'Mum!' a voice yells behind me and I turn to see Miles's white face in the corner of the room. Had he been there the whole time?

'Miles,' I cry, rushing over to him. I clutch his chest as I point at them. My raging emotions get the better of me. I'm hardly making any sense in my rush of words. 'Isabel,' I start breathlessly, 'she isn't who she says she is, her real name is Molly McKenna – she's the cousin of Gemma! Who was fired by your father. And, oh Miles.' I breathe. 'Maya... Maya... he was with her too.'

I'm sobbing now as I clutch onto his jacket. I sound crazed, but I can't see through my tears. I can't bear the weight of the truth. This wasn't how it was supposed to happen, but I'm now broken in two.

No arms wrap around me in comfort though.

Instead, as my sobbing subsides, I look up to see Miles staring down at me, and then over to Isabel and William. Hurt and betrayal etched all along his strong face.

It's only then that I notice that the door to the library is wide open. Hundreds of faces are staring at me, gaping in shock.

The last of my strength shatters when I look over to see Isabel smiling. I sink onto the floor. I am done.

Chapter Forty-Five

I sit in this library room on my own, in the dark, surrounded by the silence, and the remnants of my smashed pride, trying to figure it all out. Everything I had worked for: my reputation, respectability and standing all shattered in a few moments.

I can't remember what's happened exactly, or how long I've been sitting here on the floor in the dark.

I'd kept my eyes tight shut as I'd heard the whispers start. The sound of everyone I knew turning their backs on me. Miles, William and Isabel each went back out into the party, no doubt to try and soothe the guests. I knew what they'd be saying. Cassandra isn't well. She needs some help. They would be explaining away my actions by accusing me of madness. It wouldn't be the first time.

I thought this night was going to end differently. That I would be triumphant. Instead I'm left with nothing.

It's quiet and dark out there now and no one has come to see me. I should leave at some point and face them all. But I just can't.

I feel like I've lost everything and I have no ideas and no way to fix it.

The memory of that look on Miles's face utterly breaks my heart over and over again.

I stand up and head over to the beautiful mahogany liquor cabinet in the corner of the room. I rummage through to find what I'm looking for: the dark bottle of fine Scottish whisky sits in the middle of the shelf, as though it's been waiting for me the whole time.

I pull off the cap and take a long gulp. The burning liquid races down my throat and I almost wretch it back up, but I force it down. After a moment I feel a lighter, freer sensation take over my body. It feels good to let go, good to lose control. I've held on for far too long to this version of Cassandra King – and look where it's got me.

I collapse down onto the sofa and drink more. Everything that I've worked for has been trampled over in a matter of an evening. *All because of that girl.*

She had clearly planned it all, and much better than my now pathetic attempt. But *why*? The fury builds inside me as I rock back and forth, sipping straight from the bottle. I don't know what to do with all this anger. It's been building up for weeks now, and tonight was the final straw. She will *not* get away with this...

I must have dozed off because I wake to an eruption of noise. I'm slumped across the sofa with a thumping headache and the feeling of cotton wool in my mouth. I must have passed out from the alcohol and exhaustion. What time is it? What is going on? The noise is coming from my small clutch bag that lies discarded on the floor. It's my phone.

I scrabble to my feet and answer it blurrily. 'Hello?'

'Hello?' a crisp female voice speaks down the line. And one part of my brain thinks, this isn't William. Why is this woman calling me? 'Is this Cassandra King?'

'It is.' I bristle at giving out my details. 'And who is this?'

'This is Dr Adams, Mrs King, I'm afraid to tell you that your husband has been in an accident...' I don't hear what she says next as a roaring starts in my head. Not one of devastation, no. It's almost like a cheer.

But then it's replaced by panic. And I hear the doctor say, 'Mrs King, Mrs King,' over again.

'Yes,' I respond. 'I'm sorry, just the shock.'

'He's okay, Mrs King, but he has taken a terrible knock and he's in hospital right now. The one on the Old Brompton Road.'

'Can I see him? What happened?'

'He was knocked over by a car on the King's Road. It was a very lucky escape, but he's in a stable condition now. I can give you more details when I see you, if you want to make your way over there now. He is in the accident and emergency department. Can you make it there?'

'Yes,' I say without hesitation. 'Yes, I can.'

'Good, and the police might also want to make more enquiries into what happened. So they may be in touch.'

As the call disconnects, I collapse back onto the sofa and try to process everything that I've just heard.

William in hospital.

William in an accident.

William hit by a car.

My blood runs cold and I shut my eyes tight.

I can't believe the parallels, tonight of all nights.

Because this isn't the first hit-and-run we've found ourselves in.

Chapter Forty-Six

It's one o'clock in the morning and my head is still thumping from all the whisky. I look down at my floor-length gown. I should change – I can't wear this to a hospital.

I emerge from the study into the sitting room. A few hours ago it was filled with noise and laughter, and it is now eerily silent.

I make my way towards the staircase, listening out for any signs of life or movement.

Nothing.

Miles and Isabel are probably out or in bed. But I can't dwell on it or check. I have to rush.

Fortunately, the hospital is only about a ten-minute walk away. Five minutes if you're practically sprinting, like I am now. I cross the busy street, still pulsing with people even at this time, towards the bright lights of the large hospital in front of me. The sights and sounds overwhelm me and I blink in a daze as I enter through the revolving door. I gaze up at the huge ceiling, which is cavernous and stretches as far back and up as the eye can see.

Someone else bursts through the revolving doors, knocking me out of the way. I trip and almost fall over as unshed tears spring to my eyes. *God Cassandra, pull it together.*

I hear a voice next to me ask, 'Are you okay, Madam?' and a hand reaches out to steady me. I glance across to see a concerned nurse holding me up. Though she looks tired, bags etched around her eyes, her kindness is genuine. It almost makes me want to cry again. But instead, I do what I always do when confronted with kindness. Rebuff it.

'Yes.' I stiffen, standing up to my full height now, which is a lot taller than hers. 'It's an absolute mess in here. I have just entered only to be knocked over. It's like Bedlam, can't you all get things sorted?'

She recoils from me in shock, but I can't help it. Aggression is my only default to try and push away just how scared I'm feeling.

'Sorry about that,' she murmurs with a shake of her head and begins to walk away.

'Wait,' I say quickly. 'I'm looking for my husband who was in an accident. How do I find him?' My voice cracks at the end and I feel embarrassed as the nurse's eyes soften in understanding.

'Head over to that reception desk.' She points to a desk further away. 'They'll be able to help you.'

Rather than thanking her, I turn around. I don't mean to be unkind, but if I even said the words, I would break down.

I reach the desk and stare expectantly at the woman sitting there who is shuffling papers around. She doesn't look up, and I cough impatiently and say loudly, 'Excuse me, I'm looking for my husband, William King. He should be in Accident and Emergency.'

'One moment, Madam,' she says, still without looking up. I tap my foot.

She looks up at last. 'Yes, you'll have to go to the A & E entrance. It's next door.'

I sigh in frustration and rush out the way I came. At least I am feeling less emotional and more annoyed now.

As I emerge outside I look around again. I missed the huge sign right above the entrance in my haste. Inside, I'm met by wave of noise. Everyone is waiting with a haunted look in their eyes. I must look the same.

The queue to reception is long and I want to storm up to the desk, but I try to be patient. When I'm almost at the front, a child begins to cry and a pain pierces my heart.

'Hello, hello?' Someone from behind is tapping me on the shoulder. 'You're next,' the man behind me says, as he cradles his injured arm.

I turn back to face the front, and ignoring the screaming child and the terrible flashback, I walk forward to the reception desk.

'Hello,' I say breathlessly to the man sitting in front of me. 'I received a call from Dr Adams. My husband William King has been in an accident. Dr Adams said to come and see him...' I trail off as the receptionist turns to face his computer.

'One moment please,' he says as he taps away. 'Yes, Mr King is in room three. I'll let Dr Adams know you're here. Please can you take a seat?'

I nod and turn away, though all I want to do is scream, 'Take me there now!' but I can't. So I do as I'm told and scan the waiting area for a spare seat, finding one in a corner.

Imagine someone finding Cassandra King here; I shake my head in disgust. But then I remember that none of that matters anymore. I am ruined. Exhausted, I sit down with a flop.

I bury my head in my hands as I wait. After what feels like hours I hear my name called by an authoritative female voice. 'Mrs King?'

I look around to see a tall, young-looking doctor scanning the room, waiting for someone to identify themselves.

'Yes,' I say, walking towards her. She turns to me, a sombre expression on her face. 'I'm Mrs King,' I confirm as I reach her.

'Come with me, Mrs King, your husband has been asking for you.'

'Really?' I say, my words coming out with a tone of disbelief. After tonight, I am shocked to hear that he's mentioned me.

Dr Adams's eyebrows lift in surprise as she gestures me into a small room where there are a couple of chairs and a small, clunky desktop computer.

'Let's speak in here,' she says, and I follow her inside.

She closes the door behind her as she gestures for me to take one of the small seats. I sit down and wait in silence to finally hear what happened.

'Mrs King, William is in a stable condition and was really very lucky not to have more injuries. Or worse.'

I try to appear calm, but on the inside my heart is racing at a million miles an hour.

'It seems he was crossing the road late this evening across from a bar on Old Brompton Road, and a car swerved into him out of nowhere. He was knocked to the curb, but he's managed to escape with only a fractured wrist and bruised ribs. He knocked his head but he didn't black out and says that he feels better now, so I think we're okay to check him out if you're able to take him home? He said that you live just round the corner, so if he starts to feel unwell you can come straight back. He's a very lucky man that no further harm is apparent right now.'

My mouth is dry, my mind struggling to take it all in. My eyes dart around the room though I sit frozen still.

'Mrs King, are you okay?'

I shake my head. 'No, I mean yes, I'm just a bit taken aback.' An understatement, as I scramble to regain control.

'I completely understand,' she replies. 'I just wanted to explain the situation to you before we go in to see him because,' she clears her throat, 'he's looking a bit battered and it might be a bit of a shock to you. But I want to reassure you that everything is surface level and he will be okay.'

I nod in response, a tightening in my throat. William has betrayed me and I cannot forgive him. But I wouldn't want this to have been the way he died – I don't think, anyway.

Even though I'm relieved to hear he will be okay, after everything I've seen this evening, I'm sure that I don't want to be tied to him anymore, and I need to find a way to escape from our marriage, no matter what it costs me. Despite everything he has done to me, trying to kill him is an extreme that I could never stoop to. But would someone else?

I wrap my arms around myself involuntarily and take a deep breath. I cannot break down. I cannot lose control again. Not now.

'Mrs King,' Dr Adams interrupts my wild thoughts and I look up, concern etched over her tired face. 'Do you need some more time to process everything?'

'I think I'm okay,' I say, 'but did no one catch the number plate or the driver of the car?'

She shakes her head. 'I don't think so. The paramedic team mentioned to me that a witness thought they might even have been covered up. But I'm sure the police will look at the cameras and do what they can.' She tries to reassure me.

'Please can I see my husband now?' I ask.

'Of course,' Dr Adams responds, getting to her feet too. 'I'll take you to him. Just remember, he really is okay...'

And with that she leaves the room, holding the door open to me with one hand.

I am Cassandra King and carrying on is what I must do. So I step forward and into the bright hospital corridor and follow the doctor to find my broken husband.

But what I'm going to do when I actually see him again, I don't know.

Chapter Forty-Seven

We stride through the halls of the hospital and I try to keep pace with Dr Adams, who flows around the hive of activity like a duck in water. Soon enough she halts her march in front of a door that she opens to reveal a large ward, housing many patients all separated by curtains. It's noisy in here, but I try not to stare or think about the people in the other beds. Low voices are coming from every direction. Dr Adams walks purposefully towards the far end of the ward and stops in front of one curtained-off bed. I take a deep breath as she opens the curtain slowly.

When the figure before me comes into view I do a double take. I hardly recognise the man. He looks like my husband and yet is so unlike him. His usual larger-than-life presence is diminished in this hospital bed, where he looks small and frail. Though nearing his sixties, William prides himself on his fitness and looking 'young'. But now he looks every bit his age, even older, as I take in the lines across his face and the small cuts and gashes to his head.

'Mr King,' I hear Dr Adams murmur. 'Your wife is here.'

At that his eyes fly open, and I'm struck by the look of fear in them. I've only ever seen that look one time before, many years ago, on a night that we promised to forget. Seeing that same expression again now, it's all I can do to stop myself from sprinting right out of this hospital.

'Cassandra,' William manages to say with a croak. He sounds so weak, and that's what stops me from turning tail and running. Because he may have had the same expression on his face all those years ago, but his voice definitely wasn't weak...

'Oh William.' I can't help my voice cracking as I say his name. He has been my husband for thirty years after all. And despite everything he's done, I can't not care.

As we stare at each other, out of the corner of my eye I notice Dr Adams checking his stats.

'Well,' she says, interrupting the silence, 'you're looking okay Mr King, and so if you want, your wife can take you home. I'll make sure you have some painkillers to take away with you. But you should be just fine.' William turns to face her weakly and nods his head in thanks. 'I've explained to her about the nature of your injuries and a little of what happened.'

William sighs. He absolutely hates it here and I can't blame him.

'Mrs King, I'll just sort out the discharge papers and then you can be on your way. So unless you have any other questions, I'll leave you to it.'

'Thank you,' I manage to croak whilst William stares blankly towards the wall.

Now that I know what's happened and I am here, it's easier to remain in control of my emotions enough to actually thank her. William says nothing. So Dr Adams simply nods, and leaves us. Back to her never-ending roster and the noise of the rest of the ward.

As the curtain closes behind us, I am thankful that it's quite noisy in here. At least we'll be able to speak without anyone overhearing us. I move next to William.

'My God,' I murmur, looking down at him. 'What happened?'

He looks up at me, his face wincing in pain.

'I thought the doctor told you?' he says in his usual condescending tone. He can't be too hurt then.

'Yes. But I want to hear it from you.' As his wife, I should be crying over him, holding his hand, thanking God that he's okay. But now that the initial shock has passed and we can both see that he's alright, I can't forget what happened earlier and the betrayal that runs through me.

Maybe having him weaker for a while won't be the worst thing.

He wriggles under the heavy hospital blanket.

'It just came out of nowhere and knocked me over. I am so lucky it's nothing worse. This damn wrist is annoying though.' He draws it up to show how it's wrapped tightly, and places it back across his chest. 'But I'm very lucky, so I've been told.'

'That's good, we wouldn't want anything worse on such an *eventful* night,' I say spitefully.

'Cassandra,' William says in a low voice more like his own. 'Don't start this now.'

But I can't help it. Though my husband is lying here in a hospital bed, I can't get what happened tonight out of my mind. I have always been obedient, faithful, *controlled* – and yet it's never been enough. *I've* never been enough. I feel my mask slipping, going back to the anger I felt earlier tonight. I open my mouth to speak but William interrupts me once more.

'Cassandra,' he says in a different voice this time, which causes me to pause the angry words on the tip of my tongue. 'I don't think this was an accident.'

'What do you mean?' I say, hovering down over him so I can hear him all the better.

He blinks up at me and I see that same look of fear return. But this time I don't want to run, because he says five words that make me freeze to the spot.

He whispers in my ear, 'I think it was Isabel.'

The words start coming out of him so fast they're almost all in a jumble.

'It might seem crazy, but I think she could have organised it.' He gulps. 'After we left you to deal with the guests, she and Miles disappeared. I was left to sort everything on my own. And when all those people finally left, I wanted to just get out of the house and get a drink. I couldn't face you yet; I was so angry. In hindsight, I felt like I had a car tailing me to the closest bar I could find. But I'd forgotten about it after a couple of drinks. On my way out though... there we have it, I was hit.'

I take it all in, and then I tell him about the pictures I found in my study tonight just before I caught him with Isabel. I try to stay calm as I speak, blinking back tears through the bright lights of the hospital ward. But I have to get through this. I have to tell him everything.

And then a sentence comes out of his mouth that I never thought I'd hear him say.

'I'm sorry, Cassandra, for lying to you all these years. Some of what you've said is true and some is not. And,' he lets out a groan, 'there is one thing that I should have told you a long time ago. You didn't kill Maya. I just let you think that.'

Chapter Forty-Eight

William is lucky he's already broken in a hospital bed. Or I would have torn him limb from limb.

'What do you mean?' I growl, clenching my hands into fists.

He closes his eyes as he whispers out the words. 'You never asked, so I didn't correct you. You already believed you'd done it and I didn't want to bring it up again unless you asked specifically. I didn't want you to have another breakdown. You seemed to be doing so well.'

My nostrils flare. 'Don't make this about protecting me,' I hiss, leaning over him. 'You were just protecting yourself. Making absolutely certain I could never leave you.'

He opens his eyes, and perhaps it is just a trick of the light but a single tear trickles down his cheek. Maybe he really does feel remorse. Or maybe it's just that he's finally *has* to admit the truth.

'I'm sorry,' he breathes in a whisper. 'I should have told you. But it was complicated. You were in such a state that day. Remember, I carried you upstairs and you passed out. And when I had come back down to figure out what the hell I was going to do, she was just starting to move. I was a little relieved that I wouldn't have to bury a body – but her near death experience by your hands was less than ideal. What if she spoke about it? We could have been ruined because of your rash actions. So we came to a quick agreement, and I had to pay her off to make sure she would leave our family alone, and never bother us again. We couldn't have her causing trouble.'

If he weren't in the middle of a public hospital right now, I would punch him in the face. 'Isn't that mighty big of you!' I exclaim sarcastically. 'You made me think I killed a person!' I almost laugh in outrage. 'And of course, you created this situation by having an affair with her in the first place. You must think I'm a total idiot!'

He sighs, and I want to slap him. 'She came on to *me*, Cassandra. Not the other way around.'

'That's a ridiculous attempt at an excuse! And besides, why would I believe you?' I hiss back. 'You obviously just wanted what you couldn't have. And to hurt Miles.'

His eyes flash. 'That *boy*. You are always so oblivious when it comes to him. Trust me, he's not some sweet innocent. And she wasn't either. But Cassandra, I haven't had a single affair since then. I *promise*.'

I raise my eyebrows in disbelief. I'm sure he is lying.

But before I can say anything, he adds, 'And as for Isabel, there is *nothing* happening there. She dragged me into that study to look for you and then moved over to whisper in my ear, perfectly poised for when you entered the room. And now I can see why. We've been set up.' He says it slowly, anger radiating off him, even in this weakened state.

I think it over. It does seem possible. And that he's not just saying it to distract me.

'And the letter,' I say under my breath.

'What?' he says, flicking his eyes open with exhaustion.

'The threatening letter... now do you believe me when I say that I didn't write it? And maybe now we know who did?'

Our eyes lock and for the first time I see something there that I never thought I would see. Defeat. He nods, and if it wasn't such a serious situation I would smile at my small win.

'Yes,' he says, as if this admittance has cost him dearly. 'I believe you. But why? Who is she? And what can we do about it? How can we get rid of this monster?'

I might never be able to trust William again and I don't know what will happen next for us, but at least we can bring this viper down. Even if it's the last thing we do. We have nothing more to lose. All that's left is for us to save our son – something we can do together, can't we?

Because if Isabel tried to do this to William, what might she do to Miles in her seemingly never-ending mission to destroy us all?

Chapter Forty-Nine

I'm frantic. I've tried to call Miles a million times and there's no answer. Is he safe?

William told me that he hadn't seen either of them when he'd left the house.

Is my son lying in a ditch somewhere? I have no idea what this woman is capable of, and I'm terrified I'm already too late.

But I need to deal with one thing at a time. William needs to rest, so I've had no other choice but to return home first. And then I will do everything possible to find my son.

A thousand thoughts are racing through my mind. Shall I go to the police? But what would I say? *We think my husband was in a hit-and-run planned by our future daughter-in-law? And now I think my son is missing?* No, they would laugh in my face. Without proof, we have nothing to go on except for a gut feeling. Besides, William isn't in a state to sit in a police station for hours.

So, bleary-eyed and absolutely exhausted, we arrive home. William leans on me as we struggle up the staircase. The staircase that just hours earlier we had descended like the King and Queen of Chelsea. Now, that façade lies in tatters. Everything that we have built over the years shattered in an instant. All because we became pawns in *that* girl's game.

She has wanted to tear my family apart since she first met my wonderful Miles. Now that it's happened, all that's left for us to do is to find out why. And remove her from our lives.

But I'm terrified: Isabel tried to kill William. What will she do next?

We shuffle along the corridor, keeping a watchful gaze for any creeping shadows. I don't feel safe in my own home with Isabel possibly lurking around. But I'll go and check Miles's room as soon as I have William settled, even if there's a risk of coming across her. I'll do anything for my boy, even face an attempted murderer.

The quickness of my breathing and the thumping of my chest threatens to overwhelm me. I can't help but think back to another terrifying night, long before Isabel or even Maya came into our lives. We had to make some terrible decisions then, ones I have never forgiven myself for. But when your own family is at risk, that's what you have to prioritise, no matter what. Or, that's what I've come to convince myself of over time.

I'm relieved when we reach our bedroom door. The latch clicks and I push it open with one hand as I help William inside. He's in a daze, and for a while I let my practical brain take over, helping him to lie down comfortably. I leave the room to find some fresh clothes, but by the time I return, he's already fast asleep.

I gaze down at this man. My battered husband. A storm of emotions hits me all at once: hatred, betrayal but also, undeniably, a smattering of love. Or is it just loyalty now at this stage? I can't tell the difference. And I hate myself for being so weak.

This man has lied to you over and over again, the rational part of my brain screams at me. *What are you still doing here?*

But the other part of my brain tells me that he's protected me, shielded me from the worst and given me a life I never thought possible. But what does that all matter now?

I'm distracted from my thoughts as I see my phone buzzing – it's Miles calling. Frantically, I pick up the phone and press it to my ear, racing into the dressing room so I don't wake William. 'Hello, Miles?' I say breathlessly.

'Hello,' he responds. 'How is he?'

I'm so relieved to hear his voice that I'd barely notice the brusque edge. 'Oh, thank God, I thought something had happened...'

But he cuts me off, asking again, insistently, '*How is he?*'

'Oh your father, he's okay, we're back home and he's resting,' I say quickly. 'But I need to talk to you about that. Where's Isabel? Where are you?'

'Don't worry about me, I'll be with you soon.' And then the line goes dead.

I pull my phone away from my face to check the screen to make sure the call really has disconnected. It was such an abrupt ending. But the main thing is that he sounded unhurt. He's probably just worried about his father. And there was no mention of Isabel. That's good.

The memory of what I screamed at them all comes back to me. I *told* Miles Isabel wasn't who she said she was. And he'd stared at me, and at her, with shock and anger in his eyes.

Maybe they've actually been fighting all this time. Maybe Miles will come in and tell me it's all over. Perhaps William was delusional and the accident had been just a coincidence. Not Isabel after all.

I sit down heavily on my dressing room chaise and focus on the fact that Miles is safe, for now.

I raise my head to see that the weak dawn light is trying to stream in through the window.

Then I turn to gaze at my reflection in the mirror. I hardly recognise the person staring back at me. Dark blue circles rim my eyes, and my dyed blonde hair sticks up at odd angles. A smudge of dirt is on my cheek.

I sigh wearily and pick myself up.

A bath will help. It always does.

I enter the large marble bathroom, switching on the light. But it's too white and the brightness burns my eyes. I flick it off, opting to move around in the half-light.

Turning the tap on, I allow my fingers to skim the surface of the water, washing my hands clean. If only I could clean up my life as easily.

I'm lost watching the swirling water when I hear a loud thump from the other room. I jump up. Is that a scream? Or the sound of a struggle? It sounds like someone other than William is out there.

Oh my god. Home was probably the worst place I could have come.

Because if it was Isabel that had tried to hit and kill William, then she didn't finish the job. William is still alive. And I was the only person seen taking him home.

I might already be too late.

Sprinting across the room, I push open the sliding door to our bedroom.

But I cannot believe my eyes.

I am in a nightmare.

Because in front of me, it's not Isabel that I see bearing down on William.

It's my son.

Chapter Fifty

A scream erupts from my lips as Miles turns towards me, continuing to press the pillow down over his father's face as William's legs kick and writhe.

'Hello, Mother,' Miles says gently. 'Would you like to say goodbye to dear Father?'

It takes everything in me to go against all my instincts. To go against everything I have ever done since becoming a mother. I launch at my son.

Miles turns, releasing his grip from the pillow, and pushes me hard. I fly across the room, landing with a crash in front of my favourite bay window. I slide to the ground, my ankle twisting, and the left-hand side of my body roars in agony. I hit my head, and I'm not sure if I lose consciousness for a minute. All I can see are stars dancing across my vision.

Then I hear a wild scream.

Next, the words: 'You're too late, he deserves this!' I can't connect the voice of my son, my Miles, with whatever monster is speaking to me right now.

When my vision clears, I see that he's leaning over me. Sure enough, it's my darling boy. Except now that I look closely at his wild eyes, it's like I'm looking at a whole new face. As though the face I've known for the last thirty years was just a mask hiding this real one. A face full of hate.

'Why are you still coming to his aid, even now?' he asks scornfully, and I stare up at him, trying to search out the soft blue eyes I thought I knew.

Because this stranger's eyes are bursting with rage.

'He's thrown you aside every single time. And you've never even noticed. All he's ever done is choose himself. And all you've ever done is choose him, again and again. Over me. Even tonight when you finally learn *everything*, see his disgusting betrayal with your own eyes, you still choose to go to him. You still choose him over me.'

'Miles... please... let me g—' I try to speak, but my voice comes out in a rasp. Behind him, all I can see is a mountain of unmoving white bedsheets where William must be. Is he dead? There's a tiny piece of hope inside me that I stopped Miles just in time...

But before I have a chance to try and get up, Miles leans down and roars in my face.

'No! That man is finally DEAD – I've killed him. And it's time for you to *listen* to me.'

My whole body shrinks back in response, the curtains grazing my back. Miles's words echo round and round my head. William is dead. William is dead. No, no, no, he can't be...

Miles continues, 'You have never really listened to me. But now it's time you do! Because you were the one that left me all those years ago. You left me with *him*...' He doesn't finish his sentence, his voice breaking at the edges.

I know what he's talking about, though I truly thought we'd left that all in the past. I was wrong.

I try to stay in the present, but my thoughts can't help but wander back to when Miles was small. When I did the worst thing a mother could do.

I left. I left my little boy.

Because of what William and I had done all those years ago. It was before Maya and before any of the other terrible things I've done since. Life had become too much for me. Because what we did on that darkest night twenty years ago was unforgivable.

And I couldn't live with it anymore.

So I tried the only thing that I thought could help stop this pain.

I tried to end it all.

Even if that meant leaving my little boy.

I hadn't been sleeping, or eating. The pills I'd been given did nothing. I hadn't been able to get that night out of my head. What I'd done, what I'd witnessed, was impossible to erase. All I could see when I shut my eyes was screaming and blood. So much blood.

It was right in this very room that I'd tried. I'd been convinced that it would be better for everyone if I wasn't here anymore.

So I'd taken far too many pills. More than anyone should. And my last thoughts had been that at least someone, somewhere, would get justice for what William and I did.

A life for a life, and all that.

But the next thing I'd known I'd been surrounded by bright blinking lights. I thought, *This must be it, the other side*. Except, of course, then I'd seen William's face. His expression of absolute terror and fury told me that I was very much still here.

Maybe there'd been a part of me that didn't really want to go. That had known that as a mother I couldn't quite leave my little boy. But I really hadn't seen any other way out. Because if I were gone, at least Miles would have had his father. Wouldn't that have been enough?

I'd become convinced that he didn't need a monster like me as a mother.

But I didn't have a choice in what happened next. William booked me into the best clinic that money could buy.

Eventually, it helped me to navigate and compartmentalise what had happened. Though I couldn't ever tell them exactly *what* I'd done.

But most importantly, it had kept me medicated, strongly medicated. So much so that by the time I was allowed to come home, I would have done anything that William asked, so long as he sustained me.

By that point, I could manage the pain of what we'd done that night. Even if I was never able to forgive myself. I'd even been grateful to William for saving me, and so I did anything he asked. Believed anything he said.

All I had wanted to do when I returned was to try and earn my second chance by being the best mother to Miles possible. I thought that it must have been the only reason why I had survived, to help my son. Perhaps it could be the one worthwhile thing in my small life. I would have sacrificed my life for him if he'd asked.

But when I was finally allowed to return home, Miles wasn't there. William told me he had misbehaved badly because of what I'd done, so he had to send him to the strictest boarding school he could find in my absence. It would be good for him, William had said. Miles needed some stability after what his mother had done. And that in any case, William didn't think I'd be up to being a good mother yet. A whole year had passed by that point. And all I'd wanted was to see my boy. But William said I couldn't until I was entirely back to 'normal', and that I'd already done enough damage already. I believed him.

Now, looking up at my son, staring with such hatred down at me, I am beginning to realise that this too must have been one of William's many lies. Miles *had* needed and wanted his mother.

But by the time I was allowed within proximity of my son again, the damage had been done.

I was far too late then.

And I am far too late now.

Chapter Fifty-One

'Did you know that he blamed me?' Miles asks with such venom in his voice that it's like poison spilling into the air. 'For what you *did*? I almost *wish* that you'd died. But he blamed me, he told me that I'd put too much pressure on you. That *I'd* made you sick.'

Bile rises in my throat. How could William have said such cruel, terrible things to a ten-year-old boy?

'Don't you see?' Miles's voice is thick with scorn. 'He always wanted to control you. Control all of us. He told me that if I wanted to be a King, I needed to *learn* how to be a King. Independent, strong, powerful. He started teaching me those lessons early on while you were gone. He tried to train all weakness out of me. And then that school. Well, that was the real training ground. That's when I understood that I was a real weakling. That I cared too much about people, and that I cared too much about *you*.' He spits down at me. 'And you left me, you abandoned me!' His voice catches with a ring of hysteria.

'I couldn't afford such luxuries anymore. I needed to *stop* caring. Instead, I needed to learn power and control. And William...' He shrugs now, turning his final words into a sharp bark. 'At least he taught me that.'

I wince and squeeze my eyes shut to stop the tears that begin to seep out of the corners. I try to think back to when I was first allowed to see Miles again after my treatment. Yes, he had been quiet, and withdrawn. I hadn't wanted to push him, because I knew that I had failed him. I'd convinced myself that over time things would get better, that we'd rebuild our relationship. He'd barely wanted to see me throughout his teenage years, but over the last ten years, after he went to university, I thought we almost had. Or that at least if it could never go back to how it had been when he was a little boy, that we had something new. And I thought he'd *finally* forgiven me. Obviously not; I've been delusional all these years.

'Miles, please,' I try again, my voice coming out thick and scratchy. 'I don't understand where all this has come from. I thought we'd moved on, left that awful time behind…' I know this sounds clunky and weak compared to the magnitude of the situation. But I can't think straight.

A low choke comes out of him, and his shoulders slump at my words, his head rocking forward so his floppy brown hair hides his face.

I get an instant flashback to when he was little and I'd told him off for breaking my favourite vase. He'd looked almost identical then, but how different things are now.

'You know,' he starts, his face still in shadow. 'I thought that too, for a while. I think back now and recognise that all I *ever* wanted was to have someone I could trust. When I was little, I *thought* I had that with you, Mother. But I was wrong. After what you did, I could never trust you again.' I flinch at his brutal words as his head snaps back up, his eyes like daggers piercing into me.

'After university, I knew I wanted to create my own family – a new family – with someone though. With the right person, one person that would stand by my side, *no matter what*. And once I had them, I wouldn't need either of you anymore.' He shrugs.

'I came to terms with the fact that the only thing you two had ever given me was the promise of inheriting King & Co. From William's lessons and that school, I came to see that was all the power I would ever need. When the time was right and with the right person by my side, perhaps then I could finally build a *good* King family, a *loving* King family. One that wouldn't abandon each other.'

I rock back and forth, unable to bear his words. I try to block them out, but they keep coming.

'When Maya came into my life, I thought I'd found the one. But I was completely wrong there.' His voice is low and painful as he crouches down in front of me. 'Do you remember when you both humiliated me in front of her?'

I frown, confused, shaking my head as though that will help me find the memory he's talking about.

He laughs harshly. 'Oh of course, you don't remember. But then again, why would you? I'm nothing in comparison to what he was to you.' He nods lazily over towards William's unmoving body. 'I wanted to show Maya around your *precious* study. She told me she was interested in arts and books, so naturally I wanted to impress her by showing off your rarest collection, which I knew was in your hidden room. I'm the only person you told your favourite book to, remember, Mother? And Maya had been astounded by the secret door and the books I started to show her. But then you both *had* to ruin it. Don't you remember how you both barged in, screaming at us to get out?'

I flinch at his words as the memory rushes back to me. It had been late at night; William and I had both been in bed. So when we got the alert of movement downstairs in the library, we thought it was a break in. I had been terrified. I guess Miles forgot that part, though he was right that we hadn't been kind to him when we'd found them. Well, William hadn't been kind.

'You just *stood* there as he lost his mind, and he used every trick in the book to make me feel *this* small.' He mimes his finger and thumb closing together to demonstrate and in spite of myself, I know exactly how he feels. William made me feel like that plenty of times.

'I felt like a child again, unsure of what he would say or do next. I took it all, unable to speak, as Maya watched on...' He shakes his head, such loathing in his voice, not just for William but for himself, and sadness runs through me despite the danger I'm in. He is still my son, after all.

Although when he speaks again, his face is thunderous. 'You might have forgotten about it. But I was humiliated. And that night changed everything between Maya and me. She began to see me as pathetic and unworthy. But obviously not William... no, she did not think that of him.' He mutters darkly under his breath, 'That must have been when he decided to set his sights on her.'

I want to interrupt him, tell him that William said it had been the other way around. But did I even believe that? And what did it matter now? The damage was done.

'But,' Miles says, 'you know I never actually knew about the affair until just last week? I never knew the *whole* story about what you did for me either, Mother. How you almost killed her – and actually, the lengths you went to that day to defend me – is one of the reasons why I decided to give you another chance. Not him though. No, not after I found out what he'd done to me.'

'How, how do you know all this?' I manage to stutter out.

'Ah brilliant question.' He claps his hands together in delight. I feel sick to my stomach at his enjoyment of this torment. 'You see, all this might *never* have been discovered. We might have avoided today *completely* but Maya couldn't leave well enough alone. No, even though dear old Dad had paid her off, she felt the need to try and anonymously warn Izzy, warn girls after her, about how dangerous our family was.

'But *she* was the one who had been wrong. She *left* me; she'd been the one to break everything. But she just couldn't stop messaging Izzy for some reason – trying to warn her. And last week when we moved back into this house, she even started saying to Izzy that *I* was dangerous too, that I was jealous, controlling and unpredictable... I didn't like that.'

I stare up at him wide-eyed. These must have been the messages I'd overheard them fighting about. How things must have escalated since then.

'I didn't know for certain it was Maya of course, but I couldn't think who else it would be. And I couldn't let it continue anymore; I'd sat idly by long enough with my suspicions. I couldn't continue to let these anonymous messages potentially scare Izzy off me too.'

His knuckles turn white as he clenches his fists. 'So I tricked Maya. I'm not proud of it, but one night when Izzy was asleep, I logged into Izzy's Facebook and messaged this "anonymous" profile. And I managed to convince the user to meet at an off-the-beaten-track café in Vauxhall. Once we'd arranged everything, I deleted the messages. Izzy didn't need to know. Not yet.' He tries to look ashamed of his actions, but I know from the sing-song ring to his words that he's actually quite proud.

'It was a *very* interesting meeting,' he drawls, sitting down leisurely on the bed next to the shape that is his father. He's enjoying this.

I've managed to catch my breath again, and I try and crouch in a position I could easily leap up from – if he ever takes his eyes off me. I haven't been able to take my eyes off him.

'When I walked into the café and saw that the person waiting for me was Maya, it confirmed that my hunch had been correct. It *had* been her messaging these girls. She'd tried to jump up and leave the café when she saw me enter, but I persuaded her to give me a chance.' He smiles at the memory, as though Maya's fear was amusing to him.

I try not to shudder at this stranger in front of me. How can this be my son?

'You see I said that I was just there to chat everything through. Didn't she owe me that much? Then she'd sat back down again in that crowded café. Something in what I'd said must have rung true. Obviously I didn't know at *that* time what she'd done with William… or what you'd both done to her…'

His eyes narrow at me, as though I'm the naughty child being told off. 'I was calm really, at the start. I asked her rationally why she was trying to destroy my relationship when I'd finally found happiness. And I couldn't quite believe her story.'

He shakes his head. 'He'd paid her to stay silent,' Miles says simply. 'About *everything*. What you did, what he did – all of it. He bought her out. And told her if she ever spoke of it to anyone, he'd *destroy* her life. She admitted she'd even hidden one photograph but that she'd been too scared to use it. She said she'd started feeling guilty for accepting the money in the first place, and after how far you both almost went to get rid of her, she was terrified. She just wanted to remain anonymous and was too scared to speak publicly. But she felt she had a moral obligation to try and warn other women off the family, that's why she'd been sending those messages.'

I try to keep my breathing under control as the words sink in. I still can't believe William went this far just to keep me under his thumb. He'd told me about paying her off in the hospital, but he hadn't revealed quite how threatening he'd been if she ever spoke out. William was even more ruthless than I'd thought. Though with everything Miles has just told me about the truth of how he felt during his childhood, I shouldn't be surprised. We'd all been puppets in William's show. But that was over now. He is gone, and I am trapped here, dealing with the pieces...

Miles shakes his head. 'I was angry, *so angry* at what you'd done to me when she told me the whole story at last. But I couldn't let it show. Aren't you proud of me, Mother? For keeping control of my emotions? Another thing Dad unwittingly taught me.' He smirks, but I don't reciprocate.

'I had to think fast. I told Maya that together we could bring him down once and for all. That no one else would be hurt by you or him, if only she would share that photo with me. She was hesitant – can you believe it? She didn't know if she could trust *me* – when *she* was the one who had slept with my own father! So she made one condition. That I bring Isabel next time. And that Isabel tell her with *her own lips* that she wanted the photo too. That Isabel knew the whole sorry history. Maya wanted to make sure that either Isabel knew *exactly* the kind of family she was getting into, or the deal was off.'

His eyes darken at the memory. 'I almost lost it then. She was making such demands, of me! After what she did! But I agreed. I knew Isabel and I were something else. I knew she would understand. So Maya and I agreed to meet a week later – the day before yesterday. And I would bring Isabel.'

My mouth gapes at his words. I can't believe that Miles really told Isabel all this, and that she'd stuck around. But then again, she is the perfect liar herself...

'What, Mother?' he says, seeing my expression. 'You can't believe that two people might *actually* trust each other? Do anything for each other? Is that such an unthinkable concept to you?'

I shake my head in disbelief at his crazy logic, and even though I'm cornered here with a twisted ankle on the floor, my strong, wild son looming over me, anger flares through my body. This is *not* entirely my fault.

'What about Isabel?' I manage to spit out. 'She's been lying to you this whole time!'

I don't believe it when he smiles.

'Oh, but that's different. Izzy's the one that finally removed the wool from my eyes when it comes to you, *and him*. She's the only one who has tried to save me.'

I realise in horror that he seems to know everything about Isabel. Maybe he has known everything all along.

Has he been planning this the whole time?

'And now, it's down to me to stop you both, to remove such terrible monsters from the world. Plus, this way King & Co. can have a completely fresh start with me in charge. With you both gone, the entire Trust will naturally fall to me.'

His face freezes in a leer and my stomach rolls over. He's entirely serious.

And then I see a shadow move in the corner of the room. I've been so distracted that I didn't notice until now. I tear my eyes away from this stranger and turn painfully around to see that there she is.

That girl. Isabel.

Hatred fills my body.

I blame her for everything. Without a shadow of a doubt, everything that has led us to this exact moment is because of her.

She is pressed tight against the furthest corner of the room. I almost scream at her, but as I notice a look of fear, I stop. It goes against my instincts and everything I know about her, but I can't help but wonder if she is just as trapped here as I am.

The thought vanishes in an instant when I see her face transform into a bright grin, as though she's been in a show, waiting for her cue to enter.

No, I'm the only one trapped here.

And soon, I will probably be as dead as my lying husband.

All because I failed my son.

And deep down I know it's not Izzy's fault.

It's mine.

Chapter Fifty-Two

Izzy

I see Cassandra cowering against the window, folded in on herself like her whole existence has been knocked out of her. And I suppose, in many ways, it has. What must be William's body lies motionless beneath a mountain of white. I'm struck by how pristine and perfect everything still looks. As though a murder hasn't just taken place in this room. As though another one isn't about to occur.

I'm frozen in shock, but I can't let it show. I never thought it would come to this. I wish I could just run. But I know I can't.

I think back to everything that has happened in the last week, how much things have changed between Miles and me. The course of events that has led us to this moment.

It all started when Miles had returned from that café. He'd been pacing up and down our room in a frantic state, pulling at his hair, his bright eyes wild. They'd almost looked mad.

I had never seen him like that before.

And I couldn't believe it as he began to tell me what had happened that day. What he had done – everything from the secret meeting he'd organised behind my back to what Maya had revealed to him; what she'd asked him to do and her request for me. Everything had fallen out in a torrent.

'Izzy,' he'd pleaded when he was done, squeezing my hands too tightly. 'Please help me. I can't believe what my *parents*,' he'd choked on the word, 'what those *monsters* have done to me – what they're capable of. I mean I guess Mum defended me a little – though she still lied and never told me what she'd done to Maya. But *that* man.' He growled, not able to say the word 'Dad'. 'I can never forgive him. It's like I don't know them at all. They're just liars.' He'd said 'liars' in total disbelief.

I was reeling. His words, that his parents were liars, stuck in my throat. Because wasn't that exactly what I was too?

But he'd also called them *monsters*. And now that he'd seen this – wasn't this the time to finally tell him what I knew? What they did to *me* all those years ago?

My mind whirred, and I began to pace too.

Could I risk it?

'Please say something,' he pleaded. 'Please understand why I have to do this and why I'm asking you to help get the photograph from Maya.' He stopped me in my tracks, taking me by the shoulders. His eyes had shone in desperation.

It truly was now. Or never.

So I simply said, 'I understand and I'll do it.' His eyes had brightened for a moment before I continued. 'Because your parents did something unforgivable to me too.'

His face fell as my words hit him. But he composed himself instantly, turning back into the controlled Miles I knew. 'What?' he said, gripping my arm.

I gulped. Now I'd started, there was no way out.

So I began to tell him.

Everything.

From the *very* beginning, to even the truth that I wasn't actually pregnant.

I stared him straight in the eyes the whole time. I swear he barely blinked.

When I was done, he exhaled, looking down as though to process what I'd told him. Had I just made a huge mistake?

'I'm so sorry Miles,' I said, 'but I knew you wouldn't believe me until I had proof, or like now, when you've seen with your own eyes what they're capable of. But my love is real, so real. It's because of how much I love you that I did all this for us.' My voice caught at the end, thick with emotion.

I'd been terrified at what he'd say. What he'd do.

Because there was no denying it. I had lied to him too.

When he finally looked up there was fire in his eyes, and I thought it was all directed at me. My heart pounded in my chest.

He moved so fast I almost missed it. I was certain he was about to slap me in rage. But instead, he whooshed down onto the bed and buried his face in his hands.

His shoulders started to shake.

Oh God, panic aced through every inch of me. I'd broken him.

But as I moved over to him to try and wrap him in some sort of embrace, he looked up.

And there weren't tears streaming around his eyes.

No, there were laughter lines. He started laughing uncontrollably at what I'd just told him. This was not the reaction I'd been expecting.

'Oh, I'm sorry, Iz,' he said, getting up, wrapping me in his arms so snug that I felt like I couldn't breathe. 'I feel delusional. This has to be some sort of sick joke. I just can't take this all in.'

He let me go, drawing me out to arm's length.

'It's not a joke,' I managed to grumble out. After what I'd just told him about what his parents had done to me, and the lengths I'd gone to, I'd not been expecting laughter.

His face fell.

'I'm sorry,' I said again, trying to draw him back in. I didn't want to lose this moment. 'I never wanted to lie to you. I love you. But I thought the only way you would believe me would be if you saw who they really are with your own eyes.'

It was as though my words backfired. Because he started to pace again, and when he turned back to me, the only expression I could read on his face was anger.

I'd chosen wrong in telling him.

He said solemnly, 'We need to stop them. They've always got away with everything they've ever wanted. All they've done is hurt people again and again. It's time – it's finally time we put a stop to it. Once and for all.'

Music to my ears. Nodding, I rushed over to him.

'I understand why you had to hide these things from me. And of course we couldn't begin our family properly with them still hanging over us,' he said as I hugged him. 'We have to put a stop to them, and then it'll just be us...'

I'd dreamt of this moment for so long: when he knew the truth at last and would not reject me because of it.

'Yes. Yes, that's exactly it. It's time we show the world who they really are. And put them behind bars.' I agreed eagerly.

He hadn't looked at me as I'd said these words, though. His eyes had been staring past me towards the window, a dark, unreadable expression on his face.

'Miles,' I'd repeated, shaking him.

'Yes, it's time for them to pay for *all* the things they've done. You are my new family. And I know exactly where what you've been looking for will be, *and* what we'll need to get it...'

Chapter Fifty-Three

We'd ended up outside the same faded Vauxhall café that Miles and Maya had previously met at. I'd noticed the chipped paint flaking off the doorframe as I'd walked inside, and my thoughts filled with doubt. Maybe this wasn't the best idea. This woman had haunted my nightmares the last couple of weeks. Was this really the only way to bring the Kings down, once and for all?

But in a way it had been because of her that Miles now knew everything about me. All because of her that we were at last on the same side. Perhaps I should be thanking her instead.

I twisted my necklace in my hand – even if Maya now changed her mind and didn't share the photograph with us, I'd still have proof if I needed it of what William had done. Because my necklace from my grandmother was more than just a pretty trinket: it was also a recording device. I flicked the button to begin recording and continued to make my way through the room.

There was no mistaking Maya, even in a full café. The rumble of conversation and the stick of coffee cups on plastic tabletops disappeared to nothing as we'd locked eyes.

I'd never seen her before, but there was instantly something familiar about her. As I moved closer, I understood what it was: she looked exactly like me. From her honey-coloured long hair to the high cheekbones and large round eyes.

Except she was a more perfect version. Slim and toned, no blemishes marked her flawless skin – unlike the freckles that always haphazardly dot my nose and brow. I'd always been embarrassed by them, even though Miles said he liked them; that it looked like I'd been kissed by the sun. But how could I possibly compare to this flawless version of me that he'd lost?

Miles didn't appeared fazed and strode over to sit down in front of her. I hovered a couple of paces behind, adjusting to the shock. Her eyes swivelled over to Miles, and I didn't miss the frown of distaste that marred her otherwise smooth features as she took him in.

I moved closer, and then her eyes skated back over mine. That was another difference: her eye colour. Where mine are the darkest chocolate brown, unreadable in most lights, hers were the lightest blue I've ever seen. Close up, every flicker of emotion was visible.

When her eyes met mine, all I could see was sympathy. And maybe something else – fear? But why? She had only just met me...

Miles began to speak first, and Maya's wide eyes flickered to him once more.

'Look, Maya, Izzy is here... she knows everything and wants the same things too...' he started, but she interrupted him.

'I want to hear it from her own lips,' she said in a melodic voice. I couldn't pinpoint the accent, but it was definitely from somewhere else in this country. It was also a lot stronger and more self-assured than I was expecting.

'It's true,' I said, and tried to push the anxiety her actions had caused me far away, along with my feelings of insignificance in comparison to her. I was here with Miles. Not her. More than that, she'd shattered him with what she'd done. We were here only to get what we needed: the photograph.

Miles and I had gone over the plan. Once we had this image, he knew how to take care of the rest. This was just the first part of the puzzle to discredit his father.

And then he was going to help me get access to Cassandra's diaries – where I'd told him the proof of what they'd done would be written for all to see.

When I'd revealed everything to Miles, I told him what I'd discovered about Cassandra's secret diaries too. And he'd said he'd known both what the favourite book to open her study was and how he could get the key from Cassandra's charm bracelet.

Gemma had prepared me as much as she'd been able to. But now I needed Miles's help to finish the job.

The Kings had destroyed enough lives – Gemma's included. It was time for it to stop. With Miles fully on my side, we were *so* close to finally being able to expose them for what they truly were.

It had sent a flicker of concern through me to see how excited he was at the thought. But I'd shoved it to one side: this was what I'd always wanted after all – and I was doing this for so many more people than just myself. I had to remember that.

We were so close. And all I had to do was play my part with Maya.

I steeled myself for what I needed to say next. 'I'm here to tell you that I know everything... and that there are reasons why I also want to bring *them* down.' We'd decided to never say their names out loud, just in case of any prying ears.

Maya rolled her eyes as though she didn't believe me. 'You don't know *what* they're capable of,' she retorted, staring Miles straight in the eyes as though she was accusing him now, looping him in with his parents.

I looked askance at him, but he hadn't noticed. He was totally locked on Maya. The tight control was beginning to slip from his face.

I had to take a gamble. 'Look, whatever's happened between you two, we all want the same thing now don't we?' Her eyes swivelled to face me. 'Trust me, I know exactly what I'm doing and getting in to. You owe it to more than just yourself to help us. We have to stop them.'

She'd pursed her lips as she considered my words. And I'd taken the opportunity to study her features. And that's when I saw the other reason why Maya had looked so familiar to me. And it was nothing to do with how similar we'd looked.

My stomach had flipped at the realisation. 'Hold on... it was you...'

Chapter Fifty-Four

Her eyes had flared in surprise, and when she'd hung her head in shame, I'd known I was right.

'It *was* you I saw that morning on the river?' I confirmed to be sure.

Miles's head snapped up.

'Yes,' she said, 'you're right – I just wanted to catch a glimpse of you, that's all. Make sure you were okay after those messages I'd sent. You seemed quite spooked, and I was worried I'd maybe gone too far. I'm sorry if I scared you.'

I nodded, my momentary panic resolved – I was just relieved that at last I'd pieced that puzzle together.

'What, seriously, Maya?' Miles began, an angry tinge to his words. But I held up a hand to stop him. And he listened.

So I went on, 'Come on, Maya – it's time for you to believe me. Like I said, we're on the same side. Trust us with this photo, and we can expose the truth. Then we can all move on.'

After what seemed like forever, a determined look fell across Maya's face and I knew we'd done it. I'd convinced her.

'Fine, I guess I don't really have a choice,' she said and leant down towards where her bag must have been on the floor.

As she disappeared under the table, Miles exhaled audibly as though he'd been holding his breath tight.

Maya reappeared a second later, clutching a small photograph close to her chest. 'You promise this will do it. You'll be able to bring William down?' Her voice had descended into a whisper, and her request sounded childish and soft but there was a fire in her eyes – a hunger for this whole chapter to be over.

'Yes,' Miles and I both said in unison. And he reached out his hand to take the photograph.

Maya hesitated for a moment more before taking the plunge, flicking her wrist out to hand it over.

I trained my eyes on Miles as he rotated the photograph around. His expression turned to absolute stone as he stared at it, and before I had another chance to study his face, he stood up roughly from the table. His chair screeched across the ground under him and a couple of heads broke away from their chattering conversations to glance around at us.

Miles looked down at Maya and spoke in the coldest voice I'd ever heard him use.

'We're done here. If we need anything else, we'll let you know.' He turned away and practically sprinted out of the café. What he'd seen on that photograph had shaken him to the core.

I looked back at the woman who had done this to him, my eyes narrowing as she stared at his back in shock. Maya shook her head as she caught the judgement etched across my face. The clang of the old bell at the door signalled Miles's abrupt departure.

Then Maya said to me softly, 'You can judge me if you want. But trust me, I've already done enough of that to last a lifetime. I was lost and in a desperate situation. Look, Miles never gave me the chance to explain, but back then I needed money to send to my sister. She was the only one left in my family I still cared about.

'So at the time, I didn't think it would cause much harm selling on what I was given. And that's the thing – I didn't *steal* anything. That's what Miles never knew. William *gave* all those pieces to me. He showered me with jewellery and attention... I know now that I was stupid to believe him. But look, all I'm saying is that I made a mistake back then; I never meant to hurt Miles. And trust me, I've more than paid for it with my guilt over the years.'

I might not have believed her words but her eyes swam with unshed tears.

'We don't have long, but maybe you can tell him I'm sorry. He's refused to listen to me. He never was very good at that.' She sighed. 'But today is about trying to make amends for what I did back when I was young and stupid. I've felt so guilty at keeping the knowledge of what William and Cassandra did to me, which is why I kept trying to warn people away over the years. I see now though that my half attempts at trying to warn other people off will never be enough on their own. But I was just so scared of what William would do to me if he found out, so I hid and did what I could manage... but meeting you – I think you're braver than I ever was. And I don't know your exact reason for wanting to bring them down – but I can tell you want it more than all of us. So I've trusted you with that photograph, because you're right, it's time we stop that family from hurting anyone else for good.'

She smiled at me sadly before continuing. 'I never meant to scare you, and all I wanted to do was warn you with those messages. Before it became too late for you too. But I can see you know what you're doing. Just promise me when the time comes, if things don't go to plan, you'll save yourself too. Remember, after all, he's their son.'

Her cryptic warning barely registered before she was already up and walking past me towards the door.

'Good luck,' was all she said over her shoulder, and then she was swept back out into the sea of people on the street.

I sat alone at the table in that bustling café and felt frozen in my chair, unable to move. I don't know how long I sat there thinking over her words. *He's their son, he's their son, he's their son* echoed in my mind.

I'd always known that, of course. But there as something in the way she'd said it, as though he was just as capable of harm as they were. I clenched my hand into a fist under the table. No way – Miles had only recently found out about what had happened with Maya and when I'd told him my story, he had been shocked. Unless he was the best actor of all...

I forced my legs to move. So far, all of his actions had only been to help me. I told myself not to let Maya get into my head and make me doubt him. Besides, it was far too late to stop. Once we discredited William and had that diary, I'd be able to finish what I started: prove William and Cassandra's guilt and work to put them behind bars. Then Miles and I could move on with our lives. Together. Free at last from his toxic parents.

But now in the Kings' bedroom, as I stand looking down at William's unmoving body and Cassandra's trembling form in the corner, Maya's words come echoing back into my mind.

'He's their son...'

And now her warning makes sense. He is just as ruthless as they are, if not far worse.

I have a choice to make. I wanted William and Cassandra to pay, but do I really think they deserved to lose their lives? That had never been part of my plan – and I'd never expected Miles to go this far tonight.

This Miles is *not* the Miles that I thought I knew. Not the Miles that I thought I loved.

But I still have to ask... what do I want?

Because maybe Miles is right.

Surely they *do* deserve all of this.

Didn't I *want* revenge?

After all, they did kill my parents.

Chapter Fifty-Five

Cassandra

Isabel is staring at me with those unreadable eyes. I flinch back at the hate that must be behind them for her to just stand by and watch.

'Why don't you tell my mother dearest what she's done to deserve this? What she did to you,' I hear Miles say to her with such relish in his voice. As though he's excited. Another wave of nausea hits me, and I can barely breathe as Isabel starts to speak.

'Do you remember a little village in East Sussex?' Her voice is no more than a whisper.

It's as though she's punched me in the stomach. I know who Isabel *truly* is, at last. And she's much more than just Gemma McKenna's cousin.

I've lived that night enough times in my nightmares.

If I close my eyes, I can picture that little village in East Sussex in more detail than this very house.

Because it was the night that changed everything.

The night that almost drove me mad with despair and self-hatred.

The night that lost me my son because I couldn't recover.

The night where my whole world broke apart.

Because it was the night I killed an entire family.

But as Isabel stands before me, I realise with a strange mixture of horror and relief, that might not be the case...

CHAPTER FIFTY-SIX

ISABEL

It's funny how your whole life can change in an instant. Everything you thought you knew about yourself can just be flipped on its head in a matter of seconds. That's exactly what had happened to me that night in Chelsea. Two years ago at the Kings' famous house party. Though I hadn't known who they were to me at the time.

Now as I stare down at Cassandra, I can hardly believe it's the same woman I met then...

I'd turned up for work at the most glamorous house I had ever been in before. My cousin Gemma had helped me get the casual waiting job. It was her boss's house so she was in charge of organising it. I'd been over to travel and test out the waters, to see if I liked living in England before deciding what I'd do next in my life.

Even though I was technically British, I hadn't been back here since I'd had to leave all those years ago to be raised by my grandparents in Australia. My cousin Gemma had been my only tie back to the UK – and we'd become close when she'd come out to live with us in Australia on her own year abroad.

When Gemma had offered me the gig, I'd readily accepted. Any spare job I could get was helpful – but I never could have expected what was going to happen.

When the waiting staff had been allowed in, I was bowled over by the sheer opulence and scale of the house. We filed one by one up a narrow staircase that eventually opened up into a cavernous entrance hall. Even from this side angle, I saw how the chandelier had glistened over the white marble floor. It almost dazzled me.

But I didn't have time to admire it for long as we were put straight to work by the housekeeper running the show. She'd taken command like a general, ensuring we were all 'battle station ready'. Our silver trays ere filled to the brim with champagne flutes ready to serve as the guests entered. I wanted to do a good job for my cousin – I couldn't embarrass her. Not that anyone realised I was related to her of course.

Soon the entry hall was teeming with the most glamorous people I'd ever seen in my life. Their clothes screamed wealth from every angle. Though I still hadn't spotted the illustrious owners of this incredible home.

The guests hardly noticed me – every time I got close they looked past me like I wasn't even there, or thrust an empty glass in my face. I was invisible. But I had no time to worry. The house was packed and my sense of time evaporated in the rush of running up and down stairs to keep the drinks topped up. It was on my return from one of these trips that I heard a round of applause and a communal ringing out of 'Cheers!' – the hosts had magnanimously greeted their guests.

The room was packed, but I'd spied a sideways profile of an elegant couple leaving the bottom of the stairs: a man in black tie and a woman in a sparkling emerald green gown. *They must be the owners. How lucky they are*, I thought.

The evening continued to pass in a blur of serving champagne and canapés to practically identical people all continuing to act like I wasn't even there. I tried not to let it get to me, but as I wandered into extravagant room after extravagant room, my spirits started to sink. This was a world that I'd never be part of. How did Gemma do this every day?

It seemed like the evening was almost over, the grand entrance had thinned enough that I could make my way across it without squeezing right up against the walls. As I entered from a side door, my tray freshly filled with topped-up glasses of champagne, a raised voice hit my ears from across the room, and I spotted the woman in the shimmering emerald gown talking to Mrs Jenkins, the housekeeper in charge.

'Alice.' I heard the enunciated vowels ring out across the marble floor like a slap. 'I made it perfectly clear that we had to have caviar blinis this year, everyone commented last year how wonderful they were. And now people are disappointed, and what's more we look cheap.'

'I'm sorry, Mrs King, it must have slipped my mind on the brief,' Mrs Jenkins responded in a weak voice as she smoothed her hand through her grey-white hair pulled back in a bun.

As I continued to make my way across the room, I heard the glamorous woman – Mrs King, I supposed – give an exasperated sigh. 'We'll have to talk about this later. Things like this keep happening, Alice, and I'm afraid it's just not good enough.'

I hurried past, not wanting to be seen hearing this hard-working woman be dressed down.

But then that same commanding voice called out to me. 'Excuse me, you there.' I swivelled on my heels to look at her. 'Bring me a glass, won't you? I need some sustenance to go back in.'

I walked towards her, not taking my eyes off my full silver tray. I was so worried about dropping it.

'Ah, thank God,' she said as she picked up a full glass from the top of the tray. She barely acknowledged me as she made to turn away. And I couldn't take it anymore – it was probably going to get me fired, but screw it, these people had to be told to learn some common decency.

'Excuse me?' I managed to say loudly.

She flicked her head around to face me. Our eyes locked.

And the words I'd been about to say died on my lips. Because everything I thought I knew changed in the space of an instant. The room spun and was tipped upside down. I looked into this woman's cold blue eyes, and suddenly, I wasn't in this grand room anymore.

No, I'd flown far away to another place and moment in time. That face, those eyes, that same disdainful look was one I had seen before. One that I had seen on another late summer's evening, through glass and rubble and debris, the stench of blood and gasoline filling the air.

As I stared into this woman's flawless face, my long-buried memories of that night came rushing back to me like the speed of the car crash that had killed my parents.

This woman had been there too. Staring at me through the window of the burning car, my parents already dead in the front seats.

My vision blurred as I remembered how she had looked straight into my six-year-old eyes as I'd cried for help through the cracked glass. Those cold blue eyes had looked at me, looked straight *through* me –

like they were now. The torrent of memories overwhelmed me – as I recalled that I'd thought for a split second that I was saved. That she would help us.

But even as I'd cried for help, she had turned swiftly into the night. She'd turned and walked away from a dying child. Accepting the blood on her hands as surely as if she had killed that child herself.

All those images flashed through my mind in a matter of seconds. The large silver plate laden with glasses of champagne crashed from my hands. I'd turned and ran out of the room, unable to process the realisation of this nightmare.

But I'd sworn that one day I would make her pay.

Chapter Fifty-Seven

Cassandra

I can't believe who is standing in front of me. The child that I thought I'd killed all those years ago.

I had pushed that night out of my mind for the past twenty years. I had been forced to put it out of my mind, by William, by Dr Smythe, by the medication. And finally, when I'd written out the whole terrible saga in my diary, I thought that would be my closure. That I was done.

I'd locked it away in a secret spot where no one except me could ever find it. I thought that by locking it away physically, it would be locked away in my mind too. But now it comes rushing back to me in full force.

That dark, quiet country lane.

William had been careening down the road like a maniac, high on the success of his biggest deal yet. My family's money had funded a lot of things in our early days, including the start of his business, and he'd been riding high on how the tide was changing, luxuriating in his growing power and kingdom. That was one of the things that had attracted me to him. That he'd always known what he wanted, with such certainty and clarity. Including that he'd wanted me.

I had never had that strong assurance in anything. And after the instability of my own childhood, that's what I'd wanted in my life. Or I thought I did.

I think, looking back on it now, I could say there was a time when we were happy. I'd wanted to be a dutiful wife and a loving mother. I could put a lock on the darkness of my childhood and throw away the key.

Sure, William had a tendency to be a bit controlling at times, but I didn't mind. I wanted to be looked after, and he definitely did that.

Then, that night had changed everything for us.

I'd been singing along with him, joining in on his success. I thought I'd never seen him so wildly happy. He'd whooped with joy.

But the sound of our laughter turned suddenly into a scream. The bright glow of headlights had flashed up at us as we'd turned the next corner at speed.

Everything happened so quickly.

I flew forward against the seatbelt, as William hit the brakes hard. I braced my knees up and the belt cut deep into my chest as we screeched to a drawn-out stop. I could smell the burning rubber. Blood was roaring in my ears. I looked at William, my eyes wide with fear as I took in his pale expression. He was breathing hard too, rubbing at his own chest where the seatbelt had cut into him.

At first, all I felt was relief. We were okay. We had been saved.

But then I saw a plume of smoke erupting from behind William's head. And that's when I heard the scream. A child's scream.

I scrabbled to tear my seatbelt off, unable to stop. I think I heard William cry 'Wait!' but it was too late. I was already out the car door.

The lights of the upturned silver car continued blinking through the debris that surrounded it. I broke into a run, crunching over fragments of glass that littered the stretch between our two cars.

Desperately, I reached the windows and crouched down. I was almost sick at the sight. The glass around their heads was so smashed that it wasn't easy to see what was inside, but I could just about make out that in what should have been the front of the car, lay a man and a woman, crushed under the weight of impact.

That's when I heard the cry again.

I tried to peer through the smashed glass of the rear windows, and on the far side of the car, the side that was pressed down towards the ditch jutting out of the road, I saw her.

A small girl was trapped beneath the weight of the collapsing car, her face covered in fresh cuts and blood, but still alive. *Just.*

'Help me...' I thought I could see her little mouth form the words, but maybe it had just been my imagination afterwards. The next second, I was being wrenched away.

The broken, scared girl disappeared from view.

'Come on,' William screamed at me, 'we have to get out of here!' His grip on my wrist was so tight that when I dug my heels in to the ground, my shoulder almost popped out of its socket. A flash of pain ran up my arm but I ignored it.

'There's a girl in there!' I screamed. 'We have to help her!' I tried to pull my wrist free, but William was too strong. He continued to drag me towards the car as if he hadn't heard me, my feet stumbling the whole way.

He spun around and for a second I thought he was going to stop and help. But I hadn't seen his other arm move as the hard sting of the slap landed across my face. The shock of it made me stop struggling. Long enough for him to drag me the final steps to the car.

He shoved me in the already open passenger door and as I tried to jump out, he barricaded my way, roughly shoving me back down. My head thwacked the top of the open door, and I fell back in a daze.

It was that moment of disorientation that allowed him enough time to get into the driver's seat and lock the doors.

The next thing I knew we were driving away.

Away from the accident.

Away from the deaths we caused.

Away from the girl – who without help would no doubt die from her injuries.

We might as well have killed her ourselves.

'William, no, no, no, please, we have to go back!' I screamed at him as he continued to race away. I tried to grab at his hands on the steering wheel. I had to stop him and get out of this car again. I had to save that little girl.

We swerved and I didn't see his left fist fly off the wheel. It made impact at an awkward angle with my nose. I cried out at the pain and both my hands flew up to my face. To my horror, I pulled them away to see blood staining my fingertips.

'Cassandra, stop!' William screamed, driving faster than ever before. He didn't seem at all sorry for what he'd just done. 'Don't you see? This would ruin everything that we have achieved. We'll be charged with manslaughter. Go to jail. Everything we have worked for these past twelve years would be for *nothing*. That is *not* happening just because of an *accident*. They came out of nowhere.' I sat in stunned silence. 'It *wasn't* my fault,' he added, pushing his foot down on the pedal to speed us away even faster into the night.

'But there's a little girl in that car, she's trapped! She'll die if we don't help,' I said through the swelling that had already started above my lip. 'We have to do something. Tell *someone*,' I begged. We had already done the unspeakable. We had killed her parents. But I couldn't just leave her to die too, could I?

'No, Cassandra, we can't,' William responded, no emotion in his voice, and I watched him in complete shock. His eyes were forced on the black road in front of us, ignoring my sobbing pleas.

And so I launched at him, not caring if we crashed. I just wanted him to stop and turn around. He pushed me off again and my head smacked against the window. William screeched the car to a stop in the middle of the empty country road. I thought I'd finally got through to him.

But instead he threw himself on top of me. His hands wrapped around my throat, choking the scream on my lips into a gurgle.

'Cassandra,' he growled, staring me in the eyes. They darted around in response. But no one else was here to help me. I tried to move, but one of my arms was pressed against me, his body weight bearing down on top. My other arm hit out, but in an easy movement he loosened the grip of his right hand around my throat and caught my hand, holding my arm tight. His left hand continued to pin me down by the throat.

'Listen to me, Cassandra, I don't want to hurt you.' My shallow breathing became fast and quick. 'STOP!' he bellowed.

It was a losing battle. I relented and stared up into his blank, unforgiving eyes.

'Think of Miles. If we got charged with this, he'd have no one. We'd both be in jail. If I have this on my record, I'll never be able to do business again. Miles will have nothing. Is that what you want?'

I tried to speak. I wanted to say that it would be better for him to have parents that had tried to save someone's life. But then William said the only words that could make me stop struggling. 'Stop fighting me; do nothing and keep this to yourself. That little girl will die anyway – she's probably already dead. Put this whole thing out of your mind right now. Do as I say, or you'll never see your son again.'

Those words had been his final blow.

And I knew he meant it. William was powerful, ruthless, and he got what he wanted. I always thought we would be on the same side, but now I saw there was no other way. If I disobeyed him, he would take my son away from me, as surely as I knew William would stay by my side forever to stop me speaking of this night.

William saw the defeat in my eyes.

He let me go, pulling back into his seat. My hands flew up to my throat. It felt hot and sticky, my breathing fast.

William was already racing down those dark roads again. Away from the little girl. Away from what we'd done.

I was trapped. There was no way I could stop him driving again without getting us both killed.

And my son needed me, Miles needed me.

But so did this little girl.

My world had broken apart at the seams and there was no repairing it. So I'd made a choice. To stay silent for my son.

But I'd also made another one. I would help this little girl too. But William could *never* find out.

Chapter Fifty-Eight

Izzy

I see Cassandra's face contort in anguish. It feels like this is the first time I'm seeing the real Cassandra. The one that's truly behind the mask. But seeing her devastation is not giving me the satisfaction that I'd hoped I would feel from this moment.

No, all I'm feeling in return is raw pain, made worse when she speaks.

'I… I… tried to help, you have to know that. It was too late for your parents. But even when William forced me to leave you behind, I knew I had to help. I did leave you there, your memory is correct. But I didn't want to, not for a second.' I can see the pain written across her face. She must be telling the truth. My stomach somersaults.

'After William threatened to take my son away from me…' she continues, her eyes flickering up at Miles and shuddering, 'I agreed with him. I told him that I understood… It was the only way. He always liked being told he was right. If I hadn't told him what he wanted to hear, he wouldn't let me leave the car. It was the first lie I ever told him.

'I convinced him to stop at a service station, and I told him I needed the bathroom. I found a payphone and placed a 999 call. I gave every scrap of information I could before I had to hang up – I couldn't let William see me. But I'm sorry… I'm so sorry. I know that's not a lot. I didn't do a lot…'

Her face crumples into pieces as tears slip down her cheeks. 'But it was all I could do. I couldn't tell anyone. William kept saying that if I did, we would go to jail and Miles would be left alone in the world. And he even threatened once that if I did tell anyone, he would prove that I'd been driving.' She shakes her head. 'I guess I was trapped. But I still made a choice that day. And that's why I hated myself, why I couldn't go on. I couldn't live with it. I couldn't live with what I'd done. I had left a poor innocent girl to die.'

She looks up at me, deep loathing in her eyes, but not for me. For herself. 'And I see now why you hate me. You should. It's a hatred I have lived with every day. But it's why I've become who I am. I had to lock everything away. It's been the only way to make my life bearable.'

I stand there rigid in shock as I attempt to take in her words and the implications of what they mean. I hadn't remembered any precise details of the crash before that moment I saw Cassandra for the first time at that party. They'd been locked away in the dark recesses of my mind – until the shock of seeing those unforgettable eyes again.

I'd only known before what Nana had told me when I was old enough to ask and understand what had happened to my parents. She had told me that there had been a car accident, that my parents had died and I had survived by some miracle. That miracle being an anonymous call that tipped off the emergency services to go to Briary Road that night. I'd been unconscious when the firefighters had arrived. They'd managed to cut me out just in time before the weight of the car entirely crushed me and the ambulance services got me to hospital. If I had been left overnight and not found until morning, I would have died.

It was Cassandra's phone call that had saved me.

Ever since I saw Cassandra and my memories of what happened came back to me in a hazy blur, I have directed the entirety of my hate and anger about the loss of my parents at her. She had got away scot-free. My parents were dead – my whole life as I could have known it destroyed by her heartless actions.

My hatred had grown with an all-consuming passion since that moment. Gemma had been the only person I could confide in. She was the first person to see me when I'd returned back to her small flat two years ago in an absolute state. She'd listened with horror as I recounted everything I'd unlocked through seeing that suddenly familiar face.

Gemma swore then and there that she'd do anything in her power to try and get justice for me, and my dead parents. Her dead aunt and uncle.

I'd stayed in the UK for a while, doing the odd job, hanging around in Gemma's flat for far longer than I had planned. I became obsessed. I learnt all I could about the Kings' success and wealth. They had everything. And I had nothing. My parents had been taken away from me in the blink of an eye, and they had walked away unharmed. I had to prove who had really murdered my parents.

Gemma, as William's assistant, had started to sleuth around as much as possible over that first year, trying to become as close to Cassandra as she could. For a while it seemed to be working, and she had discovered that Cassandra kept secret diaries. We'd come so close until Cassandra had found her that day last year in her study. There's been no doubt in our minds that Cassandra had framed Gemma to get her fired.

That had been our lowest point – it felt like we'd gone back to square one. But then Gemma's friend in recruitment said that there was going to be a job opening up at King & Co., Australia. I decided that was my chance to take. Maybe I'd be able to start working in the Australian company until I could get back over here. And using my Australian name and passport had worked perfectly. No one ever suspected I was really Gemma's cousin.

Then six months ago I'd heard that Miles, the boss's son, was coming out to Australia. This could be my ticket: if I became close to him, wouldn't that help me get closer to his parents?

I suppose deep down I'd always hoped we'd become romantically close, and when we did, it meant was that there was even more reason to prove what they'd done to. I could bring down William and Cassandra, and free my beloved Miles from his parents' grasp too.

But now hearing Cassandra's story, seeing her break down on the floor in front of me as she trembles in the shadow of her son, I'm shocked to find that I feel pity. She's been a woman trapped in a game for far too long.

Since remembering that night, I'd always assumed that William had been there too. I'd been right about that, but not that Cassandra had left willingly. It had been William that had refused to save me.

I glance over at his unmoving body once more. I find it hard to feel any true sympathy.

Cassandra *had* tried to do something that night. Her actions had saved me. And the torture of not knowing if that little girl had survived had almost killed her in the end.

Hearing everything pieced together, I can see that the repercussions of that night didn't just affect me and my family. It also completely broke hers.

All this time, I had been trying to tear something apart that was already destroyed.

If that night had never happened, what position would we be in now? Would her own son have killed his father and be staring at her with such loathing in his eyes?

Probably not.

It's astonishing how every one of our lives changed forever in that instant, all because of William's actions. Everything could have been so different.

And now, what did I want? Did I still want her to pay for what she'd done? Or has she already suffered enough?

Chapter Fifty-Nine

Cassandra

I am shaking uncontrollably, the shock of the truth hitting me at once. I can't comprehend the lies and tricks William played on my mind, all the pain I went through. Here it is at last, catching up with me.

I should have fought harder against him that night. Fought harder against him on so much more than that.

But it was impossible. William was impossible.

He had me wrapped around his little finger. After surviving my breakdown, I could only do one thing: put on this mask and bury everything deep.

I'd thought if I ever came forward, William would destroy me and punish Miles to spite me, but now I see that I should have been braver, and everything I'd done had been pointless in the end. My own son stares at me with such loathing in his eyes anyway.

I should have told the truth and faced the consequences.

Nothing I did had saved my family in any way. It had broken us. I'd thought taking this secret to my grave would be the only way to save us.

But it's my secret that has destroyed everything at last.

And now, here she is, the little girl that I left to die.

I was weak. So weak. She wants her revenge, and I do not blame her. No, in a lot of ways, I welcome it. Surely I deserve what I get, don't I?

But there is still a part of me that doesn't want to give up, doesn't want to just die. Now that the truth is out there, is there not a way I can make everything right?

'That's so very *touching*, mother,' Miles says in a sarcastic voice, cutting through the silence that has grown. 'But it's really far too late for the both of us. You lied to us, you lied to us for so long. Just like him.'

My breath catches in my throat.

Miles's punishment is far from over.

No, it seems he's only just begun.

Because this is it. This is the moment I die.

Chapter Sixty

I stare up at them both. There's no way out. But even still, there is small voice in the back of my mind, begging me to try.

'What now then, Miles?' I stammer. 'What are you going to do to me?'

'Well,' he says almost with a spring in his step, coming back over to lean into my face.

I attempt to see the son I thought I knew, one more time, but I don't recognise him in this monster's eyes.

'I'm going to pin this on you, of course.' He gestures around the room as though it's obvious.

I shake my head. 'What... but how? This wasn't me...?'

His face turns into a mask of mock apology. 'Yes, I'm sorry about that. But I've decided that it's now the only option. The tidiest thing possible. You see, everyone *knows* that you and William just had a terrible fight. We made sure of that. We've been building this up for the last week. Isabel's done a beautiful job of helping seed doubt, stoking your obsessions, sending you that letter...

'But everything that happened tonight, well that was all me,' he says proudly as he begins to pace again, up and down. 'I really thought that exposing William's sordid past would be enough at first – that the press would do a piece on him and destroy his credibility. But I sent it out anonymously last week and even casually asked around. No one wanted anything to do with it. He was just too damn powerful – they were scared of him! Can you believe it!

'So next I thought if you at least discovered and exposed him publicly, that would cause enough of a scandal for the board to demand he steps down. And for *you* to reject him too.' He looks down at me in disgust.

'But no! You fell to pieces, so you didn't see what happened, but William managed to charm every single one of them into silence tonight. It was quite something to watch. And of course, what else could I do in front of them except smile and nod? I couldn't tell them it was *me* who had planted the photographs that had made you go crazy. After everyone left, I was in such a rage.'

His eyes dart across to Izzy, who remains silent. She looks ghostly pale now. I thought she would be enjoying my destruction more.

'Izzy tried to keep me patient,' Miles mutters under his breath, 'but I knew that the only way to stop him now would be through his death. And for it to look like an accident.' He shakes his head. 'I obviously wasn't thinking clearly enough though – I was too angry, and I thought a car crash would be poetic, after what he did to Izzy's parents. I hid the plates and followed him out to the bar he'd gone to. I'd hoped it would look like a drunk man had just got hit. But it wasn't quite right – there wasn't enough force behind my hit. So then I hoped he might die in that hospital tonight – then my job would be done...'

His eyes look wild with madness, and they bear down at me. 'But when I got back and I realised you weren't here anymore, that you'd gone to his *aid...*' He's shaking in anger. 'I couldn't believe it... You'd just found out he'd been cheating on you for *years* and you still go? *That* was the final straw, Mother. So then I decided to improvise and now we're here. He *is* dead. You now know everything – and so do I. You chose him over me again tonight. Just like you've done my whole life.'

I try to raise my voice to protest but he raises a dismissive arm at me. 'Save your breath, Mother, because you have a bit of a tough choice. Obviously I cannot be involved in any of this – the business and trust *have* to go to me. And we don't want too much of a scandal: it would affect business. So I'm afraid that Isabel coming forward with those diaries about what you did to her parents won't do either.' I manage a glance at Isabel and she's frowning. Had she known this part of Miles's plan?

'But I have a fantastic idea now: you admit that you killed William – that you planned the whole thing in a rage and ended dear Papa's life. If you choose that path, then for once, you'll be choosing me over him. And of course, I have an official witness to that in dear Izzy.' My mouth goes dry. 'Your other option is that you stick to your usual selfish ways and end it the way you wanted to all those years ago.' He stares at me as the horrific realisation of his words sweep over me.

He nods, grinning in an insane way. 'Yes, that's right. You can finish off what you started right here in this room. But this time, get it right,' he adds with an unrepentant scoff.

He's giving me an impossible choice – no choice, really. Lie and say that I killed my husband, or kill myself? I want to be sick.

Then he starts to laugh, a deep, throaty laugh. 'Oh Mother, your expression, you should see it. It's brilliant. Of course, I'm joking, you're not *really* leaving this room.' His face hardens now to an immovable mask, any false mirth vanishing in an instant. 'I can't *trust* you, can I? When have you ever earned my trust? Besides, I can see written plain across your face that you still wouldn't lie for me. Never a lie for me. But you would do anything for him,' he spits out.

Miles's eyes are wild, his hair dishevelled from how many times he's run his hands through it. My handsome son is entirely replaced by someone I don't recognise.

'You are going to do one thing for me. You're going to write a note admitting what you've done. And then we're going to end your sorry life, once and for all.'

He marches over to the small desk next to where I'm cowering, roughly pulling open the drawer and thrusting a notepad and pen at me. 'Now,' he says, folding his arms.

I stare up at him, at the paper and pen in his hands. When I don't take it, he chucks them down towards me. The pen hits my arm and bounces off as the notepad also falls to the floor with a thud. I glance down at it, unmoving. I'm not doing this. I can't do this.

'Come on, Mother,' he says, kneeling down before me and shoving them in my face. 'This is the *one* thing you can do for me. The *one* thing in your sorry little life.' I see the desperation on his face and a wild glint in his eyes.

I shake my head. No. I can't do this. This terrible ask, I cannot do.

He grabs my wrist and I look straight into his eyes. Before, they had been devoid of emotion, now they are full of anger. I don't know which is more dangerous. 'Do it,' he hisses. 'Don't make this worse than it already is.'

But I shake my head again and try to find my voice, even as my brain feels like it's going to explode. 'No, Miles, no.' My voice cracks as tears slide down my face. I can't believe this is happening to me, or what has become of my lovely blue-eyed boy.

'You don't think I'll do it... that's what it is, isn't it? Let me tell you, Mother,' he hisses, 'I'm on a damn roll... first Maya, then dear Papa, then you. Anyone that's ever betrayed me will be gone. I'll finally be able to start again with Izzy. The only person who has ever stuck by me.'

I shake my head, confused at his words in spite of my situation, but it's not me that breaks his monologue.

'Maya's dead?!' Izzy's cry hurtles across the room at us, and he drops my arm to turn to face her.

He looks, as though he'd forgotten she was there. Then he straightens up and turns to face her.

'Don't tell me you didn't guess,' he says, tilting his head to one side to consider her. 'When you came out of that café and I wasn't there? When I came back and told you how I'd just had to catch up to Maya to finish things off... I thought you knew.'

Isabel shakes her head, face pale.

My heart beats faster in my chest as I look around the room for any means of escape. Isabel still stands by the door, blocking the only exit.

I'm going to die, echoes though my mind.

My son is going to kill me. Just like he killed Maya and William.

Chapter Sixty-One

Izzy

I try to control the shocked expression that's flown across my face at Miles's revelation.

Maya is dead.

Miles *killed* her.

And he thought I *knew* and would be *happy*?

His earlier rage had been one thing. At first, he'd just been beside himself when his plan had failed, when he realised that the journalists hadn't listened. He hadn't brought down his father through his planted photographic evidence. I'd tried to calm him down and tell him over and over again that it didn't really matter. We had another shot with the diary – if we found it – and that we could look for it straight away while William was out if Cassandra left that room.

We still had an opening.

He said he had tried to find it when he'd planted those images in Cassandra's study earlier, when he'd stolen her key. But I see now that he'd just been lying to me – telling me what I wanted to hear so I would stick by his side throughout his far more elaborate and brutal plan. This plan that I'd had no idea about. But he'd just admitted to Cassandra that he had no intention of telling the world what had happened to my parents after all. I'd been played like a pawn.

I clench my fists in rage as I breathe through the memories of what happened next... of all the chances I'd had to escape.

Even when I'd tried to convince him to be patient, he just wouldn't listen. It was like ever since we saw Maya, all control seeped out of him. Now I knew why – he'd been spiralling after killing her. He had to bring down William, or it would all be for nothing.

When he'd grabbed the car keys and left the house, I had no idea what he was planning. He appeared just too angry to see sense. And it was the first time I'd felt a little frightened of him. I should have run then. But I'd given him the benefit of the doubt – hadn't he done that for me all this time? So I'd stayed. And as I stand trapped in this room, I realise that was my biggest mistake.

He came back in an even worse rage when he'd found out where his mother had gone. I hadn't realised it was *him* that had tried to hit William. He never said.

He'd kept me close to him in his room while waiting for his parents to return. Muttering to himself about what would happen to them next. I'd tried to coax him back to himself, but there was no stopping his obsession, so I just kept quiet and tried not to draw his frantic anger to me.

I couldn't just escape – every so often he'd look up and say that I was the *only* one that understood him. That I could never leave him. His eyes had looked so manic – I'd just nodded. At that point, I still didn't really think he'd hurt me, but his temper was so volatile that it felt like I was trying to tame a wild animal. I didn't think it was worth the risk of running. I'd hoped I'd find another opportunity to slip away. I just had to be patient.

But then he dragged me along to his parents' room. He told me he needed me there for support, and to wait outside until he called me in. This was the chance I'd been waiting for. As soon as the door shut behind him, I started to creep down the corridor. Then I sprinted. I had time to grab a small bag and coat from what *had* been our room. I just had to get out of here right now – I'd explain it to Miles later. That I'd had an emergency or something.

I'd no idea what had been in store for William though. Not until it was far too late. I only thought Miles wanted to check on them, or argue it out then and there.

Then I heard the almighty blood-curdling scream. Coming from down the other end of the house. William and Cassandra's room.

Oh my god.

I ran back down the never-ending corridor on instinct.

When I flung open the door I saw Miles batting Cassandra away, hard onto the floor like she was no more than an inconvenient fly trying to buzz around his head.

I screamed at the sight and my heart had pounded at a million miles an hour. Every fibre in my body screamed for me to run. I stared in horror as she made impact with the ground. By the time I looked up to where Miles stood over what must have been his father, he was already unmoving. I was too late anyway.

The shock of what I was seeing immobilised every inch of me. It was like being in a terrible nightmare when you couldn't move. All I could think was *this wasn't the plan. This wasn't the plan.*

This whole situation had got so far out of my control that I was spinning in space. Miles was now on an even more unstoppable path to take his parents down than I ever thought possible.

And that's when I finally understood Maya's last words to me. *He's their son.*

I tried, but I couldn't see anything left of the Miles I thought I knew. The Miles I thought I loved.

I didn't want anything to do with his actions tonight – none of this was what I'd imagined. I'd only ever wanted justice for my parents, for the world to know who killed them. I never wanted William's and Cassandra's deaths on my hands.

This all happened in a matter of seconds.

Miles just grinned, his eyes devoid of any real emotion. He stepped around the bed and grabbed me quickly as his mother lay moaning on the floor, clutching her head. He pulled me inside and closed the door with a bang – roughly placing me in the corner of the room. He pressed a finger to his lips and spun around to face his mother, walking into the centre of the room to begin his little show.

I slipped down on weak knees to the floor and curled into a ball. I was trapped. And I realised then that if I tried to run, I would absolutely be next. Miles would never let me leave this room unless I was completely on his side. The fact that he thought I was the only person he could trust was the one thing keeping me safe right now. If I ran, that would all be over. Which is why I've stood here in the shadows, letting this all play out.

Now, with this new revelation that he killed both his dad and Maya too, I see with the utmost certainty that I never really knew him at all.

I still can't make a false move. Or I'll be next. And then I'll never be able to get Cassandra out alive.

Because I might not have been able to save William or Maya, but now I'm certainly not going to let Cassandra be next. I have to play along.

'She deserved it,' I say flippantly, forcing the words out of my mouth – and they do the trick because he grins broadly in response back.

'She absolutely did. I thought you'd cottoned on when the news alert came through that there had been an accident on the line at Vauxhall.'

I think back to his words at the time that alert came through – he'd made a comment about how it's always so busy on those Tube platforms. That no one ever notices if someone is pushed or falls. And then he'd winked at me, actually *winked* at me. I'd thought he was just being silly.

But oh god... I try not to be sick as I comprehend what his words mean. As I think of that girl – the girl that looked like the perfect version of me – now shattered to pieces all because she'd hurt the man standing in front of me.

'Now then, I think it's time we finished this, don't you?'

The only thing I can do is beam back at him and nod wordlessly. I have to keep up this charade. My life depends on it.

And I need to get out of here, before he kills me too. Because when he finds out that I'm not entirely on his side – what then?

I'd thought this plan would give my parents the justice they deserve. I thought it was fate that Miles and I had come together. We had been happy in the little bubble I'd created. And when he'd heard the truth and had said that he wanted to help me get justice, that he also wanted to see his parents pay, I thought everything would be put to right at last. How wrong I was.

I had always been playing a part as his perfect girlfriend, so he would bring me over to meet his parents. I guess it had never really been *me* beneath it all. Now both our masks are off, and I see him for what he truly is.

If I don't stop him now, I won't be able to ever escape him.

But how can I manage it?

He is bigger than me, stronger than me – without any weapons, he would crush me the second I turned on him.

But there is another person in this room. Another person who has just as much to lose if Miles isn't stopped. But how to communicate to her without words, without giving myself away?

And even if I can, how can I know I can trust her to do what I need her to do? For her to stop her own son?

Chapter Sixty-Two

Cassandra

Miles has turned his attention back on me, grabbing my arm once more.

'Write the damn note, Mother.'

But I can't, I'm frozen. I shake in the horror of the moment.

He screams in frustration and in his anger pushes me hard away from him as he lets go of my wrist. The force jolts me back and I hit my head against the wall, and for a moment I see stars before Miles's hand flies at the side of my cheek. My head knocks back against the wall again and this time I bite down on my lip hard. Blood spurts out, as I also feel an intense pain at the back of my head. Am I bleeding there too? I collapse onto the ground, and a hand closes around my throat.

The next thing I know, there's a tightening, like a noose around my neck. I open my eyes and in horror, I see that is exactly what Miles is doing. He wraps the silk cord of my dressing gown tighter and tighter around my throat. He begins to drag me up, and I clutch at my throat, unable to take a single breath.

'Fine, have it your way,' he says, panting. 'No note. I'll just forge it later. We'll get right to it.' My eyes pop out wide as I take in fragments of the room, my legs kicking out.

But I can't escape him. And my legs begin to slow, giving up the fight.

This must be it, I think my last conscious thoughts.

In a way, it's probably a just end.

Somewhere in the back of my mind, I think I hear a scream – surely it's not mine?

As suddenly, everything goes black.

And Cassandra King is gone.

Chapter Sixty-Three

Izzy

As I see Miles forcing the cord around Cassandra's neck and hear her choking cries, I know I can't stand by. I have to do something.

I run at him, screaming at the top of my lungs. I try to loosen his grip and pull him away. My impact against his body causes him to let go, and Cassandra falls to the floor with a thud.

She isn't moving – am I too late?

I don't have a second to think further as Miles spins around, pushing me hard. I land on the edge of the bed and I scream on reflex as he shouts at me.

'What do you think you're doing?!'

'I... I...' I need to think quick and gain some time. Before he descends on me too. 'I just wasn't thinking, how suddenly it happened...' He cocks his head to one side as though considering my words, turning them over. Trying to decide if they're true.

'Oh my sweet Isabel, if I didn't know any better, I would say that you were trying to *stop* me.' He crosses his arms over his chest. 'And that would be a very *bad* decision for you to make.' He laughs mercilessly as he turns to look at his mother, crumpled on the ground, unmoving.

Is she still breathing? I can't tell. But I know that behind me, William King has experienced the same fate.

And Maya.

'See how weak they were, in the end. This can be it now, just the two of us, but you have to prove it to me.' A look spreads across his face as though he's had the best idea of his life. 'You need to finish the job.' He looks down at his mother, who's starting to stir on the floor. *She's still alive.*

'You need to kill her,' he says simply, grabbing me by the hand and pulling me to my feet. He drags me across to where Cassandra lies.

My jaw drops open. He can't be asking me to do this.

'Come on, Iz,' he wheedles, taking a stray piece of my hair in his hands and twirling it. He tugs on it and I stumble towards him. He whispers in my ear, 'You wanted revenge for your parents. Go on, take it.'

Her eyelids flutter before they go still once more.

I can't. I won't. I need to call the police. Get help. But first, I have to get out of this room. Somehow.

I nod, slowly. It's the only way I can think of to buy me some time. A smile spreads across his terrible face and I take a small step towards Cassandra.

As I inch forward I try and take in every corner of this room. The door is far away, across to the left. If I made a dash, Miles would intercept me within seconds. I need to get him on the backfoot. I glance desperately around the room. Near where Cassandra lies is the writing desk where Miles found the paper and pen. And on top of it is the one thing in this room that could maybe slow him down.

So as I approach Cassandra, I pretend like I'm about to kneel down but turn to grab the standalone lamp that's on the desk. I spin around and lunge with all my might at Miles. I hit him straight across the face with full force. He jumps back, screaming. I race across to the door. But just as I place my hand on the handle I feel a sharp tug on my loose hair, and my head flies back at a sharp angle.

My neck snaps in protest as Miles pins me up against him. I feel his hot, angry breath in my ear.

'You thought you could trick me, my darling? Pull one over on me? Oh my dear, you can never escape me.'

Then I'm thrown across the room, hitting my head against the corner of the bed as I fall to the ground. The next thing I know, Miles's face is above me and his hands are around my throat. His eyes pop out in anger as he throttles me. I try to kick out, try to move. But it's impossible. He's too strong. *This is it. This is how I go.*

But all of a sudden, Miles's hands go limp around my throat as he cries out, and his body slumps across me. It's only when I manage to escape out from underneath him that I notice the blood.

And the bloody knife in Cassandra's hand.

Chapter Sixty-Four

Cassandra

The knife shakes in my hand, but it's firm in my grip. I stare down in a state of shock. I have just stabbed my own son in the back.

My consciousness had returned blurrily as I heard Miles telling Isabel what she needed to do to gain his trust. My eyes had blinked open as I saw her make the choice. She'd decided to risk trying to escape from him rather than kill me. When he'd thrown her on the ground and began strangling her, I'd known what I needed to do. Every fibre in my body protested, but I'd pulled myself up and crawled along the sideboard to the bottom drawer. In it, I knew what I was looking for. It was the only weapon I could think of. The sharp silver knife turned letter opener that had been my father's final present to me.

Now, I hold the long, bloody knife in my hand as ruby red liquid drips down onto the edge of my white rug. Isabel is staring up at me with wide, frightened eyes. I throw the silver knife away and it clatters across the wooden floor.

I see her get up, ever so slowly. She tiptoes around Miles's unmoving body until she's in front of me, staring me in the eyes. For a moment, as she moves her arms, I think she's going to finish the attack. That I'd been mistaken, and I had just killed my son for nothing.

But then I'm being pulled into an embrace. And just like that, it's over.

I had to kill the person I loved most in the world to save the person I thought I'd killed all those years ago.

And as we hold onto each other, both lost in shock, one thing in this nightmare becomes clear to me.

Even though my whole life as I know it has just been ripped away from me in the space of a single night, at least my secret is finally free.

Chapter Sixty-Five

Izzy – One year later

I'm running along the beach, my toes swishing into the soft sand. It's hard going, running on the softer, looser sand, but these days I like to challenge myself. I am obsessed with being strong – I never want to be put into a position where I feel defenceless again. Even though it's only seven o'clock in the morning, the heat of the sun is starting to prickle my skin and I know it's going to be a scorcher. The ocean roars next to me and there's the sound of circling seagulls crying overhead. God, it feels good to be back in Australia. To be back home. And I'm looking forward to when Gemma moves over later this year. I won't feel so alone then, I hope.

As soon as I could after the events of last year, I'd left England behind. I'd like to think that one day I might be brave enough to return again. To rediscover the land of my birth and learn more about my parents. But not for a long while. After everything that happened, I realised I needed to embrace my current life; I couldn't live for the past anymore.

Doing so had nearly cost me my life.

I shudder to think back to that morning, a similar time of day to this – which is probably also why I always have to get up, get out and *move* or I would be lost to the terrors of my dreams. It had been a horrible day. Cassandra and I had called the police and were interrogated for hours. It had turned out that Miles was actually still alive. *Just.*

Thank *God* I had worn my necklace recording device. The small round heart that I had worn around my neck from day one helped to prove everything we said. It had been a gift from my grandmother her final Christmas. She'd been trying to prove she was tech-savvy, I think. I liked that it had reminded me of her. But I'd also brought it with me at the start because I thought it would help me catch out William and Cassandra. Turns out, I'd needed it for their son. With the proof of what he'd done spelt out loudly in his own words, there wasn't anything he could do to avoid his sentence. Even though he still tried to deny it all.

As for Cassandra's guilt over my parents' hit-and-run, after everything that had happened, I didn't want to explore whether I could press any charges. I had discovered that, in a way, she had saved me then, and when her son attacked me, she'd saved me again. And her life as she knew it was over anyway. Her cheating, manipulative husband was dead, her psychotic son locked away for a very long time after he got out of the hospital. The Cassandra King that she used to be was dead and gone too. She'd even chosen to let King & Co. be passed on to the shareholders. She'd said she didn't want to have anything more to do with it.

So everything was over.

But the scars still remained.

It gives me some comfort to know Miles is locked away for a long time, unable to hurt me. After what he did to Maya all those years later for betraying him, I shudder to think at what he might try to do to me now if he had the chance...

He can't hurt me, but sometimes I wake from nightmares at the idea of him being released. I still feel the weight of his hands around my neck and see his blood seeping across the floor. There are some things you can't forget.

I stop running and look out to sea, trying to replace the images that plague my mind.

Instead I try to picture Cassandra, over on the other side of the world in her quaint little cottage on the outskirts of a quiet country village. She lives an isolated life now, and I think she likes it. As much as anyone can after everything she's been through. We don't really stay in touch, but we've got into the habit of sending each other postcards every now and then. I think it helps remind both of us that what happened was real. That we're the survivors.

Have I forgiven her for killing my parents? I don't know. I don't think you can ever forgive anyone for causing a loss like that.

But even though her keeping this secret had destroyed me from the inside out and almost cost me my life, in a lot of ways, uncovering it also gave my life back to me. And that was something. If I had never gone through with trying to expose it, I would still be stewing over my parents' death, trying to find a way through my anger and despair. At least now, even though I am broken, I am free.

And looking up at the blue horizon disappearing over the sea, I know that's as good a starting point as any for the next chapter of my life.

My Perfect Family

Read on for an exclusive extract...

Chapter One

I wake with my heart hammering and an insistent buzzing next to my ear.

Where am I?

Blinking my eyes open, I try to take in the room through a hazy blur. A plush grey rug runs across the wooden floor towards a heavy white curtain. An assortment of clothes and shoes are strewn across a pristine sofa.

My heart begins to steady itself.

Ah, that's right. No need to panic.

I'm in a hotel room on Sydney Harbour. Today was my final morning here after closing a deal yesterday for my London law firm, and judging by the pounding in my head, I'd made the most of toasting my hard-won success. I guess now I'm thirty my body can't handle a long afternoon of drinking in quite the way it used to. Especially considering I don't drink much anymore, having experienced one too many hazy blackouts in my twenties.

I groan, sinking deeper into the soft, luxurious sheets. I know it's all my fault – but when I saw my best friend, Addie, again, she convinced me to have a bit of a celebration. I'm only back in Sydney for a short time, and I hadn't seen her in so long. I'd obviously got a little carried away in my excitement.

But now my brain feels like it's gone through a washing machine and my memories are all blurry. *What exactly happened last night?*

I squeeze my eyes shut and bury my face into the pillows, pulling my long auburn hair away from my face. I wish I could hide here and recover all day. Especially because I don't want to face where I'm supposed to be staying next: 8 Merton Street. My stepfamily's house.

I stretch my arms under the silky-smooth covers and wince at the movement. There's a sharp pain and an ache across my back. I wiggle my legs under the sheets, and they feel like lead. It's as though I did a serious workout yesterday, which is a strange sensation considering I definitely did not.

The buzzing starts again and I jump at the sound. Whoever wants to talk to me is being very persistent.

I roll onto my side and reach a hand beneath the pillows, trying to ignore the ache that rolls up my shoulder. As I pull out my phone and bring it towards me, I notice in the dim light some scratches across the palm of my hand. I must have fallen, but I have zero memory of it.

I frown as I glance at the caller ID, blinking in confusion.

Because it's someone that *never* calls me.

For a moment I consider not answering. But a reflex kicks in and I end up sliding my thumb across the screen. I press the phone to my ear as I whisper, 'Hello.'

A shrill Australian accent comes thundering down the line.

'Emiiily, it's Jennifer.' An unnecessary disclaimer: I know who she is. My step-aunt, Jennifer, who I haven't spoken to in at least a year.

Before I even have a chance to respond, her words start to tumble out thick and fast, and a cold sweat breaks out across my body as I try to follow.

'Emily, look I've been trying to reach you all morning. I'm sorry to have to be the one to tell you this... but there was an accident at the cliffs... and your mum... your mum, she's...' Her words trial off.

My stomach lurches as I manage to croak out, 'She's what?'

'Your mum. Lovely Suzannah...' Her voice cracks down the line as she finally says, 'She's dead, Emily. She's dead.'

The phone falls from my hand.

I feel like I've just been punched in the stomach, and I turn my face into the pillow to let out a guttural scream.

My ears begin to ring and my heart is pounding so fast I think it's going to leap out of my chest.

This isn't possible – my mother *can't* have been in an accident at the cliffs.

She *cannot* be dead.

Because if she is, then I think it's all my fault.

Chapter Two

My skin feels like there are bugs crawling all over it and my insides lurch. I throw the covers off me as my mind furiously tries to piece together the disconnect between my night and Jennifer's words.

She can't be dead, she just *can't* be dead. It's just not possible.

Because I swear I saw her last night.

I have one clear memory of my mum's face as I said goodbye to her yesterday after lunch. But after that, from when I met up with Addie, my recollections become a blur.

I know I promised Mum that I would stay with her at my late grandparents' house last night. My grandparents' house in Dover Heights, overlooking the cliffs...

And yet, here I am – in my hotel room. Did I still go and see her?

Hazy images of my mother's face flash through my mind, so I'm sure I did. But the order of my night won't come back to me. I can't get a grasp on the full picture.

I put my head in my hands. My thumping headache continues as I attempt to force my brain to retrace my footsteps. But I can't – it's a kaleidoscope of mismatched memories.

'Emily?' I hear Jennifer ask from a distance.

I'm speaking aloud, mumbling, *No, no, no* through my fingers, and whispering, *She just can't be dead* over and over. Bits and pieces of Jennifer's words reach me through my stupor.

'Emily!' she tries again shouting down the phone. 'Just listen to me; come on over, we'll talk it all through. We can explain properly what happened – or what we think happened.'

I scoop the phone back up. 'Wait, Jennifer, come on, tell me now – I don't understand. It just *can't* be true!'

I grasp at that explanation; maybe this is all some kind of sick joke. I leap out of the bed now, even as my body screams at me. But I have to move around, I have to do *something*.

A sad sigh hits me down the line, and I stop myself from throwing the phone across the room. Jennifer can't be this resigned to doing nothing.

'I'm so sorry, Emily. And you just got back from London. But I really think it'll be better to see you in person – so please come over. All I know so far is that a dog walker spotted something on the edge of the cliffs where they meet the water very early this morning – just below your grandparents' house – and they called the police. Glenn was alerted and taken over there; he's been there for hours. Then, well, it was a bit tricky but he has just identified the body as your mum's. God, I'm *so sorry*.' She's silent before she adds in a small voice, 'But you know how dangerous those cliffs can be.'

I pace up and down the small room as I try and process what I've just heard. My long, lightly freckled legs cover the distance in a matter of steps before I have to turn and start again.

I picture those exact cliffs that make up Dover Heights, my grandparents' house one of many nestled above them. I'd always loved that their back garden beyond was wild, that there wasn't a fence blocking the incredible natural view of the Pacific Ocean, unlike many of the other newer houses that had started to pop up along the cliffs. But I knew, we *all* knew, the danger of venturing too far out towards the edge. Because it leads straight out onto that sheer, unforgiving drop – an impossible fall to survive.

A bubble of anger rises in my throat as Jennifer keeps talking. The police had called *Glenn*, my stepfather, over me. *He* identified the body – not me. Not her only daughter.

My stomach churns. Why haven't the police bothered contacting me?

'So what are they saying? How did she end up there?' I'm shouting now, and I sound near hysterical. But I don't care – I can't believe these words are even coming out of my mouth.

'I don't think I'm the right person to tell you everything, Emily. But they're saying it's a terrible accident. Please come over and speak with Glenn. He can properly explain what he's been told—'

But that's the last thing I want. If Glenn tells me, I'm certain I'll break down in front of him. And I won't let that happen. I can't see him until I'm more in control of my emotions – and my memories.

'No,' I interrupt her before she can get another word out. 'I have to know now. Tell me everything.' I'm gesturing wildly even though no one can see me. But as soon as the demand is out of my mouth a flash of a scream flies into my mind. It's hazy, and dark. But it's there. And I'm certain it's a memory of last night.

I freeze, still as a statue as I hold onto the moment, bringing my free hand to cover my eyes as though that will help me. But it's gone before I have a chance to grasp it. I let my hand peel back, and that's when I notice the scratches again. The scratches all down my palm. They send a shiver down my spine as I recall that earth-shattering scream again.

I fall with a thump onto the sofa as my legs give way. And that's when I see them: the angry red marks all over my knees, a light purple bruise blossoming like a flower in early spring over my pale skin. My stomach twists.

I have no idea why I'm hurt, and no idea how or why Mum could have fallen off the edge of the cliff last night. But I do have a memory of a scream, and cuts and scrapes on me as though I fell in some scrub.

Scrub that could have been at the edge of my grandparents' house.

As soon as I brush on the thought, I shove it away hard. I couldn't have had anything to do with this. But I know I'd promised Mum that I *would* come and see her yesterday. And I've never let her down before.

I'm breathing in and out in shallow puffs, my heart thumping faster than I've ever felt it before.

I need to think. I need to remember. This can't be my reality.

Jennifer's voice echoes down the line, pulling me out of my frantic thoughts.

'Emily, I don't know why she was there. This is as much as I know right now. So please, come over. Glenn can tell you more.'

My body is going into shock. I have to get off this call. So even as a thick tightness in my throat threatens to choke me, I manage to say, 'Okay Jennifer, I'll be over soon.' I don't give her a chance to respond before I end the call.

The instant it's over I hurl my phone across the room. It thwacks against the wall with a resounding thud.

I don't care if it's broken. My heart has already shattered into a thousand tiny pieces.

A shuddering howl escapes from the very centre of my chest and sobs wrack my aching body. The words *she's dead, she's dead* echo around and around my mind.

I fall sideways on the sofa and roll my thin body into a tight ball. I try to make all five foot ten of me as small as possible, tucking my knees into my chest, as though curling up will protect my heart.

But it's not a soft pillow I land on.

My face makes contact with something wet and slippery, the shock of it halting my choking tears. I slip my hand out to pick up the cold, soaked item. And my stomach plummets to the floor as I realise what it is.

My top from last night.

Completely soaked in water.

And blood.

***

Dying to discover what really happened to Emily's mother? Pick up *My Perfect Family* on Amazon today.

A Big Thank You!

Dear reader,

Thank you so much for choosing to read *The Mother-in-Law's Secret.*

This is my debut novel, and it's just so incredible to finally be able to share it with all of you!

I really hope you loved discovering all of Cassandra's and Izzy's secrets, and if you did, I would be so grateful if you could share an honest review online, and with your family and friends. I can't wait to hear what you think, and it makes a such a big difference in helping new readers to discover my book too.

I'd also love for us to stay in touch, so if you'd like to stay up to date with all my newest releases, you can sign up to my mailing list on my website, below. You will also receive an exclusive short story, absolutely free! Your email address will never be shared and you can unsubscribe at any time.

Sign up here: www.melaniepricebooks.com

And don't forget to follow me on social media. I respond to all my messages and would absolutely love to hear from you!

facebook.com/melaniepricebooks

instagram.com/melaniepricebooks

twitter.com/melanieRprice

Thank you,

Melanie

Acknowledgements

The Mother-in-Law's Secret has been a labour of love and dedication over the last couple of years, and it wouldn't have happened without the help of so many people.

It's hard to know where to begin as there are *so* many people to thank! But I'll start with my wonderful fiancé: Seb. I couldn't have done this without his constant support, advice, and patience. We make the best team and I can't wait for our future. Also a big shout out for his help in being my audio editor!

Plus alongside Seb, thank you to his mother and father, Fiona and Ian. Firstly, thank you for being the complete opposite of Cassandra and William King(!) – you have both been kind, supportive and excited for me, and I can't wait to join your family.

On a practical level, this story would never be what it is today without the insight of my editor, Eve Hall. Your brilliant notes helped me to transform *The Mother-in-Law's Secret* into something I'm really proud of. And a huge thank you to Natasha Hodgson for her sleek copyedit and proofread. Finally, a big thank you to my cover designer Lisa Brewster: for her amazing concepts and final design.

I'd also like to particularly thank Myrto Kalavrezou, Amy Batley and Maddy Marshall for being my number one cheerleaders and advice-givers. I am so lucky to have you all in my life. Plus a big thank you to my author group Mikayla Davids and Kelly Golden – you have both been amazing sounding boards, and I'm so grateful.

There are so many more friends and family to thank – but certainly too many to list or it'll become a whole additional book! So all I'll say is that you know who you are, and I'd like to thank all of you for every conversation and word of encouragement. It means so much.

And last, but absolutely not least, my Price ladies: my mum, Jessica, and my sisters, Angie, and Lulu. I am so lucky to have such a supportive family and to count my mum and sisters as my best friends. Mum, I'd like to especially thank you for giving me my love of books. You opened this whole world to me and I could never have done it without you!

I wish that my dad, Geoff Price, could be here to celebrate too. I lost him far too soon and there's not a day that goes by when I don't miss him or wish I could talk to him. But, I also would never have been able to finish this book without him either. Both he, and Mum, instilled in me the belief that I could do anything I put my mind to. And this book definitely falls into that category – trying to write two books alongside having a life, a full-time job and planning a wedding has seemed a bit impossible at times to say the least – but with their words echoing in my ears, I knew that if I kept chipping away I'd get there. And here, at last, I am! So a big thank you to him – I know that wherever he is, he is cheering me on as he did every single day of his life.

Finally, thank you to all of you for reading! I hope you loved *The Mother-in-Law's Secret* as much as I loved writing it.

About the Author

Melanie Price is the author of *The Mother-in-Law's Secret* and *My Perfect Family*. She grew up in Sydney but now lives in London. All of her books explore the intricacies of living between Australia and the United Kingdom – with twists and turns galore. *The Mother-in-Law's Secret* is her debut novel.

Printed by Amazon Italia Logistica S.r.l.
Torrazza Piemonte (TO), Italy

56791296R00199